Llywelyn

Llywelyn

JOHN·HUGHES

y Lolfa

First impression: 2014

Cover design: Sion Ilar
Cover picture: © Depositphotos

ISBN: 978 1 84771 832 7

Published and printed in Wales
on paper from well-maintained forests by
Y Lolfa Cyf., Talybont, Ceredigion SY24 5HE
e-mail ylolfa@ylolfa.com
website www.ylolfa.com
tel 01970 832 304
fax 832 782

CHAPTER 1

First week of January 1277

IT IS FREQUENTLY believed that women who are pleasing to the eye have difficulty in establishing stable and enduring relationships with men because they are so admired for their appearance that all their other virtues are ignored.

They are desired and sought after sometimes as a mere challenge, sometimes as objects to be conquered and sometimes to make attractive ornaments to be displayed to friends and acquaintances. Such women are, sadly, often neither developed to their full potential nor to their own desire.

The beauty of some women may be renowned, discussed, compared, admired and envied. But such beauty can form a barrier for those who wish to make a happy and a wise choice of a partner in life, and can allow the effect of their own appearance to have too great an influence on their wisdom.

For pretty women the choice of a partner appears to be wider than it is for the merely average looking, but it is not so because many a wise man will shy clear of such a shiny gem knowing that others will be attracted by the glow and that the precious stone could fall from its setting at any moment of weakness.

Beth was such a woman. Twenty years old and endowed with arrestingly good looks. Her face was framed on perfectly angled bones with her attractively high cheekbones being not a fraction too high as to render her eyes sunken nor, in any way, detract from those never-to-be-forgotten eyes.

Her blue eyes, with their streaks of green – depending on the angle of the light, were inherited from her Viking ancestors and many believed that they were her most distinguishing feature with their hypnotic, yet vivacious, appearance, until of course their own eyes were diverted to some of her other jewels.

Her black hair, passed on to her by her Celtic forbears, together with her firm chin, gave her face strength and beauty. Her full lips were of exactly the correct dimensions and perfectly balanced and contributed to her attractive face.

She was taller and slimmer than the other women of her generation; undoubtedly a result of her father's Viking roots.

She was, to most men she met, perfection personified.

Beth was noticed wherever she went and, once met, sought after. The most confident of the district's males believed they were in serious contention for her hand. The sons of the nobility and the fathers of those sons looked out for and desired her attention.

The power of beautiful women over men is as strong as the magnetic pull of powerful men for women. But Beth was too young and inexperienced to appreciate and judge the relative strengths and weaknesses of these forces of attraction.

To Beth it was all fairly simple, she had always, from the time she was a very young child, dreamt of marrying a prince and becoming a princess. Her heart was set on it. It was her wish at all the wells she visited. Thus, no ordinary suitor stood a chance, which was both a hindrance and a blessing. It kept her out of harm's way in her youth and, in that way, was as useful as many a plain face or set of rotten teeth.

Beth lived in a dream. She was aware of her beauty but carried it well by being pleasant to every man she met, yet avoided giving anyone any hope of capturing her heart. Even at the age of twenty, she was beginning to be considered strange in that she was not yet attached to a man of some importance and wealth.

Her father, Gruffudd ap Owain, could have tried to force her into a relationship with a local nobleman of good prospects likely to inherit a large estate. There were many young, middle-aged and even old men who would have fitted his hopes but he was not that type of father. He was not that type of man either and that's how he had survived in such a hostile environment as the Marches. Further, he somehow sensed that Beth would not easily be cajoled into such a contract and so he had tended to leave her to her own devices.

To Beth it had to be a prince. However, all the princes in her dreams had been mature men much older than herself, who had already achieved fame and the admiration of their contemporaries. She, Beth, would then acquire that same level of fame through her association with her imagined but much admired prince.

This was Beth's state of mind when in January 1277 a message arrived at Gruffudd's castle in Aberedw, that Llywelyn, the Prince of Wales, was on his way to visit them. Gruffudd had remained loyal to the prince over many years and in very difficult times.

Relations between Llywelyn and the king had been deteriorating for months. The king was making demands of Llywelyn that he could not meet without seriously undermining his own position. War seemed inevitable and Llywelyn was securing his borders before it broke out.

Preparations for the visit started immediately and the pace of life at the outpost accelerated dramatically. Any minor building works left so far undone were undertaken; whatever needed an additional coat of whitewash was given it and whatever needed repairing by the blacksmith was undertaken. Of course extra food and drink was ordered.

The day following the arrival of the message had been a cold, January day and the blacksmith's workshop below the castle had been busy. The place had been busy, with a number of horses shod and tools for the land sharpened and re-tempered.

Even with the extra activity caused by the impending visit some still found time to lounge about aimlessly just inside the wide entrance, trying to keep warm and indulging in gossip and speculation. It is fair to say that, in the main, they were the men, with the women being far too occupied with their tasks at home. The occasional woman had appeared from time to time either to look for her husband or to request the blacksmith to repair an implement.

The castle, at the confluence of the river Edw and the much larger Wye, was built backing on to a high cliff above the Edw with two points on the cliff linked by a semi-circular wall and ditch facing the gentler slope to the north and west.

Strategically it was an important castle for Llywelyn at the southernmost point of his lands and adjacent to Mortimer's estate to the east. It was held firmly by his strong and loyal supporter Gruffudd as it had been by his father before him.

Exactly at the time stated in the message, Llywelyn and his entourage of mounted troops and an array of carts could be seen approaching Aberedw Castle following the eastern bank of the Wye.

At the base of the castle hill the itinerant court was met by Gruffudd. Llywelyn greeted Gruffudd warmly as the latter paid homage to him by bending down on one knee before his prince.

Llywelyn was escorted up the hill past St Cewydd's Church, passing also on their left the stables, the blacksmith's large workplace set into the rocks and a number of other essential establishments, including the bakery.

Beth was at the castle gate to meet the prince and his party. Llywelyn, now in his mid-forties, had not seen Beth since she was a child and was clearly amazed at how she had developed into such a beautiful young woman.

She curtsied to him when he approached her and took her hand, smiling and looking at her as if she was the only person there, giving her his full attention. His natural charisma impressed her instantly and boosted her confidence.

All she could do was smile at him and it was all she needed to do. She was captivated by his genuine charm and the delight he showed at meeting her. He somehow made her feel very special in those first few seconds of their first encounter as adults.

"This is Beth," he announced with confidence. "I've heard so much about you."

To Beth no-one had ever said her name with such feeling and as she bowed her head again she whispered, "Prince…"

"I'm Llywelyn to you and as I am to your father," he helped her.

She responded with a smile that would have melted any heart.

"I was warned about your beauty," he said. "But the warning was totally inadequate. I am poorly prepared to meet such a beautiful woman."

Holding on to Beth's hand he turned to her father saying, "I'm told your beautiful daughter is not married. I'm delighted of course, but you must have been negligent in your fatherly duties."

Llywelyn laughed at Gruffudd as he searched for a reply and after glancing at Beth he turned back to her father, "Gruffudd, you have hidden your daughter well. How have you managed to keep her unmarried this long?"

Gruffudd told him the truth. "She's far too choosy and I do not believe in forcing her to marry against her will." He hesitated for a second and added jokingly, "I'm not confident that she would obey me anyway."

They both laughed and Llywelyn turned again to Beth whose hand he still held firmly. She looked embarrassed and blushed which further endeared her to the prince.

Gruffudd stepped in to relieve the mounting pressure on his daughter and told the gathering, "We have prepared a glorious feast in honour of our prince and his illustrious courtiers and arranged a competition between his poets and ours. As the home team we have given ourselves the advantage of being allowed to choose the titles of the first ten poems to be composed. You will find us tough opponents. Our best mead and wine is laid out in honour of our most high and noble guests. You are most welcomed here. Llywelyn, it's an honour to have you and the royal courtiers visit us here at Aberedw."

Beth's father needn't have been concerned about his daughter. She was revelling in the attention she was having from her prince. Her dream was becoming a reality and the prince was very much up to her expectation.

Turning to Beth, Llywelyn said, "I request that you sit next to me at the table."

She could not have asked for more.

Despite having travelled far during the day, including attending mass at Cwm Hir Abbey they were ready for the feast and the merriment.

They gathered in the castle hall and jugs full of mead were handed out. The food was laid out on large oak tables. A pig was roasted to perfection above the hearth and the hall was full of its mouth-watering aroma.

Llywelyn and his most important nobles were seated at three long tables, with Beth on the prince's left and her father on his right hand side. The castle hall was packed with many sitting around the sides and others standing.

The food, the drink and the assembled company were quickly blessed and the eating, drinking and music started immediately and noisily.

There was great hilarity in the hall. Llywelyn talked politics to Gruffudd as others approached him to discuss various issues and get his views on matters that vexed them, asking for his advice and support. But, however occupied he was, he ensured that Beth was an important part of his conversation, frequently asking her for her opinion, her take on an issue.

He frequently turned to her saying something that caused her to laugh; other remarks made her pensive and others left her hopeful. In short, he kept her enthralled and was every inch the prince of her dreams.

Beth had taken to Llywelyn instantly when she met him at the gate, not least of course because he was a prince but also because of the attention that he bestowed on her. She was flattered by this and spoke to him freely about how she wished she could see other parts of his realm.

"If you wish to see other parts of Wales then I can help you," he said enthusiastically.

She was by then perfectly relaxed in his company and told him, "I have never seen the sea, although I've heard a lot about it from the visiting poets. I've heard about the waves and tides and bays, but I've never seen any of those things."

"You must visit the royal court at Garth Celyn. It's by the sea with excellent views of Anglesey across the Menai. You would love it at Garth Celyn."

"I certainly would love to see more places, especially the sea."

"Well why don't you come back with us to Gwynedd and Garth Celyn for a while? You can live there as my guest and as part of the court."

It might be that he just enjoyed her company but he was also probably thinking that Beth's presence at the royal court would further cement the bond that existed between him and her father and strengthen his hold on this crucial area of Wales, particularly as conflict with the king was intensifying.

Beth was delighted by the offer and the genuine smile that spread over her lovely face showed she wanted to go with him before she said, "I would love to go to Garth Celyn."

She was so pleased with the invitation that the immediate acceptance was inevitable, but Llywelyn, witnessing the strength of will in the young woman, nevertheless stressed the need for him to talk to her father about it all.

"Talk to him now," she said nodding to her father sitting on his right.

Llywelyn turned and spoke to Gruffudd briefly and then turned back to her, "That's settled then. You are coming back with me to Garth Celyn."

"Thank you. I'm so pleased."

Nevertheless, Beth had actually already decided that she would be going up north with her prince. She was aware that Llywelyn had many years earlier promised to marry Eleanor de Montfort, but she also knew that Eleanor was held captive by King Edward and was not likely to be released soon. In fact, probably never, as the king was well known for his determination to have his own way regardless of the personal suffering of anyone, including a relative, such as Eleanor.

While, the court members were entertained by the bards and singers gathered by Gruffudd, Beth hardly noticed them as she was so engrossed in her conversation with the prince.

The meal over, the drinking and merriment continued and Llywelyn took the opportunity to talk to Gruffudd about the upcoming conflict and the state of affairs in the Elfael area.

Gruffudd was, on balance, encouraging and felt that most of the Welsh in the area would be supportive of their native lord. However, by nature, he was an optimistic man and Llywelyn gave great heed to his views and never questioned the situation further.

Beth's father was also happy that she was going north with Llywelyn, knowing of course that Llywelyn was a single man and that Eleanor was out of circulation probably for many years. He knew that Edward's prisoners normally died in his prisons.

Prominent members of Llywelyn's court who wanted him married with an heir, were pleased to encourage him to find a wife and Beth suited their wishes, though she had few political connections to help his situation.

The revellers went to bed late having drunk well, but the following morning they were ready to leave. Beth set out with the court on her way north, in one of the many wagons, bidding farewell to her family at Aberedw.

From her position on the wagon she could see Llywelyn near the front of the group, sitting comfortably and confidently on his horse. She admired his broad back and his riding skills. She knew that he was entertaining to be with and made her laugh as experienced the previous evening. She knew she liked him and the fact that he was over twenty years older than her, possibly, made him more attractive.

Llywelyn and his court travelled up the east bank of the Wye with the intention of crossing into Ceredigion before proceeding northwards to Garth Celyn. The group was stretched out for about half a mile along the track which followed the river bank.

They knew that they had to be careful on their journey until they were out of the area under Roger Mortimer's influence. Llywelyn had no wish to take up too many issues with Roger at this stage and it was decided that a visit to Cwm Hir and Aberedw was significant enough.

However discrete Llywelyn was about the journeys he took out of Gwynedd, it was inevitable that news of his movements would be leaked and become known to Roger Mortimer and many others. Also, regrettably, there was always the possibility that among his own men there was one who could not be trusted.

The journey north was without incident and Beth was delighted to see the high, snow-capped mountains of Gwynedd, and happier still to be with her prince.

Chapter 2

Garth Celyn: February 1277 to 13 October 1278

T HE ROYAL COURT was perched on a promontory extending from a hill and pointing over marsh land and the sea towards Anglesey. It was a well-chosen location with the hill, known as Dinas, used centuries earlier as an Iron Age fort and now as an observation post with an unrestricted view of the bay, the Lafan sands and Anglesey.

Beth was very impressed by the scenery surrounding the court as she approached from the west. On her left she could see the coast of Anglesey across the Menai and the high majestic mountains on her right.

The rectangular outer wall of Garth Celyn was built mainly of wood with its longer sides parallel to the seashore. This wall was the first line of defence but was intended more to deter animals than to keep out any determined foe. The buildings she could see inside the wall were more substantial, constructed out of light grey stones.

They entered through the main gate facing the sea. Inside the perimeter wall she could see there were numerous stone buildings including the main hall and, she assumed, the attached royal apartments. Other buildings, including the smithy, bakery and stables, had been built within easy reach of the hall. She turned around to look back through the main gate at the sea and the Anglesey coastline on the horizon and she knew her life had changed forever.

She shifted her attention from the wonderful scenery

surrounding the court to the buildings inside the outer perimeter and more specifically now to where she would be living.

Llywelyn wasted no time, having acknowledged the welcome, and dismounted. He directed a servant to take Beth to the room allocated to her.

To her great joy, the room had a window facing the sea and she had a magnificent view across the straits. Llywelyn had remembered that she wanted to see the sea and its fascinating ebb and flow.

Beth settled quickly into the life at Garth Celyn. She enjoyed the bustle of the royal court. She loved the view from her window, which was stunning and different every day, depending on whether the sea was in or out or on its way in one direction or the other. When the sea was out she could see the Lafan sands stretching across to the far shore. On a clear day she could almost make out the individual buildings on the Anglesey shore and could see the friary at Llanfaes and, to her right, Ynys Siriol, the small island at the far end of the promontory pointing towards the Gogarth.

She saw Llywelyn daily and was delighted to be in his presence but the relationship did not develop and they remained only very good friends. The close relationship she wanted with her prince did not come about as he became more and more engrossed in the affairs of state as a war with King Edward was becoming more inevitable.

The prospect of a major conflict was clearly distracting Llywelyn from other matters though his close advisers were pressing him to marry someone and produce an heir. Many, if not all at the court, thought Beth would make an ideal wife for him. She was young, beautiful, and very well liked at court.

During the first weeks of 1277, Llywelyn was in constant indirect communication with the king. The king was demanding that Llywelyn paid homage to him, but Llywelyn was reluctant, believing that he was his own master in his own country. Edward, however, was determined to subjugate Llywelyn and his people, so no agreement was achieved, despite great effort by many.

Anian, the Bishop of Bangor, who was acting as the main intermediary, went to meet the king on Llywelyn's behalf to try to arrive at some agreement that would avoid a war. He failed in his mission and the political situation looked very gloomy.

Beth and Llywelyn were constantly in each other's company and very friendly and happy together but their talk was about the political difficulties facing him and his court.

A few days before Palm Sunday 1277, the two met early in the morning and he told her that the Bishop of Bangor and Madog, the Archdeacon of Anglesey, were to visit about midday to discuss the impasse between himself and the king. He warned her that he was very concerned that there would be little room for compromise and that it was very unlikely that a peace treaty would be accomplished.

"I am not looking forward to this meeting. While I am glad that another effort is being made, it's very difficult to see what progress can be achieved, particularly with Anian involved. I know he wants me to pay homage to the king – he's made that clear. If I do, then that will be the end of any Welsh independence. He will destroy our way of life, our laws and culture."

"Surely the bishop realises that."

"Yes, but he does not seem to care. He is determined that I and the whole of Gwynedd surrender."

"What about Madog, the archdeacon?"

"He is, I'm convinced, on our side. I was hoping that he would influence Anian, but it seems the bishop is very strong willed."

"He argues that this king is very determined, has the will and the ability to defeat us. He advises that I pay homage to him now so that Wales survives and we wait for a better opportunity in the future to regain our independence."

"I see."

"I don't trust Anian. He's two-faced and will do anything to save his own skin, even if that means getting me to my knees before Edward."

"So in these talks and negotiations you don't trust Bishop Anian to be totally impartial."

"No, I don't. But I do trust Madog because I've found him to be a man of his word. He supports my point of view and isn't afraid of saying so."

"So you're pleased that Madog will be accompanying Anian on the visit?"

"I'm very pleased about that, but I'm not very hopeful of success. Edward is determined to conquer and destroy us."

Beth hoped that Llywelyn could make the most of the meeting and that he could then disengage a little from the political concerns facing him and think more about everyday life, children and hopefully her.

At midday the bishop, the archdeacon and their attendants, including an armed guard arrived and were met by Llywelyn and his advisers just outside the main gate.

While both men were of similar height they were of very different build. Anian, the bishop, was a slim man, clearly a reader and a deep thinker. He had a hatchet face and carried a permanently grim look under a good thatch of hair on which his mitre sat rather precariously and uncomfortably. He mistrusted everyone and was distrusted by many.

Madog, the Archdeacon of Anglesey was well built, enjoyed his food and life. He was as bald as a coot and it was a wonder that any headgear stayed long on his head. He was of a jolly and sunny nature. He was relaxed and smiled charmingly at everyone he met. Clearly, he was the type who thought well of everybody.

Llywelyn called to them as he approached them. "Welcome

to the royal court. Did you have a pleasant journey on such a fine day?"

"I don't see why we had to come here. You could have come to Bangor. I hope you appreciate the effort we've made," was the typical Anian response.

"Good afternoon Llywelyn," Madog intervened.

Anian had not finished griping. "It was very hazardous crossing the rivers this morning. The Ogwen crossing was particularly dangerous."

"I would have thought both rivers were low."

"We could have drowned."

Llywelyn was becoming annoyed by the bishop's comments already and replied, "Surely bishop, there was not enough water in it today for even a weasel to swim across."

The bishop was not amused and continued with his cantankerous comments. "We could have been attacked by bandits."

"Unlikely, in such a well-ruled country."

"That's your opinion," was his sour reply.

Madog made no comment but smiled amicably and motioned with his hand suggesting it was time to move on.

Llywelyn took the hint and suggested that they went to the hall to have food and drink before starting on their negotiations.

At the mention of food and drink, Madog set off towards the hall, beaming from ear to ear. Anian followed reluctantly, mumbling his discontent.

They disappeared into the hall out of Beth's sight and hearing. Like the others who had witnessed the meeting at the gate, she realised that the prospect for successful negotiations was grim.

The meeting went on for a while and Beth became hopeful that progress was being made, but her hopes were dashed when the church delegation came out. It was obvious that it had not been a fruitful meeting. The bishop looked sour and angry, while the archdeacon looked disappointed, but he did manage to exchange pleasantries with Llywelyn as they departed. The bishop, however, left as grim faced as when he arrived, and barely bid Llywelyn farewell.

Later, Llywelyn told Beth that it had not been a pleasant meeting and that the bishop had been very difficult, argumentative and unwilling to move from the position that he had described to her that morning. Beth was very disappointed, as she realised that this would almost certainly lead to a war with Edward.

While Llywelyn, and therefore Beth, was glad to see the back of Anian, there was an air of depression at the court during the following days because people realised that the bishop did offer a path to some kind of agreement for peace, though they didn't want peace at any price.

On Palm Sunday, Bishop Anian at the end of mass at St Deiniol's Cathedral Church, announced Llywelyn's excommunication and promptly left Gwynedd for a monastery at St Albans.

This was devastating news for Llywelyn and a great blow to any hope of peace. But some at the court, including Llywelyn, saw the benefit of Anian's departure in that it left Madog, the Archdeacon of Anglesey, as the senior cleric in Gwynedd. They saw Madog as a more trustworthy person and likely to be more helpful in bringing about a peace agreement. They saw Anian as a hindrance to peace and a coward who had departed to save his own skin.

But Llywelyn had enough enemies; even his brother Dafydd was already firmly committed to Edward, having already shown his treacherous side by plotting to kill Llywelyn some years earlier, and now the church was lined against him.

War was now a certainty and the excommunication signalled the start of a war. The siege of Dolforwyn Castle, in

Montgomeryshire, started by Roger Mortimer soon reached a successful conclusion for Edward when Llywelyn's supporters at the castle surrendered.

More bad news reached Garth Celyn when it became known that supporters of the king had marched on Brecon and the Tywi valley and cleared Llywelyn's forces from those areas. By May 1277 the king had control of most of Wales except Gwynedd.

On the twenty-fifth of August, Edward moved his main army to Rhuddlan and soon after on to Degannwy and from there attacked Anglesey, destroying the harvest.

It was now possible for Llywelyn and his soldiers to see, from the hillside above Garth Celyn, the English soldiers burning the crops on the opposite Anglesey shoreline.

It was then that Beth began to hear whispers in and around the court that some of Llywelyn's own supporters were deserting him. First, it was his noblemen in areas like Powys and Dyfed, but worse was to follow when in September information arrived at Garth Celyn that some of Llywelyn's own strong supporters in Gwynedd were leaving him to face the king on his own.

At this time Beth and her prince were close. Despite his military concerns and despair, he took time to be comforted by her as his true friend whom he knew would never desert him. She did not even try to take advantage of his loneliness – though frequently tempted by her own desires – she remained a loyal friend only.

It became apparent that Llywelyn had no option other than to come to some kind of understanding with the king and, as a result of his weak military position, he accepted the Treaty of Aberconwy negotiated by his representatives most trusted men: Tudur ap Ednyfed, his chancellor and brother to the highly respected Goronwy ap Ednyfed, and Goronwy ap Heilyn on the ninth of November 1277.

As a result of the treaty, Llywelyn lost control of large areas of Wales, but held on to Gwynedd. His brother Dafydd was given possession of lands in north-east Wales. Anian was to return to Bangor and Llywelyn's excommunication was revoked. Significantly, as part of the treaty, the king agreed to release Eleanor de Montfort so that she could marry Llywelyn.

This was a severe blow to Beth and her dream. She became very unhappy and thought of returning to her family home, but as she had no news of her family in Aberedw and with the country in such a state of unrest, she felt it was safer to stay at Garth Celyn and make the most of life there until things settled.

As the day of Llywelyn's wedding approached she gradually became resigned to the inevitable fact that she would not marry her prince after all.

Chapter 3

13 October 1278 – the wedding at Worcester

Llywelyn spent Christmas day 1277 in London with King Edward, following the signing of the Treaty of Aberconwy. The king arranged a feast for him and all those who had accompanied him there. Beth had remained at Garth Celyn and was again considering going back to Aberedw in the new year because there was talk now of Eleanor being released from prison soon and marrying Llywelyn. She thought she would delay her departure until Llywelyn returned and then she would talk it over with him.

Following his return in early January, it became general knowledge quickly that the king had entertained the Welsh nobly and had agreed to release Eleanor so that Llywelyn could marry her, but no specific date was agreed. However, the gloom that had hung over Garth Celyn for the past year had lifted and Llywelyn was clearly a happier man.

By then Beth had resolved to simply tell him that she was leaving. After all she would not be leaving his side at a time of trial for him and she felt there would be no place for her at the royal court.

She decided that she would not approach him for a day or two regarding her decision but she knew that she could not leave it too long in case he would travel to one of his other courts to explain the treaty and what had been agreed in London.

Therefore, two days after his return, she made her way towards the hall where she knew he would be getting ready for the day. It was clear that it was his intention to go hunting because the huntsmen and the dogs were already milling around ready for the start. As she approached the main hall, Llywelyn came out obviously in good spirits and ready for the hunt. She was disappointed that she would have to disturb his day of enjoyment because she was well aware that he had not enjoyed many days over the last twelve months and more.

He saw her and immediately expressed his delight, making it more difficult for her to raise the issue with him.

"I was coming to see you before going hunting," he said with a broad smile on his face, clearly pleased to see her in the early morning with frost still thick on the ground.

"Where will you hunt today? It looks cold out there," she said pointing up to the hills and mountains beyond. "The dew is frozen up there. It's white. Please be careful, we all rely so much on you."

"Don't worry Beth. I've been hunting up there in much worse conditions than these. I wanted to talk to you following my visit to London. Eleanor will be released soon and we will marry immediately afterwards. I want you to be a companion to Eleanor when she comes to live here. She will have her own servants and helpers, of course, but I want you to be her close companion and help her to understand our ways of doing things. Our customs and laws will be strange to her and she will need all the help you can give her. Of course, my advisers will be available to her but I think it would be easier for her to understand and come to terms with things if they were explained to her by a woman, particularly a sensitive and sensible woman like you."

Beth was taken aback by his request. Was it a request? Or just a nice way of telling her what she was to do. She had no alternative but to say yes.

"I am delighted. I will tell you more at the feast tonight when I return from those dangerous icy hills," he said laughing and walking towards the dogs.

"After Eleanor has settled I would like to return to Aberedw," she called out after him, but there was no possibility of him hearing a single word as it was all drowned by the baying of the hounds excited by their master and the thought of the hunt ahead.

Beth realised that he had not heard her and murmured to herself, 'I will have to raise the issue with you again once Eleanor has settled at Garth Celyn.'

It did cross her mind that this was the reason he had brought her to Garth Celyn in the first place, but she did not dwell on the idea for long as she thought too highly of him.

Month after month went by, but there was no Eleanor and no wedding. Llywelyn was getting more and more disappointed and despair was setting in. Many at the court began to think that Eleanor would never be released and there would be no wedding. But then, in late September, the invitations arrived. The king had decided to have the wedding at the priory in Worcester on the thirteenth of October.

This was a significant date for Edward because it was St Edward's Day. It showed his magnanimous side to his supporters and his evil side to his opponents. He was wielding his power with great skill and controlling every aspect of the situation.

Preparations began immediately and spirits at the court rose again to new heights.

Beth was to accompany the court to Worcester. She would be introduced to Eleanor before the wedding and so she would have time to talk to her about her role at the royal court of Garth Celyn.

They left Garth Celyn in plenty of time to arrive at Worcester the day before the wedding was due to take place.

The king, Eleanor of Castile, his queen, and their followers had been there for a few days as had the King of Scotland and his wife.

Llywelyn was allowed to meet Eleanor the day before the wedding and both made further commitments to each other during the brief private moments they had together. Edward, the unrelenting controller, arranged everything according to his own wishes.

Beth had her first glimpse of Eleanor in the late afternoon when all involved in the wedding were shown around the cathedral. Edward, a tall man towering above everyone, was also there deciding where everyone was to be seated and keeping a close eye on all that was happening and intervening when he felt there was the slightest deviation from his expressed wishes.

Everything was meticulously planned, like his military campaigns, with Edward's aids rushing about showing Eleanor where she would be standing, showing Llywelyn where he would be and what was to be said by all the parties present.

Beth was standing outside the main entrance where Edward had decreed the marriage would be conducted so that all the witnesses could see that it had actually taken place. He was clearly concerned, in his obsessive mind, that in the dark cathedral people might claim, for some unknown reason, that a trick was played and that the two had not actually married. By conducting the wedding on the steps of the main entrance there would be no doubt.

The marriage, Beth knew, would be conducted by the prior, but many in Llywelyn's court were wondering if the Bishop of Bangor would be there because he had returned to his post at Bangor a few months earlier, though there had been no communication between him and Llywelyn.

The bishop and Llywelyn were very suspicious of each other, but Madog, who had stayed at his post in Gwynedd throughout the troubled time, had travelled with Llywelyn to Worcester.

Beth guessed that if the bishop were there he would not appear until the next day.

Once the preparations were over and the key players had dispersed, Beth and others from Garth Celyn entered the priory church. She had been most impressed by the magnificent building. However, inside it was surprisingly dark and it took a while for her eyes to get accustomed to the gloom.

She walked down the north aisle. It was dark with little light entering through the high narrow windows. There had been a recent mass, probably arranged by Edward, and a significant amount of incense had been burnt. The smell, though pleasant enough, was catching her in her throat and making her mouth dry. She ambled slowly in the direction of the altar, peering through the gloom and the smoke from the burnt incense.

A side door opened and a ray of bright light penetrated the cathedral piercing the smoke and there appeared near her and immediately in front of one of the larger pillars, a man in a white habit, which looked grey in the dark cathedral.

She was surprised by the man's appearance and was aware of the fact that she was glowering at him in the gloom. But he kept her stare and did not flinch. He was elderly with grey hair and a pale, translucent skin. He had a pleasant kind face and his eyes sparkled.

He whispered to her, "You look unhappy. Why don't you sit on that bench?" He indicated a small seat attached to the outer wall.

"Sit there for a while and contemplate what saddens you. Then, when you are ready, join the others praying before the altar."

She looked at him puzzled, as though requesting an explanation, but walked slowly to the nearby bench as the man moved away and melted into the darkness.

Do I look sad she asked herself? Am I sad? As these questions troubled her, she became aware that there were tears forming in her eyes and before long they were running down her cheeks.

Yes she was sad; she was very sad, but had not been able to show it to anyone not even admitting it to herself. She had no-one to talk to about the loss she was experiencing.

She loved Llywelyn, but here in the cathedral the next day he would be married to another woman. The reality of what was happening to her was making her sad, very sad. She would never marry Llywelyn; she would never marry her prince. She was crying uncontrollably now and it continued for a quite a while until she had cried out her grief.

When eventually she began to control her sobbing, she dried her eyes and took the man's advice and went to pray near at the altar.

She prayed that she would overcome the grief of losing her prince, and for the strength not to hate her rival Eleanor. Then, as she grew stronger, she prayed for strength to bring her to like Eleanor.

Having exhausted herself in prayer, she rose from her knees and slowly walked out of the cathedral into daylight, at the same time looking for the man who had helped her.

As she stepped out of the door a shiver went through her body. She realised how cold it had been inside the cathedral and blamed the temperature difference for the shivering.

The next day, Bishop Anian did indeed appear for the wedding. He was not one for missing a free meal thought Beth. The ceremony took place on the cathedral steps in the sunshine, exactly as Edward wished.

Eleanor wore a stunning white gown – more dazzling than anything Beth had ever seen before; clearly there was a strong French influence. She was given away by Edward, witnessed by the King and Queen of Scotland. The Archbishop of Canterbury officiated but Anian was there, highly visible, obviously not on the top step, but far too high up for Beth's liking. She was beginning to loathe the bishop.

Following the wedding there was a very impressive feast provided by Edward. There were opportunities for the guests to circulate and talk. Beth spent most of her time with others from Llywelyn's court, discussing the wedding and how awestruck they had been with the clothes and the ceremony.

Beth did keep an eye out for the elderly monk who had spoken to her in the cathedral, but didn't see him. She was a little surprised because she had felt sure that he was at Worcester for the wedding. The more she thought about it, the more shocked she was at the thought that a stranger had seen how sad she was, even in the dark cathedral.

However, she was relieved to see that he was not at the gathering, because she was afraid that she would succumb to weeping again if she saw him. Instead, she was able to relax and spent some time with Llywelyn and Eleanor.

Of course, it did flash through her mind more than once how she would have enjoyed being the bride and she was without doubt jealous of Eleanor, though the bride didn't have her beauty.

Many at the feast admired Beth and the way she looked. The Scottish king, a dour-looking man, had a glint in his eye when he saw her and it was just as well for Beth that the Scottish queen knew her husband well and kept a close eye on him.

Llywelyn and Eleanor and their entourage returned to Garth Celyn and he settled into married life well, particularly considering his age and the age of his wife. His land, though much reduced, was at peace again and now there was a Princess of Wales. A title, of course, that Beth had hoped to call her own.

CHAPTER 4
March 1279 to July 1279

To her surprise and relief, Beth enjoyed her work of easing Eleanor into the workings of the court. She knew all the personnel well and knew exactly what each did and the part they played in making the royal court function. Eleanor was not a fast learner but a very willing one.

Beth, in turn, learnt about France and the French way of doing things, including dressing of course.

Following the wedding the relationship between Llywelyn and Anian improved slightly. It had to. The king looked after his supporters and had decreed it.

As difficult as it was, Llywelyn had to accept the bishop whom he viewed more as a viper than a prelate, and he had to put a brave face on the matter.

The two had to work together and it was suggested that an envoy, appointed by the Bishop, visit Garth Celyn at regular intervals with a view to avoid conflict and improve the understanding between the prince and the bishop. Llywelyn objected to this arrangement because he was of the opinion that he, Llywelyn, should choose the envoy, while naturally Anian was strongly of the view that the envoy should be appointed by him.

Letters were exchanged between them and representatives negotiated on their behalf. However, little progress was achieved until the intervention of Madog, who suggested that he would put forward a neutral name that would be acceptable to both parties. Anian agreed and after a brief period of consideration Llywelyn agreed too.

In March 1279 the new envoy arrived at Garth Celyn. Tudor was a young man in his mid to late thirties, with good qualifications in the law and the affairs of the church. Tudor had trained as a priest but had not followed the calling. He had found the priesthood too confining for his liking and had instead lived well on services rendered to the nobility. The fact that he could read and write had, not surprisingly over the years, made him useful to the higher echelons of society and he had been employed with the nobility in England.

He was intelligent and good looking and, surprisingly, not yet married. His role was a simple one, in that he was to visit Garth Celyn for some days every few weeks, and meet with Llywelyn and his advisers. It was intended that he would express the bishop's views on issues that might involve the church and the state, and that he could present the bishop's petition on behalf of some of Llywelyn's tenants. He was to help interpret the law as it was to be applied to the church and its tenants. The latter was already becoming an increasingly important issue due to the conflict between the application of Welsh and English law.

Tudor would similarly talk to the bishop about issues that concerned Llywelyn and try to resolve difficulties before they became issues of conflict causing the parties to resort to the courts and the king.

Tudor's pleasant and gentle nature assisted him greatly in his tasks.

Beth had now spent three months in the enjoyable task of helping Eleanor and her servants understand the Welsh ways of doing things. She was wondering at this time what would she have to do when Eleanor became fully acquainted with the routines of the court and Beth's thoughts once again turned to the idea of returning to Aberedw.

In the depth of the night, when she could not sleep, she accepted that things had not turned out as she had hoped. She had been in love with Llywelyn and had hoped that, while it seemed that Eleanor was to be kept in prison for a long time, Llywelyn would have chosen another partner.

But he had remained true to Eleanor despite enticement from other women at the court, who were brazenly courting Llywelyn's attention and favours. Beth knew that she had also given him indications on more than one occasion that she desired his attention, but felt on each occasion that he had somehow failed to notice this.

She knew that other women at the court felt so sure of themselves that they explained their failure by pronouncing that his love for Eleanor was too strong for him even to notice them, or that his loyalty to Eleanor was total. Beth's view at times was that his love had not yet been fired for anyone and that he would one day be inspired to fall in love and that's what kept her happy in herself during her first months at Garth Celyn.

Beth felt good about the fact that she had kept her own council on her relationship with Llywelyn, despite what was said behind her back. Also, she felt vindicated in that she had never openly courted him nor thrown herself at him like many of the other women.

She was, however, accepting that she would never have a romantic association with him. She knew he was lost to her.

Of course, the fact that she secretly loved Llywelyn meant that it was very difficult for her to set her desires on a less noble person. She did not find it easy to redirect her love. Other men at the court were below her reach and most of them knew that, particularly those who had witnessed her close friendship with Llywelyn in the past. So, Beth had no viable suitors.

Her desire to return home was then very understandable. She

knew that she would have to talk to Llywelyn first and was rather reluctant to do so because it would probably be hurtful to them both. So she delayed for a while, but was resolved to leave the coming summer and planned to talk to Llywelyn at Whitsun.

Then, no sooner had she set her mind to leave than Tudor arrived at the court. They would see each other from a distance. As he arrived Beth might be out walking with Eleanor. At other times he would be leaving as she was talking to others by the gate. She knew who he was and she could only presume that someone had told him who she was.

She had certainly discussed him with Eleanor and both found him a good-looking man who always found time to smile at them.

Then, one day in early May, while Beth was walking along the edge of the woodland just above Garth Celyn pondering how to break the news to Llywelyn regarding her decision to go home, she saw Tudor walking towards her. He clearly was not in a hurry, no more than she was but, unlike her, he seemed more interested in his surroundings and the views across the Menai.

They greeted each other and she expected then that he would walk past her and down towards the court, but he didn't.

"Isn't this a wonderful place? I enjoy coming here every time I come to Garth Celyn," he said.

"Yes," she replied.

"This is such a wonderful view," he continued pointing towards Anglesey.

"Yes," she replied again.

"You're not here to enjoy the view are you?" he asked.

"No," she said honestly, but did not want to explain to him exactly why she had come there to ponder and added quickly, "I was daydreaming."

"Oh! What were you thinking about?" he asked.

"I can't remember," she replied defensively. "I'm always

daydreaming. It was nothing of any importance otherwise I would remember what it was I suppose."

She did not wish to be questioned on her private thoughts and perhaps sensing this he moved on, saying as he descended the slope, "Perhaps I'll see you here again then. And next time perhaps you can tell me what you're dreaming about."

He then bent down and picked up a bluebell, took a few steps back up towards her and gave it to her saying, "There, take that to remember this meeting. It's the best of the May flowers, as this is the best of meetings."

Beth was shocked by the speed of his action and the flow of his words and could not match his alacrity with words of her own and could only reply with thank you.

She had thought of him as a ponderous man, happier in his study, his books and letters. To her he had been older than his age, both in appearance and manners. She had viewed him more of a type to trip over the bluebells than someone who was able to pick one so quickly and present it so well.

She stayed glued to the spot as he descended towards the outer perimeter of the court. She stared after him and was still looking at him when he was about thirty yards away. He turned back to look at her and even waved at her. She was horrified with herself for not continuing her walk, instead watching him, but she did lift her hand with the bluebell and wave it at him. The next instant he was through the back gate in the wall and out of her sight.

She blushed and felt a pleasant tingling in all parts of her body.

She followed him slowly to the gate, crossed the yard and went up the stairs into her room. Immediately she picked up a leather jug and went downstairs again to fill it with water. Once back in her room she placed the bluebell in the jug, which she positioned on the low table by her bed.

What did he mean by the 'best of meetings' she wondered, sitting on her bed. He had been very forward she thought, but not too much. He had been very sweet but not sickly.

She decided to forget the whole incident and concentrate on how to tell Llywelyn of her intention of going home. But that was difficult with the bluebell standing upright and bold, yet beautiful, by her bed.

It was not long before they met again at the edge of the wood. This time the conversation lasted much longer – almost as if they had planned to meet. They talked about their roles at the court and their likes and dislikes, their favourite poets and songs, their favourite places and anything else that came to their minds.

They met frequently at the edge of the wood and found a fallen tree trunk to sit on as they whiled the time away chatting. Beth still had not spoken to Llywelyn regarding her intentions.

Tudor was at least ten years older than Beth, but to her this was an attraction. After all Llywelyn was far older than her, over twenty years, and she knew that she had fallen for him.

It soon became apparent to Beth that Tudor was showing interest in her in a way that Llywelyn had never done. Tudor would touch her tentatively on her hand occasionally during their meetings as though to test whether she would object. She did not object but found herself liking the touch and wishing he would touch her again and more often. But Tudor took things gently and at a pace that he knew Beth could cope with and yet leave her hoping for more contact.

On her own she did think of Llywelyn, he was the prince that she had always dreamt of but was now out of her reach. Tudor was no prince but her love had been ignited by Llywelyn. She still dreamt of him but less frequently than before, simply because her mind was becoming increasingly occupied by Tudor.

Beth was pleased and flattered to have Tudor's attention and the two became close with the relationship developing gradually, carefully nurtured by Tudor into a loving one.

Though nothing happened quickly with Tudor (and there were times when she did think that he was the ponderous person that she had at first thought he was before he gave her the bluebell), she knew that they were making progress and it was in the direction she desired.

One day in June they were standing in their favourite spot at the edge of the woodland where they first met, when Tudor nervously put his arm around her waist and guided her gently and carefully saying to her softly, "Let's go behind this tree."

By now she had total confidence in him and willingly went behind the great tree. There he kissed her in a way that gave her more pleasure than she had ever experienced before.

They parted with Tudor returning to the court and Beth remaining in the woods to savour the moment that had just passed. She did not wish to return to her room and walked uphill further into the woods. The further she penetrated the wood the darker it became but she did not fear the darkness caused by the thick canopy of leaves.

Facing downwards she stepped carefully over some fallen branches and twigs and, after walking like this for a few yards up the slope, she stopped to rest and lifted her gaze and stared into the darkness ahead of her. It was silent, dark and foreboding ahead when she heard a voice inside her head asking 'was that a passionate kiss or was it just a peck?' She knew she was only at the early learning stages of love and perhaps, on reflection, the kiss did lack passion, but for her it was a start.

Beth turned on her heels and went back down the slope determined to ignore what she might have thought earlier.

However, soon after that kiss in June, Beth and Tudor were engaged to be married and within a short time the two were married by the bishop himself at the cathedral church in Bangor in the presence of Llywelyn and Eleanor, the Princess of Wales.

Llywelyn was delighted by the match, as was the bishop and those two were seen to smile in each other's company for the first time in years.

Beth and Tudor made their vows to each other publically at the ceremony and additional vows in the evening privately to each other, coming to their own understanding of married life. They settled down to live at the court continuing with their separate lives but now shared the same roof.

Tudor would occasionally visit the bishop.

Every evening Tudor would show great interest in Beth's conversations with Eleanor during the day and in all the court's gossip. She had plenty to relate to him as she was privy to much of the court's business through her association and friendship with Eleanor. She knew the advisers and their views on all matters of state. Tudor was keen to hear everything and always listened carefully.

Chapter 5
August 1279 to May 1281

B ETH HAD AN important role at the court, with Eleanor requiring considerable support in her duties – Eleanor was accustomed to the courts of France where she had spent most of her life. Her imprisonment, for nearly the best part of three years after leaving France, was humane relative to what Edward normally handed out. Even so, it would not have been a pleasant experience for a young woman and had frightened and damaged her confidence.

Even walking freely in the countryside was a privilege for her and she did a lot of it. During her imprisonment, walking was something she had missed. So walking in the woods above Garth Celyn, and up to the ancient fort was a new experience for her and the views on a fine day were breathtaking and had a calming effect on her soul.

Frequently, she and Beth went down to the beach to collect shells and bathe their feet in the gentle waves. Sometimes they would go onto the sands when the sea was out and even run races with each other across the flat sandy banks.

Beth had told her the story of William de Braose who had an affair with Joan, Llywelyn the Great's wife, and how William had been hung in the marshy land between the court and the sea. Every time they passed the place where the hanging took place, they would cross themselves, but immediately afterwards would exchange naughty smiles at the thought of the infidelity.

Beth would accompany Eleanor to the church daily and they

would pray together. Eleanor relied on Beth for interpretation of language idioms and ideas. Thus they became good friends and within a short time the two had become inseparable. Llywelyn was pleased with the relationship because he knew that Beth was a reliable companion for Eleanor. While Eleanor's own servants were dependable and good to her, he encouraged the friendship with Beth and when he had to be away from court he knew that his wife was in good company.

Everyone hoped that she would become pregnant and produce an heir as soon as possible. Wiser heads knew that it would take time for Eleanor and Llywelyn to get to know each other and for her to relax in her new home.

Beth hoped that Eleanor would not get too pressurised by what was expected of her. However, the fact that nothing was happening for Eleanor was helping to draw attention away from the fact that nothing was actually happening for her either.

The relationship between Beth and Tudor was very good and they were very happy in each other's company, which was obvious for all to see. They talked a lot every evening and were very thoughtful of each other. But while they lived under the same roof and shared the same bed she knew there was no possibility of her becoming pregnant. She very much regretted this but was determined not to let it spoil her relationship with Tudor, she knew in her very being that it was only a matter of time before Tudor's confidence grew.

She could remember their conversation on their wedding night as though it were only yesterday and not, by then, close to two years earlier.

Tudor had sat with her in the evening on the edge of their bed and said to her, "I want us to share everything; I want us to tell each other everything and to be honest with each other about everything."

It was easy for Beth to agree because it was exactly what she wanted and so her reply was, "Yes, yes, please let us be like that with each other."

Tudor had picked up on the last few words and said, "Yes. Let us share everything with each other only. We will have many secrets, trivial ones and important ones, but we will not share them with anyone else – they will be just between the two of us."

"Yes," she said again with enthusiasm.

It was then that Tudor had gone to his black box which he kept under the bed and brought out a few pages of scripture which he had himself copied.

"Let us make a vow on these pages that we will tell each other everything, but never tell any of our secrets to anyone else and if we do so may God strike us dead."

They had both vowed those words with their right hands on the pages. Beth remembered seeing the relief on Tudor's face after they had made that vow to each other.

Under the terms of that vow, they lived happily together: Tudor spending most days helping to read and write letters for members of Llywelyn's court, though he did not attend meetings where matters of state importance were discussed or decided upon. Beth attended to Eleanor and her servants, and what was needed to keep her and Tudor contented at the royal court.

Life continued in the usual hectic manner with the hope rising daily that Eleanor would become pregnant. The older women were looking for signs of changes around the eyes. The phases of the moon were studied carefully for any signs of cause and effect. Eleanor's servants, two elderly spinsters well versed in the ways of the world, were dedicated to her and gave nothing away.

Beth, on her part, genuinely knew nothing, and could

honestly say to those who quizzed her that she and Eleanor did not discuss such matters and that she just wished Eleanor well and that she was confident that, given time, there would be a happy outcome. Of course, these same words applied to her position as well. Beth would also like to become pregnant.

The months went by and 1280 came and went with no change in Eleanor's or Beth's conditions. Beth had been married since July 1279 but Eleanor, however, had been married since October 1278 and by the spring of 1281 had been married for over two years. The pressure on her, though never expressed directly to her, was mounting and she felt the weight of expectation on her shoulders.

On the second Sunday in May 1281 a messenger arrived at Garth Celyn. He had arrived by boat on the shoreline to the east of the court. The man had sailed from the Brittany coast having travelled from Rome where he had met the Pope on Llywelyn's behalf. He had spent years as Llywelyn's envoy in Rome and was accustomed to putting Llywelyn's case to the Pope. His task was a vital one and when Llywelyn had been excommunicated, he had worked hard to stop it, but the king's representatives, who had more political weight and money, carried the day.

Even so, the work in Rome was very important and the envoy was highly regarded and respected at the court and was warmly welcomed with a feast prepared in his honour. No-one at the court, not even Llywelyn, would have known when he was due to arrive, not even that he was on his way.

Llywelyn's court had learnt its lessons since the capture of the ship bringing Eleanor from France. The king and his agents must have known of the crossing in advance and arranged for the interception, capturing Eleanor, her brother and two friars accompanying her, throwing Llywelyn and his court into disarray and despondency.

Beth met the messenger at the feast that night and found him to be a very serious man, but he was not named when introduced to her, only referred to as our man in Rome. Beth slept alone that night, because Tudor had gone to the cathedral in Bangor and stayed the night there dining with the bishop and other priests.

The next day, shortly before she was due to meet Eleanor, Llywelyn came to visit her. He was accompanied by his new chancellor, Goronwy ap Heilyn, and Beth knew that something was wrong and immediately thought that Tudor had been injured or, even worse, had been killed.

After exchanging pleasantries quickly, Llywelyn said, "Beth, you met our Rome ambassador last night."

A strange question she thought which immediately put her on alert while she answered affirmatively.

"Well, he has come back from Rome with a strange story. What he said was that when he went to plead our case over the dispute over land in mid Wales and to argue that Welsh law should prevail, he found that the Pope had somehow had a prior warning about our case and had been well briefed as to the main points of our arguments. It was clear to our ambassador that someone had informed the king's representative in Rome on what arguments to use to counter our claims. As a result our ambassador failed to obtain the Pope's support, but did some private investigation and found that indeed, the king's representative in Rome was fully aware of what case we were to make before it was presented to the Pope. In other words he had been informed beforehand. We would like to know by whom, so as not to make our ambassador's work more difficult than it is already. We had suspected a leak to the king's representative in Rome earlier concerning land that belonged to Eleanor in France, but it was not as obvious as in this case."

Beth knew immediately that she was a suspect; otherwise she would not be questioned like this. Eleanor had told her what the ambassador was trying to achieve in Rome regarding the case and about her own claim to land in France.

Beth, of course, as part of her vow to Tudor had told him what she had been told by Eleanor.

That much she knew had happened. What she did not know was whether Tudor had told someone else. Had he broken his promise to her?

She was now torn between her allegiance to her prince and her vow to her husband. She remained silent thinking what to do and hoping Llywelyn would give her time to ask Tudor before she had to confess anything to Llywelyn.

But the chancellor, seeing Llywelyn and her hesitate, asked the key question directly, "Did you know the details of this case Beth?"

She had no alternative now other than to answer directly; any hesitation would be disastrous and she would lose Llywelyn's confidence and Tudor would be in great trouble whether he was involved or not. Visions of William de Braose hanging there in the marshland came to her mind.

Only honesty would now work for her and Tudor. "Yes," she said. "Eleanor was worried about the case and discussed it with me a few months ago."

The worst was over perhaps, she hoped. But it wasn't.

The chancellor asked keenly, "Did you tell anyone what you knew?"

She had to be honest. "Yes. I told Tudor."

Both Llywelyn and his chancellor seemed relieved if not pleased, which surprised Beth.

Then came the next question, again from the chancellor. "Did Tudor tell anyone?"

"I don't know," she replied honestly. "He made a vow to me

as I did to him that what was said between us would remain between us only. So he should not have told anyone. I did not think there was any significance to what I told him. If he has told someone else then I am very sorry and can only think he has slipped it out by mistake. He is a good man, Llywelyn," she pleaded with visions of a hanging clear in her mind.

Llywelyn nodded his head as though he agreed with her, but the chancellor made no such movement and said nothing but looked grimly at the two of them.

Llywelyn made to go out of the room saying as he departed, "We need time now to think things through. Stay in your room until I or someone will come back to talk to you."

They left her sitting on the edge of her bed, with tears rapidly building under her eyelids before bursting down her cheeks. She was lonely, upset and afraid of what was going to happen to her and Tudor as she heard the chancellor ordering a guard for her room.

Alone, she began to wonder had Tudor told anything about the case to anyone. Had he broken his vow to her, his wife. She assumed that Llywelyn, as soon as he heard from the ambassador about what had happened, had questioned all who had knowledge of the case, which would probably be about half a dozen people at most. He must have questioned them all or was about to do so.

Eleanor would have told him that she had told her but was she the only one to know the details outside Llywelyn's inner circle? She desperately hoped not.

She remained on the edge of the bed and looked sideways at the jug containing bluebells she had collected earlier in the day. She bent her body forward and covered her face with her hands, her spirits broken; she cried without restraint.

Time went by very slowly and eventually she heard the bell that would normally signal the time for her and Tudor to go to bed. They were obviously going to leave her to worry all night in the hope that she would divulge more in the morning.

CHAPTER 6

May 1281

About an hour after the bell had rung, Llywelyn and the chancellor returned to her room but behaved in a less friendly manner with Llywelyn demanding to know when would Tudor be returning.

"Late tomorrow morning," she replied. "I am so sorry, so sorry, Llywelyn," she pleaded through her tears.

Neither man replied.

"Am I your only suspect?" she asked.

Both nodded, confirming her suspicions.

"I am going to be honest and open with you, hoping that will save lives and help us to resolve this affair," Llywelyn said grimly.

He was deadly serious now and Beth knew that it was a matter of life and death.

"When it was first mooted that Tudor was to come here, I was not very happy to have an envoy of Anian's working here in the court. But, when he arrived I found him a pleasant and honest person as indeed we all did. Then he very quickly swore allegiance to me and to the court. This gave us confidence in him and I welcomed him to our midst and he certainly has helped with the relationship between me and Anian.

"Then to top it all he married you. I know you are loyal to me just like your father has been over the years and under difficult circumstances at times. I trust you implicitly and I therefore trusted Tudor implicitly."

He paused for a second or two before continuing. "I know I sometimes tend to place my trust in people I should not trust and, even now have difficulty in not trusting my brother Dafydd, though I know him to have been untrustworthy in the past. But that is my weakness; it is a fault of mine. However, we are now fairly certain that Tudor has passed the information to Anian who then passed it to one of the king's agents in Bangor. The information went to the king's ambassador in Rome so that when we presented our case, the king's ambassador had all the relevant answers at his fingertips and won his case. Too much information and detail was passed on for it to be an accidental slip of the tongue. It must have been a deliberate act. I will have to regard it as an act of treason and there will have to be dire consequences." The chancellor nodded gravely in agreement.

"Beth, if he has done it, do you think he will confess?" Llywelyn asked.

"I don't know," she said through tears. "If he has done it then the bishop must have some strong hold on him."

"If he has done it, he will be hanged tomorrow," replied the chancellor.

Upon hearing this Beth burst out sobbing. "What can I do?"

The chancellor had overplayed his hand, and to a very intelligent young woman. Through her tears she looked up at him and said, "If you hang him and he is working for Anian, you will incur the bishop's wrath and the wrath of God on yourself. They will excommunicate you again and your relationship with the king will deteriorate faster and further than before."

Then looking directly at Llywelyn, she added, "People want peace not another war, Llywelyn."

Looking at his chancellor he asked, "What's to be done? She has a point."

Before they could say any more Beth said, "Let me talk to him tomorrow when he returns and see if I can find out what he has done and try to find a way out of all of this in a way that will be to your advantage. If we can get him to spy on the bishop for you, then you can at least gain an insight to your opponents thinking and possibly their plans."

After much thought they agreed, but the guard would stay on the door until Tudor came back and she was to be given no more than half an hour to talk to him on her own.

They left her to her own thoughts and tears for the night. She slept not a wink but puzzled on the problem. She was fairly convinced in her own mind that, for some reason, it was Tudor who had passed the information to the bishop or some agent of the king.

She wondered if Tudor could be convinced to become an agent for Llywelyn to avoid the rope around his neck and possibly her own at the same time. If he could be, then he would be of value to Llywelyn and his cause.

She trusted Llywelyn above all but there were grave doubts in her mind now about Tudor – had he broken his vow to her? If she had had any idea that he would have passed the knowledge on to Anian, she would not have told him anything.

After a sleepless night, she was disturbed early by the guard with her breakfast and Llywelyn and the chancellor returned. She had hoped to be left to her own thoughts until Tudor returned, but clearly they wanted to make sure that she had not changed her mind and would get Tudor to tell the truth.

Having established this, they left. She felt confident of Llywelyn's support and was aware that what she had proposed was very attractive to them. She hoped it would work out as she waited for Tudor.

It was a long wait. He was not back at Garth Celyn until mid afternoon. When he was escorted into Beth's room he realised that there was something wrong and asked, "What's the matter?"

She hissed to him under her breath, "Wait until we are alone."

The soldiers left. "What's wrong?" he asked.

"Some six months ago I told you that Eleanor had a case that was to be presented to the Pope and I told you the details of her arguments. You promised that you would not pass that type of information on to anyone. Have you kept your promise or have you told someone?"

He hesitated slightly, flustered ever so slightly but then replied firmly, "No, I haven't. Definitely not. What makes you ask such a question? You know I wouldn't say it to anyone."

She'd had much longer than him to sort her mind out and was prepared with her questions.

"Llywelyn knows that someone has passed on the information and he knows it's you or I. I have told him what I told you about six weeks ago. I know I have not told anyone else, so it must be you. To save your neck, you need to be honest about it and admit if you have told someone because there is a possibility that Llywelyn will hang us both at the same place his grandfather hanged William de Braose."

She was losing patience with him and continued, this time, shouting at him, "Stop and think. Did you tell anyone? Be honest. Remember this is a dangerous game. They may know more than they are telling me. They can catch us lying and if they do it's amen for the two of us."

His colour had drained. He was pale and she thought that she could see that he was at last frightened. "I am a fool," he said. "I said it by mistake to the bishop hoping that he would be able to assist Eleanor's case. It just slipped out. I was trying to be helpful."

Beth was not crying; she had cried enough. "What about your vow to me? I trusted you. They will not believe that you said it by mistake. I can tell you they think it was done on purpose and that you did it because you are working for Anian and so indirectly for the king. Llywelyn thinks it's treason and we will be fortunate if we see tomorrow."

He shuffled uncomfortably.

"Now," she said. "I want the full truth. Are you a spy for Anian or the king?"

There was a hesitation again before he opened his mouth to speak. Beth did not give him a chance this time. "You hesitated to think what lie you can tell me. It won't do. I need to know the truth before I can plead your case with Llywelyn. The chancellor, I can tell you, wants us both strung up."

She allowed him a few seconds to think and then asked again, "Are you Anian's spy at this court?"

"He does ask me to tell him what is going on and what the thinking here is on various issues," he said sheepishly.

"That's it then. You are working for Anian and therefore for the king."

"I don't see it that way Beth," he pleaded.

She was having none of it.

"You are a spy and the first thing is for you to admit that to Llywelyn."

Looking at her he said, "But that means he would hang me."

"Possibly," she said. "But if we can show that you will be more use to him alive than dead, he might spare you and me."

"How can I do that?"

"Promise to work for Llywelyn. Get information for him about what Anian is thinking and doing. You could try to find out what the king's intentions and plans are. They must trust you because the information you gave about Eleanor's land in France was correct and of use to them."

"Would that work? I'm willing to do anything."

"You would have to produce some good information – something that's of value to him."

"I could do it."

"You need to think carefully about it. There is no point saying something now to save your neck today. It's got to be workable and Llywelyn and the chancellor will have to be convinced that, if they accept your offer, you won't escape to England the next time you meet the bishop."

"I see," he said, more pensive now realising that it was not going to be simple to get out of the mess he was in.

"Your biggest problem is to convince Llywelyn that you will be acting for him and not the bishop. You must give Llywelyn something substantial that will convince him it will be worth him keeping you alive."

"What do you know that would be of value to Llywelyn, but that if the bishop knew you had divulged he would want you killed?"

"Like what?"

"I don't know what information you have. But I know you had better think of something quickly," she pleaded.

"The king is constantly asking about the strength of Llywelyn's forces."

"I would have thought that Llywelyn is well aware of that," she said with disdain. "Can you name his agents in Gwynedd? Is there anyone else working at Garth Celyn. I think if you are to save your own neck, you will have to put someone else in peril of losing theirs."

He hesitated, realising the seriousness of what she wanted him to do.

"Don't just name anyone you may dislike because you will need proof."

"Proof?"

"Yes Tudor, proof. They are not fools, no more than you are. Please remember my neck is on the line also."

"Well I can name Anian."

"They know that and he unfortunately is untouchable."

Just then they heard the guard addressing Llywelyn outside the door and a second later Llywelyn and his chancellor barged into the room, just like Llywelyn's grandfather had barged in on his wife decades earlier.

They were in no mood for any compromise. Llywelyn blurted out, "Has he confessed?"

Beth and Tudor answered together with a resounding yes.

This took the wind out of Llywelyn's sails and he mumbled, "I see."

"Who are you working for?" he asked.

"Anian," said Tudor going on his knees and begging for mercy.

"And who is he working for?" asked the chancellor.

"The king, I think," came the nervous reply.

Beth could see that the chancellor wanted an instant hanging. She could see that even if Llywelyn would spare her, Tudor was to be hung. "It's worth thinking things out," she said. "There is nothing to be gained by acting in haste. Tudor tells me that he is willing to work for you Llywelyn, and get information that will be of value to you. It would be like having a person working on your behalf in the king's court and supplying you with valuable information."

"It's worth a try, I suppose," said Llywelyn glancing at his chancellor.

"How can we trust him? He can turncoat again once we release him," said the chancellor.

Beth intervened quickly again. "Tudor surely knows the names of the other agents working for the king in Gwynedd and elsewhere," she said. "Surely that would be very useful information."

"I suppose it would," admitted the chancellor. "What are their names?"

"If you can name some agents I will spare you," said Llywelyn. "I need convincing that you are truly repentant."

Tudor realised how well Beth knew Llywelyn. He knew he had to give some information away to save himself, and he had to do it quickly to avoid raising any suspicion that he was making it up and lying.

"Anian, as you suspect, is the king's chief source of information in Gwynedd. He had me placed here through his influence over Madog, the archdeacon, who is totally unaware of what is going on. I do, however, know of another agent."

"And who is he?" asked the chancellor.

"If I name him to you, what's stopping you hanging me after I've named him?"

Beth stepped into the breach again, "If you can get Llywelyn to trust you now by giving him information that is of value, then he will spare your life in the hope that you can give him more valuable information in the future. Don't you see you are in an ideal position to do that."

The three men appreciated the logic of her argument and the possible benefits.

"Now name an informer. There is much sense in what Beth says and I will go along with it if you name the correct person," said Llywelyn, hinting that he already knew the name and was testing Tudor.

"Well," Tudor procrastinated. Clearly he didn't wish to give any name but with the thought of a noose tightening around his neck he said, with great uncertainty, "I see Hywel ap Gruffudd at the cathedral when I am there waiting to see Anian."

His voice was breaking as he ended the sentence and realised the enormity of what he had done.

There was silence. It was not a name they expected.

Tudor added quickly, "I don't know any more. All I'm saying is that I have seen him there."

Llywelyn and his chancellor were dumbfounded. They knew that if it was true, Hywel betraying Llywelyn was very serious indeed. Hywel ap Gruffudd was from a trusted family and a grandson of Ednyfed Fychan, who had served the Gwynedd dynasty loyally and brilliantly.

"Oh my God. What have I done? Are you going to kill him?" asked Tudor. "I just see him there and I think he is there to give information to Anian. I don't think you should trust him, that's all I know."

"It's no longer your worry," said the chancellor. "It's up to Llywelyn what happens to him and what happens to you."

"Yes. Your concern now is to find out as much as you can about Anian and the king's plans in Gwynedd and elsewhere," said Llywelyn.

He continued, "So as not to cause suspicion at the court here, you and Beth are free to live your lives as you did before. But be sure that you will be watched carefully Tudor. If you double-cross us you will be dealt with without any mercy. We are giving you a second chance."

"Thank you my Lord," said Tudor going on his knees and kissing Llywelyn's hands.

Beth looked at Llywelyn and said, humbly, "Thank you, Llywelyn." She felt confident that Llywelyn appreciated what she had done and felt his anger was directed at Tudor. She was not so sure of the chancellor, but knew she could rely on Llywelyn to put him right.

Just as Llywelyn was leaving she said, "I will need to talk to Eleanor about all this please."

"Yes," he replied. "She wants to talk to you also. Go and see her in about half an hour. I will have spoken to her by then."

Left alone Beth and Tudor had to resolve their differences and arrive at a new understanding.

She was furious with him and made it clear to him that the

vow to share everything was broken and she would no longer tell him anything of what she heard about the place and certainly not what she was told by Eleanor or any of the key people at court. She was not sure in herself that she would ever be trusted at the royal court again and knew that she would have to work hard to regain the courtiers' trust in her.

Having vented her full anger at him and knowing how close they had come to losing their lives she, this time, set out the new terms of their marriage. She made it clear to him that, having saved his life, she expected him to tell her everything of what happened between him and Anian and everything that was said by Anian.

She reminded him that their relationship had been like that between a brother and sister and she made it clear to him that was now how she wanted it to continue.

Tudor accepted her terms for their relationship and that he would report everything that was said at the cathedral to her and to Llywelyn.

After her tirade at Tudor, Beth calmed and went to see Eleanor. Llywelyn was there too and was expecting her.

He welcomed her into the room warmly.

Beth instantly apologised to Eleanor for divulging their conversations with Tudor.

Eleanor was crying but accepted the apology and said that she should never have given such personal information to Beth. She said that she always shared everything with Llywelyn and understood why she shared everything with Tudor. She knew all that and felt she should share some of the blame.

Eleanor was very keen that their relationship continued. She valued their discussions together and their friendship, and she would be very lonely without Beth's companionship.

With Llywelyn's blessing they agreed that things would continue as they had been for everybody's benefit.

Beth told them what agreement she had come to with Tudor, but avoided mentioning the intimate details. She was convinced that Llywelyn knew that Tudor was the rotten apple in the barrel and she hoped that the decisions taken that afternoon would be the right ones and that Tudor would to be kept under close observation in the future.

What feelings she had for Tudor had been decimated in a matter of a few hours.

CHAPTER 7

May 1281 – after Tudor's confession

Llywelyn insisted that the guard remained at Beth's door and that Tudor was not allowed out.

Instead of returning to her own room, she went walking down the gentle slope towards the beach, passing the marsh without giving it a glance. She did not want to see Tudor for a while at least; she wanted time and space to think. The room, Tudor, and even Garth Celyn was not the right place to be and the woods above the court reminded her too much of Tudor and the way she had been deceived by him.

It was cold for May and the clouds were rushing from the west across Anglesey towards the Isle of Man. She thought they were too high for rain and looked backwards at the mountains and saw that the clouds cleared the hills above Garth Celyn and felt confident that there was no rain imminently. She wrapped the shawl around her head and increased her pace towards the beach.

She could see Anglesey clearly in the distance and the sea she knew, from her experience of living so close to it, was gradually ebbing away from the high tide line which it had reached less than half an hour earlier.

Down on the beach, the breeze worked its magic on her breathing and her mind. The sound of the waves dulled her nerves. She began to breathe the salty air deeply into her lungs and could physically feel her shoulder muscles relax.

Her initial thoughts were to leave and go home to her father in Aberedw, but they did not last long as she walked along the beach in the direction of Aberogwen and Bangor. As her mind focused on her position, that of being married to a traitor whom Llywelyn could hang any day, she realised that Llywelyn would not let her leave without knowing what had recently taken place. Neither would she wish to leave him in his hour of need. He still meant too much to her.

Having decided that she would have to remain at Garth Celyn, her thoughts turned to find a solution to her predicament with Llywelyn and Tudor.

She was relieved that Llywelyn had taken heed of what she had said about Tudor's betrayal. She felt confident that she had gained influence with Llywelyn and that he respected her views and advice, now on a semi-political level. This gave her hope, encouragement and an ambition to be more involved in the court's decisions. Having tasted power, she wanted more. After all, she had saved Tudor's life.

And as for Tudor, she now despised him and did not want to share her life with him. She felt betrayed and let down by him. Betrayed by the fact that he was a traitor and let down by the fact that he had not given her the love that she wanted, having promised so much.

He had been a good companion but she wanted more. She wanted to be loved and she wanted children.

She resolved that if these needs were not to be satisfied, she would make her own life and being a support for Llywelyn could replace those basic needs of her body.

She then turned her mind to Tudor's behaviour the previous day and it kept recurring to her that his pointing a finger at the bishop was too simple. Tudor knew that Llywelyn disliked Anian and that accusing him of cooperating with the king would go down well with Llywelyn.

It dawned on her that there might be another person who

could be getting the information from Tudor. Many people visited the cathedral at Bangor and Tudor could be meeting any one of these at any time. They could even meet casually in the street outside the cathedral. She and Llywelyn had been far too naive. During his visit to Bangor he could be meeting Anian and meeting another person separately – there were many possibilities.

She decided that she would go and see Llywelyn as soon as she could and warn him of the possibility that Tudor was lying. She would try to convince Llywelyn that it was best to keep to the agreement with Tudor and allow her to elicit the truth from him, restrict more severely what he would learn and feed him false information.

When she returned to the court she went to seek out Llywelyn, but he had gone out hunting for the afternoon to the hills. He wanted a break from the treachery that he had discovered and, like Beth, wanted to clear his head to consider more fully what steps to take.

Beth, in the meantime, spoke to Eleanor and expressed her new ideas. Eleanor, who was still raw from the whole affair, managed to smile and say, "Llywelyn and I discussed the very same thing in bed last night and I believe the chancellor is of the same opinion."

Beth nodded her head and thought if everyone had come to the same conclusion then it must have been right.

Eleanor continued, "When Llywelyn comes back, I will ask him to call you here and he can talk about how to extract the truth out of Tudor."

Beth was pleased and said, "Good. I'll give it some further thought."

She got up to leave Eleanor but was asked to sit down again because Eleanor had more important things to tell her.

"Don't leave just yet. These affairs of state can be so tedious.

Let me show you a new dress I've had from France. It was brought here with the messenger from Rome."

Beth was delighted with the dress and stayed to admire it for quite a while.

The guard was at her door when she returned and remained there until he was relieved later in the afternoon. Beth and Tudor had little to say to each other. He occasionally tried to apologise to her but she refused to listen to his weak excuses and spent time at the window looking at the sea gradually ebbing away and wondered how she could stay in the same room as her husband during the days and weeks to come. However, the sounds of the hunting party returning livened up the court and Beth.

It was not long before she was summoned to meet Llywelyn and, as she entered the hall where he sat with his chancellor and Eleanor, Beth with a forced smile asked, "Did you enjoy the hunt?"

"Yes," he replied and the chancellor agreed heartily.

"Oh good," she commented, worried that the meeting might not go well for her.

"Come and sit here Beth, next to Eleanor," Llywelyn said in good humour beckoning her to sit.

"I take it that Eleanor has told you what my thoughts are and I think you are of the same opinion," she said, looking at the two men in turn. They nodded agreement under her gaze and she continued quickly, "Then, I believe there is more to be gained now by letting Tudor think we have believed him, but we keep a close eye on him and feed him with false information when possible."

"We agree with you and are very impressed by your thinking and advice on this matter," Llywelyn said, smiling at her. "It is better to be cautious and not act too hastily in this case."

"Thank you," she replied, letting her gaze fall to the ground for an instance. Then picking her head up and glancing at

Eleanor for approval she said, "Llywelyn, you know that, like my father I will be loyal to you and our country through thick and thin. Please believe me, I am very disappointed with myself that I did not question Tudor's loyalty to you and to me long before now. He was in an ideal position to carry gossip, if nothing else, from here to Bangor."

The chancellor agreed with her and said, "We have all been naive Beth. We must be more aware of our enemy's power of espionage and intrigue."

Eleanor agreed with him and said, "Just think of the way the king captured me and my brother. He must have been informed somehow by an agent working here or in France. He or his officials must have known exactly what our plans were. I can't bear to think that someone I knew and trusted in France would do that and it must be equally difficult for you to imagine the same here. Some people are horrible."

Towards the end of these words Eleanor started to cry and Llywelyn put his arm around her and Beth placed her hand in hers from the other side.

"Yes," said Llywelyn. "We need to be more careful and aware that there are agents around us who wish us harm."

Eleanor asked rhetorically, "Why do people behave so dishonestly?"

The chancellor, however, attempted to answer her and replied, "There are probably possible many reasons; they might want rewards, money or favours; they may be blackmailed to do it or they may want revenge for some reason or another."

Before she could stop herself Beth added, "Ambition for power may also be a strong reason for such behaviour."

"Have you anyone in mind?" asked Llywelyn quickly.

"Not really," replied Beth hesitantly.

"Come on Beth. Tell us. I've always admired your honesty from the first time we met."

She hesitated again before saying, "I think we should consider all possibilities. Your brother Dafydd has always wanted to be the Prince of Wales. He has always wanted to lead the Welsh and he has already shown that he will go to great lengths to achieve his ambition. I need not remind you of his plot against you with Gruffydd ap Gwenwynwyn not so many years ago. Then in the last war he was against you and, of course, gained the land east of the Conwy as a result of the treaty."

She stopped and looked at Llywelyn expecting to see great anger on his face, but he was calm.

"Carry on," he said.

"No," she said. "I have already said too much and I know how fond you are of Dafydd."

"I need to know everything. Tell me your whole view on the matter."

"Well," she ventured. "I believe that Dafydd wants to rule Gwynedd. I believe that he is driven by that single but overwhelming ambition. If that is the case, he will want to know exactly what you are thinking and doing. He will have his own men watching every move you make."

"But if I don't have an heir, Wales will be his anyway," he said looking at Eleanor and holding her tight. "But we are hopeful, aren't we Eleanor?"

Eleanor smiled and whispered, "Yes."

Beth stepped in, "It's early days and we are all hopeful for you."

"Yes indeed," agreed the chancellor.

"I would have said the same thing for you only a few days ago," said Llywelyn looking at Beth. "But now I don't know what your wishes are."

"My troubles and burdens will have to be my own, at least for a while longer," she replied sadly.

"Let us return to my brother, Dafydd. Beth, you think that he has agents working for him here at Garth Celyn?"

"I don't know," she said. "But common sense tells me it's possible, indeed likely."

Llywelyn was silent for a while and Beth was afraid that she had gone too far in her assertions. But, looking now at the chancellor, he asked, "Do you think it's likely?"

"I think it's possible, Llywelyn. I think we need to bear it in mind and be careful."

"But what gossip would be of value to him?"

Beth was ready with the answer. "Suppose that Eleanor becomes pregnant, then Dafydd would not follow you and he could again try to have you killed. All information is valuable to him and the fresher it is the better, giving him longer to plan."

Llywelyn was silent.

Beth continued, "Dafydd could be working with Anian and others. We don't know. But I believe it's very important that we try to find out."

"How can we find out Beth? Have you any ideas?"

"Yes," she said. "I think that I should try to get Tudor to think he can trust me and hope that he will divulge, in time, who is involved, who is pulling the strings and why?"

They all looked at her.

"Well? Do you approve?" she asked.

The two men looked at each other and seemed to be of the opinion that there was nothing to lose.

"I need to know that you are in total agreement with my plan because it could appear that I am disloyal to you, Llywelyn, which of course I never will be. But, others may think that, if they are to trust me. So, it's vital that I have your agreement."

Llywelyn was firm, "You have my full agreement provided you keep me informed, which I am confident you will."

Having agreed, the chancellor raised the question of what was to be done with Hywel, the man named by Tudor.

Beth suggested, "We need to find out exactly what the truth is and, with your agreement, I can accompany Tudor on his visits to Bangor and see for myself who meets whom and report to you here in Tudor's absence and we can take it from there."

"As you know," Llywelyn said, "Hywel is a powerful man. He is related to my previous chancellors, Goronwy ap Ednyfed and Tudur ap Ednyfed, and has attended the court here many times. He is not a person I can take action against without there being serious consequences and this is not the right time for that. If what Tudor says is true, then we need to know what he is doing in the cathedral at the same time as Tudor."

The chancellor added, "I don't understand why Tudor would name him unless he knows more than he is admitting."

CHAPTER 8

May 1281 – later same day

BETH RETURNED TO her own room prepared to challenge her husband. She acknowledged the guard and entered.

Tudor was glad and relieved to see her and mumbled a greeting sheepishly.

She did not answer.

"Are you still very angry with me; I can understand if you are. I have been very foolish putting both of our lives at risk."

"Hmm!"

"I should never have married you," he said. "They made me."

"What?" turning to face him. "What did you say?"

He repeated his statement and she replied fiercely this time, ignoring what he had said, "If you and I are to survive this we must work together and we must trust each other. Unfortunately I can't take your word on trust any more. I will need proof frequently that you are telling the truth and the whole truth."

"I should never have married you Beth," he said again. "They made me. They forced me. I had no choice. "

"You shouldn't have married me? What you mean is I shouldn't have married you."

"I will never lie to you again Beth," he said earnestly. "I will tell you everything. You can trust me from now on."

"Good," she said. "Who forced you to marry me? Tell me, because it certainly wasn't me nor my family and I don't believe it was Llywelyn. So who was it?" She was livid with him and her anger was forthright.

He kept quiet not daring to face her fury.

"Tell me, who was it Tudor? Who told you what to do?"

"The truth is, I don't really know. I was sent here to get information about Llywelyn, his advisers, their views and any court gossip and to take it back to Bangor. At the beginning I only met Bishop Anian and discussed with him issues which vexed Llywelyn. He would ask me what things were like here and he showed some interest, but that's all. But that did not last long. After the first few meetings, I met another man wearing the habit of a black monk and he questioned me about all the comings and goings at this court. I honestly don't know who he is, Beth. But I have been telling him everything I'm afraid."

"Who is he?"

"I don't know. He wears a habit with a black hood and always speaks from behind a screen."

"Why are you doing it? Tell me honestly why? You must have a good reason."

"As you know I learnt my skills of reading and writing as a monk with the Cistercians in the abbey at Aberconwy. I left there to work for some of the nobility in England, but I was paid very little more than getting my food and lodgings and it was an endlessly boring task. All I did was read and write letters for them. Can you imagine it?"

She did not answer and waited for him to continue.

"What I didn't tell you was that I was approached by a man in Chester and asked if I wanted to do a more interesting job and get paid much better. I have no idea who the man was. I expressed interest and he sent me to meet Bishop Anian at the cathedral in Bangor, which I did. I was then appointed to help smooth the relationship between Llywelyn and the bishop. You know the rest. I started here and within weeks I was reporting on everything I saw and heard to the black monk at the cathedral. I can tell you, once you start on that task you can't get out of it. They get their claws into you."

He stopped but she just waited for more information.

"Remember," he continued. "Once you have given them some information they have got you hooked. You have committed treason and the punishment for that is death. So, every time I said I wanted to stop, they threatened to tell Llywelyn what I had done. I was stuck and I couldn't get out of it."

"But who are they that want this information from you?"

"I don't know them, other than I know that the black monk is one of them, and I know they want to know everything about Llywelyn, about Eleanor and what's happening at the royal court. So they must be enemies of Llywelyn."

Beth was not sure if she was getting the whole truth from Tudor and decided on a different line of questioning, hoping to get closer to the truth.

"Why did you marry me, Tudor?" she challenged him.

"The answer to that is simple," he responded without hesitation as though he had rehearsed the answer. "I saw you here at the court and told the black monk about you. I told him that you were not married. He wanted me to get closer to you because of your special relationship with Llywelyn. He told me that his friends wanted me to marry you because they thought I would be of more value to them married to you. They also promised that they would pay me more, if I was married to you."

"I see. You were paid extra after we were married then. Was it worth it?"

He was embarrassed by the question. "I should not have married you. I have felt awful about it all. We should not have married," he said facing downwards and shaking his head, clearly ashamed of what he had done.

"You did not have to marry me because someone told you. Come on Tudor, tell the truth."

"It is the truth. I had to obey them. Also, you are a very beautiful woman and I wanted to be with you. I wanted people to be jealous of me having you in my room. It made me feel important. I wanted to display you, like I would fine clothes or an expensive silver cross around my neck."

"You wanted to possess me for others to admire and for them to envy you?"

With his head down he whispered, "Yes, yes. I started off as a monk and would like to have stayed a monk, but I became greedy for possessions and wealth and it's been my downfall."

"Is this the truth Tudor?"

"Yes, the absolute truth. It's the reason for everything. It's why we live like we do. I could not lie that much to you," he said with an appealing voice. "Please forgive me, Beth."

She did not reply to his wish for forgiveness, mainly because she was not inclined to forgive him for months of feeling desperately guilty. At least she had some explanation now and she did experience some relief.

Beth changed her line of questioning again, taking advantage of his weakness. "Were you telling the truth about Hywel ap Gruffudd?"

"When I named Hywel last night I was frightened and felt sure I was to be hanged and I said anything to try to save my own skin, but it is true that Hywel is at the cathedral when I am there."

"Are you sure that is the whole truth?"

"Yes. If I were Llywelyn I would not trust Hywel. It's just a feeling I have."

"How can Llywelyn find out if he is plotting against him?"

"That's going to be difficult. I don't know the answer to that question."

"You could follow him and see where he goes and what he does and whom he meets in Bangor."

"I have tried."

She pondered on his answer for a moment and then stated, "I will come with you to Bangor in future. You don't mind do you?"

"No," he replied lamely. "I don't suppose I have any options."

"None," she said firmly. "When are you expected next?"

"In two days' time," he replied.

"That's soon isn't it?" She didn't wait for a reply but continued, "Good. I'll see Llywelyn for his approval and then we'll leave together in two days' time."

Beth met Llywelyn early next day and obtained his approval.

CHAPTER 9

May 1281 – two days later

B ETH DEPARTED FOR Bangor with Tudor as planned.
They rode in the company of an ox-drawn cart and travelled at a leisurely pace on another bright, windy day with only the occasional cloud dashing across the sky from the west.

The track they followed brought them to the river Ogwen which had little water in it and was easily forded by the horses, and posed hardly any difficulty for the ox and cart. They climbed the bank opposite slowly before turning north to bring the sea back into view with the Anglesey shore appearing very close by. On reaching the brow they could see the small estuary of the river Cegin below them. There were numerous boats and fishermen's huts around the estuary and stretching along the Hirael beach.

They forded the river Cegin and left the cart to go down towards the beach while they continued their journey westwards towards the cathedral.

As they turned to their left along the edge of the hill, the cathedral gradually came to view. First the top of the bell tower, followed by the presbytery until finally they could see the whole building in all its glory. It was surrounded by smaller buildings of all shapes, arranged in a most haphazard way.

"I will come into the cathedral with you," Beth announced. "If we meet anyone, just introduce me and tell, whoever it is, that I have insisted on coming here today. There is no need to explain in detail, but if you are asked tell them I was bored at Garth Celyn and wanted a change. I won't gate-crash your meetings but will go down to the beach for a walk and come back to the cathedral later in the afternoon."

Tudor was content with that arrangement. They had not discussed the details of their visit to Bangor because Beth was unsure in herself exactly what her objectives were, other than to find out what was going on and put faces to names.

After dismounting and passing their horses to safe hands, they went towards the cathedral together. A short distance from the door, Beth picked up courage, changed her mind and said to him, "I will enter first. Come in a few minutes after I've entered and join me in the nave."

She entered through the main south door into the darkness with the tower on her left. It took a while for her eyes to get accustomed to the darkness.

The inside of the cathedral was spacious with the altar at the eastern end below a window with a rounded arch. At the western end there was the bell tower with a stone base supporting a timber structure with a stairway leading to the upper rooms. The stairway was located immediately to the left of the south entrance.

Beth walked past the stairs to the far side of the building, opposite the entrance.

Shortly, she saw Tudor enter. He looked unsure of himself. She watched as he walked slowly towards the main body of the cathedral looking for her. She watched everything from her position just beyond the edge of the light entering through the open doorway. There were many Bangor commoners inside, coming and going to pray and state their wishes. The few priests about the place all seemed to be doing specific tasks. She was observing them very carefully and wondered which one would be meeting Tudor.

No-one came to meet Tudor when he arrived but she thought that she saw that he was indeed noticed by one of the cathedral helpers as he entered, and that person immediately went to the stairs at the base of the tower and glanced around furtively as he ascended the stairs.

Tudor had, by now, reached the central nave and was looking for Beth. She came out of the darkness and moved towards him. She could see that he was very nervous.

When she was within earshot, she whispered, "Where do you normally meet your contact?"

"In the belfry."

"Stay here near me and see if your contact comes down to look for you. He surely knows you have arrived by now. One of the helpers went upstairs soon after you arrived."

"He just expects me to go up. Sometimes, when we have finished, he does escort me down the stairs but not all the way to the bottom. He normally stays out of sight."

Beth considered this for a moment and Tudor asked her, "What do you want me to do?"

"Do as you normally do. Go up the stairs if that's what's expected of you."

"I'll leave you then?"

"Yes. I'll go out for a while and come back later to pray here and see if I can see him leave. I'll move away from you now. Keep your nerve and remember you have a lot to lose if you double-cross Llywelyn or me." She glared at him as she moved away, threatening him with her eyes.

She watched him ascending the stairs to the belfry and disappear into the darkness.

Beth decided that she would stay a few minutes in the cathedral and then walk around the outside. Its location, at the foot of the wooded hill, made it look smaller than it was but that was the intention of its builders – to keep it hidden from Viking raiders. She saw the tombs of Gruffudd ap Cynan and Owain Gwynedd, both Gwynedd kings and ancestors of Llywelyn.

The cathedral had played a significant part in Welsh history over the centuries and she was pleased to have an opportunity to absorb the atmosphere of the place.

Having seen as much as she wanted of the inside, she came out of the open doorway just as an elegant-looking man, in his late thirties, was about to enter. He was well dressed and proud, walking with confidence and clearly a member of the Welsh nobility.

Beth knew that she had met him before at Garth Celyn but, with the hundreds of people visiting the court every year, she was not sure of his name but guessed that he might be the Hywel named by Tudor.

She turned on her heel and followed him back into the cathedral. He knew exactly where he was going and, after nodding his head briefly in the direction of the altar, made his way past the stairs leading to the belfry and entered a narrow door in the corner at the opposite end of the tower.

He had barely looked at her and she knew he definitely had not recognised her.

She stayed in the cathedral and found a bench to sit on, in a position which gave her a good view of the belfry stairs and the doorway the nobleman had entered. She waited and wondered what was being said upstairs. She wondered if Tudor had spilled the beans and told them that he had been exposed as a spy by Llywelyn and herself.

So far he had told her the truth she believed, and there was no reason why he should not keep to his word. Over the last few days she had come to realise that he was not a very strong character. It had surprised her that she had not noticed it before but she had been a little in awe of him and his ability to read and write so cleverly.

She again became conscious of her surroundings and suddenly aware that there was a monk looking at her. Feeling very uncomfortable, she glanced sideways at others nearby and slowly got up from the bench. She could hear the monk saying to her and to others in that part of the holy building, "People come here to pray and praise God. Those who come here for other reasons are not blessed."

She turned to face the monk to get a good view of him but he had turned his back to her and was walking away from her. She was shaken by his words and felt guilty about misusing the cathedral. However, she sat back on her bench, determined to see her mission to its conclusion.

Sooner than she expected, Tudor came down the stairs unaccompanied. She was disappointed not to see the person whom he had met in the belfry.

He went straight out of the cathedral without noticing her, probably thinking he'd meet her where their horses were tethered. She decided to wait for the nobleman to appear because she had already decided to follow him.

Barely a minute after Tudor went out, the nobleman appeared in the doorway in the corner. He bowed his head towards the altar and made for the doorway. Beth got up from her bench and followed him out of the cathedral. He was about ten yards ahead of her when she stood in the doorway. She delayed a little to give him a better start and then followed him, making a slight detour to whisper to Tudor by the horses, "Is that man Hywel?"

Tudor was surprised but managed to nod his head to her indicating that it was indeed Hywel.

"Does the door in the far corner lead to a staircase to the upper rooms?" she enquired quietly.

"Yes."

She whispered again, "Did you tell them about me?"

"No," he whispered back.

"I hope not for your sake," she said. "Stay around here somewhere. I'll be back shortly," and she hurried after Hywel.

He had gained more distance on her as a result of her delay but she was comfortable with the lead. He was following a rough track along the banks of the river that ran below the cathedral towards the sea. She could see him stop and enter a small tavern on the banks of the river.

Beth was uncertain what to do. She wondered if she should stop and go back to Tudor after all she had achieved a lot or should she strike while the iron was hot and brazenly enter the tavern. There were quite a few men and women drinking outside.

She decided to pull the scarf tight around her head to cover more of her face and entered the tavern. She was faced with one dark, dingy room. Hywel was there, being served a flagon of ale.

She pretended to look around for her husband and took in the tavern scene quickly. She decided Hywel was not meeting anyone there and left.

She stayed within view of the tavern door, hoping that he would emerge from the gloomy place and she could follow him again. She didn't have to wait long; he came out, went to the nearby stables and was soon mounting his horse and riding off at a slight trot towards the sea, fording the small river about a hundred yards below the tavern and turning to his right.

Beth made no attempt to follow him. It would have been impossible anyway and so she made her way back to Tudor and their horses, a little disappointed. But, as she drew on the successes of the day, she became more satisfied with her achievements.

It was not long before she found Tudor who hadn't strayed from the horses. As she approached him, she again realised the power she had acquired over him in recent days and wondered if that power had always been there but that she had never had cause to use it. He was a man and physically much stronger than her, but now she was stronger mentally than him. She wondered if it was the recent events that had changed the balance of power or had it always been the case between them, but that before she had not been aware of her own strength.

She asked him as she approached, "Have you eaten."

"No," he replied.

"Oh good," she said, wishing now to show him some kindness. "Let's eat here and you can tell me what they asked you and what you said."

As they ate a piece of salted ham and bread they'd brought with them, he told her that the meeting had been exactly like all other meetings. He had not mentioned a word about being found out by her and Llywelyn but had, as they agreed, told monk of the arrival of the messenger from Rome. The monk had been, according to Tudor, pleased with his account and telling him about Eleanor's new dress from France had been of great interest to him, as Beth had suggested it would be.

He had asked him about Eleanor's condition, that is, was there any indication that she was pregnant and Tudor had said that there was no mention of it and that he would know soon if she were because Beth would be about the first to know.

Tudor felt the meeting had gone well.

Beth had a string of other questions ready prepared in her mind for him. Was Hywel there? What did he say if he was there? But the chain of questions were broken at the first link when he told her that Hywel was not at the meeting and that he had never attended any of the meetings.

He explained to her that he had followed the normal routine and had gone up two flights of stairs to Anian's library where he sometimes met the bishop. He reminded her that Anian was a very academic man and had many manuscripts which he kept there and allowed Tudor to borrow. There was a good view of Hirael bay and the sea beyond from that room. He had met

Anian in the library and had discussed a few inconsequential things with him there before he had gone down one flight of stairs to the room below where he had met the black monk behind the screen.

She asked him if he had seen any distinguishable mark on the black monk and he replied that with the screen between them and the man wearing the black hood he had not been able to see anything that would help to identify the monk. Further, he told her the fact that he spoke through his hand muffled his voice and had the added effect of covering his face. The combination of all these facts in a dark room had made it impossible for Tudor to notice any distinguishable features in the man.

Beth concluded from this account that Anian did not wish to tarnish his own image, nor dirty his own hands by dealing with spies himself, but she had no doubt now that he was the string puller, the controller.

After finishing their food they started on their return journey. The cart was waiting for them at the south end of Hirael beach and the group were back at Garth Celyn long before nightfall.

On their arrival Beth went immediately to find Llywelyn, who was with Eleanor. The chancellor was not present because he had sustained a minor injury while hunting, but would join them later. She reported to them everything she had seen and what Tudor had told her.

Like Beth, Llywelyn was disappointed that she had not seen Tudor's contact in the belfry and he knew that he would have to somehow identify the black monk and find out what Hywel ap Gruffudd was doing in the cathedral.

Beth asked, "Who exactly is Hywel? I know he is from a highly-respected family and is a nephew of your previous chancellor and I know that he has, at times, been a member of your council here at Garth Celyn. Can you tell me more about him?"

"He is a grandson of Ednyfed Fychan and has a brother Rhys and another called Llywelyn, who is the prior of the Dominican friary in Hirael. He is from a highly respected, clever and astute family and they have held esteemed positions in Welsh life particularly here in Gwynedd."

Then a smile flickered across his face as he said, "Hywel's father, Gruffudd was not as highly respected as his brothers Goronwy ap Ednyfed and Tudor ap Ednyfed, both of whom were excellent chancellors. Gruffudd ap Ednyfed fell out of grace with my grandfather and had to escape to Ireland until my grandfather died."

"Why was that?" asked Beth curiously.

"The story I've heard is that it was to do with some slander involving Joan, my grandfather's wife. Of course Joan did disgrace herself with William de Braose and was caught. I don't know if she was also involved with Gruffudd or if it was just a rumour about them."

They all smiled and Llywelyn shrugged his shoulders before he continued, "I can't afford to have Hywel plotting against me. I need to know if there is any substance to Tudor's suspicions of him."

Beth agreed, "I think the first step is to find out what Hywel is doing at the cathedral and then find out what he is planning, if anything."

"Yes," said Eleanor. "He could be planning a revolt against us. We do need to know. We must not underestimate these things." Eleanor was clearly alarmed, having suffered enough as a result of the work of secret agents. Someone had betrayed her during her sea crossing from France and she was not going to forget it easily.

"What's to be done?" asked Beth.

"Can't we have him followed?" asked Eleanor. "He is bound to lead us to his contacts ultimately."

Llywelyn replied, "His contact may be the person he meets at the cathedral."

"Also," added Beth. "It's not easy to follow people, as I found out today."

"We'll ask the chancellor when he joins us. He shouldn't be long now."

Beth said thoughtfully, "What if I were to befriend Hywel and try to find out what he is up to?"

Llywelyn was surprised. "Beth, you have changed. You are a different person from the one I knew but a week ago!"

"Yes, indeed!" said Eleanor.

"I've learnt my lesson. I've learnt not to be so trusting and I've learnt that to stop people doing evil things you must do something about it yourself and not rely on God."

They could see that she was very serious, but Llywelyn cautioned her against doing anything dangerous. "You need to be very careful before you get involved in these matters," he said to her. "You could easily put your own life in great danger."

"My life is in danger through my association with Tudor. He could easily ask them, whoever they are, to kill me to get me out of the way. I am already in danger. I need to find out what danger I am in and if, at the same time, I can help you and Eleanor, then all the better."

"How exactly would you befriend Hywel," asked Llywelyn.

"I don't know. I need to be introduced to him. I can't ask Tudor."

"I could invite him here, with others from Anglesey, on the pretence that I need advice on how to improve this year's harvest on the island, and you could be introduced to him then."

Beth brightened up immediately and said enthusiastically, "Let's do that."

"I will set the date for early next week and send the messages out tomorrow. You have less than a week to prepare yourself. What will you tell Tudor?"

"Absolutely nothing," she said firmly.

"I will inform the chancellor when he returns."

She returned to her room that night relatively happy that she was going to play an active role in identifying Tudor's contact at the cathedral. She was still very apprehensive about her future and her relationship with Tudor in particular. She would have to keep a firm grip on him and remind him, whenever it became necessary, that she could bring their marriage to an end in a way that would be humiliating for him.

Beth did not talk to Tudor about anything to do with her meeting with Llywelyn. She hardly spoke to him at all, other than to tell him that she had told Llywelyn everything which in itself he must have felt was a threat. Sharing the same room with Tudor, whom she now despised, was a burden but was aware that there were no alternatives for a while.

She felt some pleasure at the thought of meeting Hywel at the royal court, admitting to herself that she'd had found him instantly attractive when she saw him at the cathedral door, with his nobility and power forming an intriguing aura around him.

He would be a challenge – she knew that much and she also knew, as she wondered if he would find her attractive and interesting, that she would have to prepare her mind carefully for their meeting.

CHAPTER 10
Early June 1281

B ETH RECEIVED A message from Eleanor noting that Hywel had turned up for the meeting and that, as soon as it was ended, she would be called to the hall for the feast and merriment.

She was very nervous, but determined. She was dressed simply but attractively with the help of Eleanor's skills. Beth, an exceptionally attractive woman had on previous occasions dressed down so as not to overshadow Eleanor but, for this event, she was to be at her most stunning and Llywelyn knew that she would be admired by Hywel and others.

She had been instructed by Eleanor to make an entrance by being a little late. Every aspect of the plot was orchestrated carefully and so as not to be hindered by Tudor. Beth had arranged for Tudor to be out drinking with friends. This last arrangement had not been difficult because drinking had become an increasing habit of Tudor's in recent weeks.

There was a party atmosphere in the hall when she arrived. Llywelyn had ensured that the drinking of mead was well under way. Even those who knew Beth well turned their heads when she entered, and those who did not know her were immediately impressed. The one for whom the effort was made did not fail to notice her and it was not long before he had mingled his way through the throng to be next to her, so that when the dancing began he was in a good position to request a dance with her.

Soon they were dancing happily together. He wanted to know everything about her but she was cautious about what she said. She did say that she was married but she said it in a flippant fashion and gave him to understand that there were other important things in her life, not least enjoying herself and dancing. She did not mention her husband's name and nor he did not ask for it.

At a break in the dancing she spoke briefly to Eleanor who was generous with her praise and encouragement.

Hywel was soon returned to her side. They danced again a couple of dances and then he suggested to her that they should go out for some fresh air and she of course agreed.

They stood next to each other about ten yards or so from the hall. There was a sliver of a moon – just enough to make it possible to walk carefully but not enough to recognise anybody in the gloom.

She knew what she wanted and took a slight stumble against his strong frame and he held her for a second or two, slightly longer than was really necessary.

"We had better not go much further," he said.

"I suppose not," she agreed, though wishing for a fuller moon.

"You can steady yourself by holding on to me until we have cooled down enough to go back indoors. Your dancing is excellent," he said. "You move most gracefully and yet so fast."

She knew that he was vulnerable to her looks and figure, and holding his arm she said, "You are a very energetic dancer. I had difficulty in keeping up with you but I enjoyed every second of it."

His reply was to hold her tight and turn her face so that he could kiss her squarely on her lips. She responded as was her duty, she rationalised, yet realised immediately that she enjoyed the experience.

"Shall we go to a quiet place somewhere?" he asked. "Surely you know of somewhere?"

Things were moving too quickly for her. It was, she thought, probably in the right direction but she needed time to think things out.

He kissed her again passionately on her lips.

She would have been willing to be carried away by this man's power and attention but her sense of duty prevailed and she managed to say, "It is very risky here and I don't know exactly where my husband is at the moment. We had better go back. Also, I don't want Llywelyn or anyone else to become suspicious. Eleanor is watching everybody and telling Llywelyn about everything she sees and hears around the court. Between the two of them I feel like a prisoner."

Tudor had never kissed her so passionately. She was struggling to cope while Hywel asked her, "How can we meet again?"

"I don't know. I don't know where you live? I can go as far as Bangor," she volunteered before he could answer.

"I'm in Bangor frequently," he said. "Can we meet there next week?"

"I think so," she said hesitantly. She wondered if Tudor would be going there but she knew that Llywelyn would help her. "Which day?"

"I need to go there on Wednesday. We could meet at midday if it's possible for you."

"I'll meet you on Wednesday then," she said, grateful that he could not see the broad smile on her face and the glow in her eyes.

"Just below the cathedral at midday. Can't wait," he said.

"Let's go back in and we mustn't dance together again otherwise we will make people suspicious."

"Give me a last kiss then until Wednesday," he said.

They kissed and returned to the hall separately, but he did not keep his promise of not dancing with her again that night.

Later than Beth, Tudor returned drunk to his room, but

sober enough to confirm to her that indeed he was expected to go to Bangor the following Wednesday.

The next morning she waved to Hywel as he disappeared through the gates of the court. She was on her way to report everything to Llywelyn, including the bait she had used to hint that she could be disloyal to him. It was a difficult task, but she did it.

CHAPTER 11

A week later in June 1281

ON THE WEDNESDAY, Beth and Tudor went to Bangor. She did not go into the cathedral this time but went for a short walk towards the beach until she could see the Dominican friary about a hundred yards ahead of her. It was a peaceful looking building, squatter than the cathedral but in a better location closer to the sea and shadowed by a hill through the winter months, unlike the cathedral. She turned back and ambled slowly towards the north side of the cathedral for her midday meeting.

She had instructed Tudor to stay with the horses when he came from his meeting and to go for a drink if he wished to wait for her, because she intended to explore Bangor, the friary at Hirael and the beach.

She sat below the cathedral and waited. Many thoughts went through her mind and also many questions: Would Hywel turn up? Where would he take her? What would he expect of her? What could she possibly learn from this? Was she doing the right thing? How would it all end?

She was tempted to go back to the horses and wait for Tudor, but she knew there was no future in that part of her life and that she had to see this through.

Hywel appeared, smiling and clearly delighted to see her, while she was still deep in thought. So she failed to notice which way he had come out of the building.

"I've got my horse at the tavern down there," he said pointing to where she had seen him a few weeks earlier. "I've hired a horse for you. I was thinking we could go over the brow of that hill and down into the woods above the Menai," he said pointing to the low hill separating them from the straits. "I've got food and drink for us."

She realised that Tudor was going to have a long wait but all she said to Hywel was, "I can't be very late."

He reassured her with, "I know."

They climbed the path up the side of the Fron looking down on the small settlement, the cathedral and the friary. Bangor looked quite beautiful from above now that they were out of the stench of the narrow passageways and river.

In a short time they were sitting in the trees above the sea but within hearing distance of the sound of the lapping waves below them.

It was a romantic, isolated location. They were alone, far from Hywel's estates and Garth Celyn, in a world of their own. She seemed to know that he would kiss her and was prepared in her mind and body.

When he turned to her and started kissing her, she knew what was expected of her and she provided, bringing to an end a stage in her life. He never noticed, and she hid it well.

They spoke about many things afterwards but kept clear of politics and loyalties. She kept those topics for another day because she was confident that they would meet again.

They returned to the tavern and she went to meet Tudor who had been drinking and had not noticed the passage of time. They were quite late arriving back at Garth Celyn but no-one made anything of it and Beth was able to give a full report to Eleanor, but a slightly abridged version to Llywelyn.

She had achieved what she had set out to do that day and was satisfied that a big fish had been hooked and an ambition fulfilled.

Chapter 12

Late June 1281

TWO WEEKS LATER Beth was once again in Bangor and waiting for Hywel below the cathedral. Tudor had been given the same instructions and was not displeased at the opportunity to wet his thirst after his stressful meeting. He hadn't asked her what she was doing while not with him last time, and she hoped he wouldn't ask this time either but she always had a prepared answer.

Hywel appeared at the time expected and they picked up their respective horses and again headed for the woods above the Menai. The weather this time was not as good and Beth wondered what he had in mind. She did not have to wonder long because he told her he was going to take her to a small cottage that he knew of, not far from where they were before.

They arrived at the door of a small cottage with a wooden barred window. They tied their horses. Hywel seemed to know exactly what he was doing but Beth was a little nervous wondering whose house was it.

It was obvious that the cottage was lived in by someone. It was equally obvious that Hywel did not live there, he would have a grand dwelling with many servants.

Beth could not contain her curiosity and asked him, "Who lives here?"

"It's someone I know, but they have lent me the house for a few hours this afternoon."

Beth was taken aback by this but did not say anything and

entered the cottage behind him. He was confident in his entry, as though he was familiar with the place, and Beth had the impression that he had been to this house before. She put the thought out of her mind and concentrated on the task she had allotted herself of finding out who were the agents working against Llywelyn in the Bangor area.

The cottage had been arranged for their arrival. There was a table laid for two with ham, bread and mead. He went to the far end of the room and drew open a curtain to reveal a bed.

Beth, surprised by it all asked in bewilderment, "Have you prepared all this?"

"Don't worry," he answered. "It has been arranged by friends of mine. They want us to have a pleasurable time."

She overcame the shock slowly and took the opportunity to lay another bait for him by saying, "I hope that Llywelyn is not involved and won't get to know of this. For all I know you could tell him or let slip that I have been here with you. I'm nervous about all this."

"Don't worry Beth. Llywelyn will be the last to know about us."

"Hmm! I'm afraid of him these days. Ever since he agreed to that treaty with the king he has been very difficult and I would like to move away from Garth Celyn to get away from all the tension."

Hywel became very pensive, clearly thinking what was the best response to her comments and asked tentatively, "Don't you like Llywelyn then?"

"It's not that I don't like him. I just think he is not himself and so not doing the right things."

"Lots of people feel the same," he said.

While not treachery yet, it was getting closer she thought.

"How's Eleanor these days? Any signs of pregnancy?"

"Not to my knowledge," she replied.

"But as her friend you would be in a good place to know wouldn't you? So, I assume she is not."

"I suppose so," she said as unconcerned as she could sound but she realised he was fishing. This information, she knew, was invaluable to Llywelyn's enemies and she would be the one giving it away, if their affair continued. But she had already worked it out in her mind that Tudor would soon discover if Eleanor were pregnant and would pass the information on to his black monk. So, she did not feel that she had actually divulged a state secret, not yet anyway.

"Taking their time aren't they? I would have thought Llywelyn would want an heir as soon as possible."

"I don't know. I think it's early days yet." At this point she saw a chance to widen the conversation and set up another trap by saying, "I suppose he feels he has an heir in his brother Dafydd and his children."

"Do you think so? Does Llywelyn think that way? I would be very surprised if he did."

"I'm not so sure." Then she thought a lie here might bring something out of him. "I've heard him saying that he looks to Dafydd and his family for the future of Gwynedd and Wales."

Hywel looked at her, clearly judging if he could trust her. "I suppose Dafydd would make a good leader once Llywelyn has gone."

"Yes," she said abruptly.

"But does Llywelyn trust him? He tried to have Llywelyn killed a while back and he supported the king in the 1277 war. And after the Aberconwy Treaty he has acquired Llywelyn's lands to the east of the Conwy. Surely Llywelyn has not forgiven him for all that."

Boldly, she answered him by asking him directly, "Do you think Dafydd would make a better leader?"

He was thrown by the question but knew he had to give some

kind of answer. "Well, I know of many people who think so," he said.

Rightly or wrongly she took this as an indication that he was supportive of Dafydd but could not say so directly because he didn't trust her enough yet. So, how could she get him to trust her and say more she wondered.

"Are there many people who think like that?" she asked, faking mild surprise.

"Many," he answered. "They think Dafydd can work better with the king and so avoid another war."

"Do you think like that Hywel?" she asked putting on her charm, smiling and placing her hand on his chest over his heart.

"If I were to answer that truthfully, I suppose it could be treason," he said. "But with you I can say it because you have expressed your dislike of Llywelyn."

"Yes," she whispered reaching for his lips with her own. The difference between them she thought was that she had Llywelyn's permission to say such things while he hadn't. She was surprising herself as to how good she was in getting information out of this man.

"Is it time for bed now?" she asked.

He did not need to be asked twice. They were relaxed and happy together and later were woken gently from their exhausted state by the sound of birds and squirrels rustling the leaves and scratching outside.

On the journey back to the cathedral he travelled by her side or slightly ahead of her when the track was narrow. On those occasions, looking at his broad back and strong frame, she wished the two of them had met in different circumstances and on the same side. But they hadn't and she had to strive to keep things that way. She knew then it could be quite a struggle.

She left him at the tavern by the river and made her way

to meet Tudor, whom she found finishing off a drink near the horses. He didn't ask her where she'd been. Her prepared answer was that she had been walking on the beach and time had passed quickly. Tudor's drinking habit was working well for her. He wasn't drunk but quite merry and the journey back to Garth Celyn went smoothly with Beth left to her own thoughts.

She was convinced that Hywel was working on behalf of Dafydd but aware that this was a rash conclusion and only time would reveal the truth. She remembered her conversation with Hywel, analysing it so that she could repeat it to Llywelyn and get his views on Hywel's allegiance.

Towards the end of the journey home and when Tudor was a little less merry, she managed to get his report on his meeting. The monk had asked him about Eleanor's state of health but nothing else and he hadn't volunteered any additional information.

At Garth Celyn, Beth repeated her conversation with Hywel directly to Llywelyn, in the presence of Eleanor, and the more intimate happenings to Eleanor on her own later. Beth believed that her friend would undoubtedly pass some of the details on to Llywelyn.

Llywelyn had made more enquiries about Hywel and was able to confirm to Beth that he had been married for a short period but that his wife had died. He also confirmed that Hywel had lands in Anglesey and the Cantref of Arfon, some acquired through his father and some through his dead wife.

It did not take all three of them long to agree that Hywel was not to be trusted, though there was no specific proof of disloyalty against him. He visited the cathedral, but so did many others. The fact that he visited at about the same times as Tudor, was odd and suspicious. His verbal support for Dafydd was a wider concern. All Hywel could do was pass information to Llywelyn's enemies, but Dafydd could lead a serious rebellion against Llywelyn.

That Dafydd was causing unrest was no great surprise to Llywelyn. It was a disappointment but he had, over the years, been disappointed by Dafydd on many occasions – it was what he had learnt to expect.

Llywelyn's friends, including Beth, and his many advisers were warning him that he had too many enemies and that he needed to neutralise some of them and that it would be prudent to start with Dafydd.

Under pressure from these friends and advisers, Llywelyn agreed to start negotiations with Dafydd and arrange a meeting between them to try to resolve the issues that caused the animosity and distrust.

CHAPTER 13
Late July and August 1281

B ETH MET HYWEL again in late July in Bangor and went to the same cottage they had visited in June.

The house was laid out exactly as during their previous visit. Their conversation again turned around Eleanor's pregnancy. Hywel said that people were now convinced that she would not conceive, but Beth was still arguing that it was early days for them because they had not met before they got married and it took time for them to get to know each other.

They discussed Dafydd and his strengthening position. Hywel was convinced that more nobles, even those in Gwynedd, were turning to Dafydd's cause and abandoning Llywelyn – if not in deed, then certainly in thought. It further convinced Beth of Hywel's support for Dafydd.

They talked politics, discussed relationships at court, ate, drank, spoke sweetly together, kissed, embraced and went to bed and Beth was sure that she had heard him whisper in her ear that he loved her and it was as much as she could do not to whisper the same words in his ear. Their intimacy was drawing them closer and she was further under his physical spell. She knew the danger but felt she was duty-bound to continue the developing relationship.

They had talked freely with nothing to disturb their time together other than the scratching and rustling sounds made by the wildlife outside their little cottage.

Following this meeting she convinced Llywelyn and his

chancellor that Dafydd had to be neutralised and a meeting was arranged between Dafydd and Llywelyn in late August.

Negotiations had been conducted throughout August between representatives of both sides to ensure that there would be a successful outcome.

It was agreed that the setting for the meeting would be the church at Trefriw in the Conwy valley, near the eastern border of Llywelyn's Gwynedd. This was the church that Llywelyn Fawr, their grandfather, had built fifty years earlier, and where he had worshipped with his wife Joan when they stayed at the hunting lodge. The two brothers were to meet in the old church and sign a peace agreement.

It was regarded as a suitable venue because it was a church setting associated with their grandfather and conveniently located near the Gwynedd border so neither party had to travel far into each other's territory.

The ceremony would be blessed by the Bishop of Bangor, much against Llywelyn's wishes, but his advisers insisted that he had no choice. They argued that Madog the archdeacon would also be present on such an important occasion, affording support for Llywelyn.

Beth was to accompany Eleanor and her servants.

Llywelyn felt obliged to invite Hywel, so that there would be no suspicion that he was suspected of any treachery or the planning of anything sinister, and Beth was pleased that she could see him in a different setting. They would be able to talk which would be most pleasant and she looked forward to it.

They started on their journey some days before the meeting was due to be held. Starting at daybreak, they climbed to the upland moors and followed the old Roman road through Bwlch y Ddeufaen, before descending into the Conwy valley and arriving at the hunting lodge in the early afternoon.

The lodge was ready for them, with the additional tents and food all laid out well in advance of their arrival.

In the days leading up to the meeting they enjoyed themselves in the area. Most followed the river down to the estuary to view Deganwy Castle on the opposite shore. The bards were full of enthusiasm for the glory of past kings ruling from this stronghold across the river.

The day before the meeting, Llywelyn and a small group of his closest associates visited the remote ancient church at Llanrhychwyn, high in the hills above the Conwy valley.

Beth was in this select group who visited the old church for a private mass given by a local priest solely to pray for Eleanor, her fertility and that she conceive a child soon.

Beth also prayed but her own prayers were for the opposite.

Following the mass and special prayers, Beth thought that both Eleanor and Llywelyn looked relieved, which convinced her of the enormous strain they were under.

Beth knew that Hywel would not arrive until the morning of the meeting but would stay that night and she looked forward to seeing him again.

When Hywel did arrive it was early and when the opportunity arose they exchanged meaningful glances.

Dafydd and his entourage arrived later that morning having crossed the river higher up the valley and followed the west bank down to Trefriw.

Beth, standing near Eleanor, witnessed Llywelyn's welcome of Dafydd and was pleased that it was indeed warm, whatever his real feelings were.

She was certain in her own mind that Dafydd's ambition was to rule over the whole of Gwynedd and probably the whole of Wales. The two were smiling in each other's presence and generally happy together, but Beth could not help thinking how long it would last before Dafydd would turn against him again.

The leaders and their families went in procession to the church for the signing of the agreement before the altar. Beth noticed that Hywel made a show of being firmly in Llywelyn's camp, but she was almost certain that she knew better and that he was, in fact, a supporter of the younger brother.

The most obvious difference between the two brothers was that Dafydd was accompanied by his wife and a brood of children while Llywelyn only had Eleanor. Dafydd was in a strong position at that moment, but Beth knew that if Eleanor were to give Llywelyn a baby boy, the balance would change dramatically and she hoped that their prayers at Llanrhychwyn would be answered soon.

The document, by which the two agreed to respect each other and to avoid conflict, was signed at the end of a mass for peace, with the princes' own royal chalice and plate, brought from Cymer Abbey especially for the occasion. The brothers and their courtiers trooped out to join the crowd outside and announce to the surrounding throng that peace had been achieved and praised God. They then walked in a procession behind the Cross of Neith (Croes Naid) with Llywelyn and Eleanor leading, and Llywelyn wearing the Prince of Wales' crown giving a clear message that he was the most senior brother and prince.

Following the ceremony they returned to the nearby royal hunting lodge for the feast and the party began in earnest.

Beth kept an eye out for Hywel who was mingling with the crowd but throwing the occasional glance towards her. As darkness fell and the dancing and drinking continued in torchlight, Beth knew that this was the time for her to meet Hywel if she was going to meet him at all.

She saw him looking at her in the gloom and he indicated to her that he was going to go out through the main gates. She guessed that most, if not all, of the guards were drunk and she knew that Tudor was drunk because she had made sure he was.

Once she saw that Hywel had moved away from the dancing she gave him a few minutes and then slowly walked in the direction of the main gate glancing occasionally to see if anyone was watching her. Apart from Eleanor, who always kept an eye on her, no-one was taking any notice of her. She did not know if Eleanor approved deep-down – probably not – but she gave the appearance of being in agreement, which was all Beth wanted. Beth believed that what she was doing was for Llywelyn and Eleanor, and she kept reminding herself of this, possibly to cover her own sense of guilt as she left to meet Hywel.

She passed through the main gate without, as far as she could judge, being seen. There were a number of people standing just outside the gate, some clearly escaping from the noise of the party, if only for a short break. Once she moved away from the light by the gate she entered total darkness and, at that moment, she felt a hand holding her arm. She was relieved to see it was Hywel.

"Let's go behind the court onto the hillside," he said. "There will be some light there but no-one will be able to see us and we can sit on my cloak."

Keeping a firm grip on her arm he led her round the back of the court and up the gentle slope behind it to the edge of the trees. He was right, there was enough light there for them to see where they were going thrown from the court festivities and the torches on the walls.

He spread his cloak on the ground and they sat on it close together, with his arm holding her tight.

"Well," she asked. "Do you think this 'bonhomie' between these two will last?"

"Llywelyn will have to make it last or his supporters will drift to Dafydd's side. He has much more to offer."

There was nothing new in this for Beth but she was still surprised by his forthright criticism of Llywelyn. Perhaps this was a time for her to probe a little further. She still had no idea who Hywel was meeting at the cathedral in Bangor. Llywelyn and Dafydd had even agreed that they would work together and exchange ambassadors. If things were now so sweet between Llywelyn and Dafydd, what was the point of these clandestine meetings?

With this in mind and with her own self-confidence growing constantly she asked, "Will you continue to attend your meetings in the cathedral?"

This was the first time she had tackled him directly about the meetings.

"Meetings?" he queried.

His hesitation in answering only encouraged her to question him further. She did not give him a chance to lie but, instead, led him to believe that she knew that when he went to the cathedral he met someone. It was a reasonable assumption she thought and, in any case, he might think that he had mentioned meetings to her and so she asked him, "Who do you meet there anyway?"

His unease became discernible, even in the darkness. He was shuffling his feet, a sure sign of his uncertainty she thought.

"Truthfully, I don't know who it is," he said. "His face is well covered by the hood that he wears. He is dressed as a black monk and sits behind a screen and in the gloom of the belfry it is very difficult to make out any of his features and I have never seen him standing up."

This was identical to the description given her by to Tudor, so she assumed that they were meeting the same man.

She had learnt a lot while looking down at the jovial party below them and now had to play the other part. At that instant if flashed through her mind that she was not just playing a part any more, but that instead what was happening between her and Hywel was becoming important to her and her thoughts and emotions were getting increasingly tangled with him. The acting was turning into reality.

They were happy in each other's company and provided something for each other that was otherwise missing in their lives. It wasn't one surrendering to the other, it was more like they were joining forces but for different purposes.

They returned to the party separately; Hywel having escorted her to the main gate. She was happy and contended with her life at that moment.

Beth found Tudor far soberer than she wished and he wanted to dance with her. She obliged, knowing that after the one dance he would be exhausted, which indeed he was. While supporting him to a bench after the dance, hoping to take advantage of the state he was in, she asked him, "What does the man you meet in the belfry look like Tudor?"

His reply was instantaneous, "As I told you, I can't say because I've never seen his face. He is always in a black monk's habit with the hood covering most of his face and behind a screen. He looks like what you'd imagine the devil does."

She thought he was too drunk to lie and so believed his story. Also, the fact that it matched Hywel's was further confirmation that what Tudor described was true.

Beth reported everything faithfully to Llywelyn the next day. He was naturally particularly interested in the black monk in the belfry. He was not aware of there being any Benedictines in Gwynedd, so he had to conclude that the monk was a Dominican friar.

Hywel left the following day and he and Beth did not meet again at Trefriw. They had agreed that they would meet the next time Tudor would go to Bangor. Doubtless the black monk would wish to know how the events at Trefriw had gone, unless, of course, he was there himself.

Llywelyn and his party returned to Garth Celyn about a week after the agreement was signed.

Chapter 14
Mid-September 1281

E VEN JUST TWO weeks without seeing Hywel was now getting to be a long time for her. He was, against her own will, becoming an important part of her life. There were times when she longed to talk to him, sometimes just to ask him what his view was on this or that or even just to see his smile. She was aware that she was falling under his spell. Then, one day, she woke earlier than usual and Hywel came to her mind and a voice inside her said, 'The truth is you are in love with this man.'

She had to admit that he was frequently on her mind but that did not mean she had fallen for him. He was just like a job for her, like any other task undertaken by others except that her task was different and possibly more dangerous. Perhaps it was the excitement produced by the danger associated with him that made her think about him frequently. But not only did she think of him often, she also desired his presence whenever she thought about him.

When Tudor first confessed to his role as an agent of one of Llywelyn's many enemies and she agreed to try to find out who was involved in Bangor, she thought it would take a month, at most, and then everything would become clear. But, here she was, five months on, and not really any closer to resolving the mystery.

At the start she had no idea that she would become so involved with another man. She knew nothing of Hywel then and didn't know much more about him now either. The more she thought about it, the more she realised there were countless things that she needed to know about him.

He possibly knew much more about her than she knew about him. He knew she was married, but it made no difference to his attitude towards her, and he also knew her background in Aberedw because she had told him.

He never spoke about himself when they were together, but that time passed by so quickly that there was never enough time to talk about everything. She knew that he was one of the Gwynedd nobility and a descendant of Ednyfed Fychan and had land in Anglesey.

At the beginning it didn't matter who he was, but now she needed to know more. She could ask him questions about himself but could she trust him to tell her the truth? However, when she remembered some secrets they knew about one another, a smile came across her face.

Concerned that she was coming under the spell of a man she knew too little about, she resolved to follow him after their next meeting and devised a plan that would allow her to do just that. She would have to go to Bangor on the same day as Tudor but not at the same time. She would ask Llywelyn to provide her with an escort and go a little after Tudor had left, meet Hywel, and then follow him afterwards to wherever he went and then return to Bangor and be escorted home. This would allow Tudor to return whenever he wished and not have to wait for her and he could be told when he returned that she had changed her mind and gone to Bangor.

Intertwined with her thoughts about Hywel was the haunting image of the monk in the black habit. There was something very sinister about him. Though she had not seen the black monk he was vivid in her mind's eye. She could picture him, just as poor Tudor had described to her many times under her questioning. She could visualise him through the screen, sitting there with his black hood covering his face in the gloom of the belfry with the shutters of the single window closed.

Tudor had constantly told her that he had not seen a single facial feature of this man. He said that he was very careful in keeping his face covered. From the monk's voice Tudor thought he was local but with his accent greatly modified, and probably proficient in many languages.

At times Beth was inclined not to believe Tudor but would remember that Tudor and Hywel's descriptions matched each other accurately, and would then accept that both must be telling the truth.

On another occasion she followed the line of how did the monk get in and out of the cathedral without being seen or recognised. Surely she thought if someone stood outside the entrances for a while they would see the monk coming out, but if he left the black habit in the cathedral he could emerge through the door wearing anything he wanted.

She had made no progress in identifying the black monk and decided to question Hywel again.

Thus, as September was drawing to a close, Beth, with Eleanor and Llywelyn's connivance, left for Bangor with her escort, a trusted servant, about an hour after Tudor. She was beginning to feel sorry for Tudor and did not wish to keep him hanging on too long for her in Bangor and so encourage his drinking habit.

Her escort left her when the friary came into sight, having agreed that he would stay in the vicinity until she returned. Beth made her way towards the area below the cathedral where she was soon joined by Hywel following his meeting in the belfry. Together they climbed the hill to the cottage that had become their love nest.

The tide was in and, with no breeze, the Menai looked like a perfectly still lake surrounded by wooded banks. Only the sound of gulls floating noisily over the water brought it home to them that they were looking down on a tidal waterway.

Everything inside the cottage was laid to perfection as always; another mystery for her to try and solve but she had other priorities that day.

She was determined to question him again on the identity of the black monk. As soon as she was inside, she soon came straight to the point, "What can you tell me about this black monk who is giving us reason to meet, yet is keeping you away from me all morning?"

No sooner was the question out than he had his arms around her and was carrying her to the bed.

His action took her breath away and immediately she thought he was avoiding the question, but she did not regret that her question was not answered. Indeed she soon forgot all about the question.

When they emerged from their doze to do justice to the food provided, they started talking again with Hywel displaying a broad grin saying, "You were asking about the black monk. Do I know who he is? No I don't know who he is and I can tell you very little about him. I can't see any of his features. I'm convinced he is from Gwynedd, though he is very successful at disguising it and he is fluent with words. He is an educated man, that much I can tell you."

"Is he Bishop Anian?"

"I can't tell you. He could be I suppose, but I have met the bishop many times and I think I would have picked up some clue or other if it were him."

"Who on earth is he then?" asked Beth rhetorically.

"A mystery," he said. "The screen hides his face well and with his hood on it's impossible to see his face. He whispers, which makes it difficult to identify his voice."

"Would you like to know who he is?"

"Yes, of course, but how can I find out?" he asked. "Instead of accepting the situation I should have tried to find out who he is. I must admit, however, that he is a sinister character and you know you've got to be careful of him if you value your life."

"Oh my God," she said putting her hand to her mouth. "Do you think he's had us followed?"

"No," he replied. "I'm very careful. I've made sure that we have not been followed. Did you see the man sitting on the river bank by the tavern?"

"Yes, I think so," she said, not sure if she had or not.

"You can't miss him." She nodded her head and he continued, "I pay him to let me know if anyone has followed us from the inn. I look back from the brow of the hill and I can see him sitting by the river. If we had been followed he would have waved a white piece of cloth as though he were blowing his nose or wiping his forehead. He hasn't in the past and he didn't today, so I know we were not followed."

She was impressed and relieved but said, "Someone, if they knew where we were going, could come here by the steep path to the west of the Fron and would not be seen by your man."

"But how would they know where we were going?" he replied. "I think we are quite safe Beth. I have thought of everything."

"I know. You are very good. Thank you."

After a thoughtful pause he added, "That's odd you should have raised it now, the black monk asked me about it today. He wanted to make sure that no-one was following me in and out of the cathedral. I told him months ago that I had the arrangement in place for a long time. I just wish I could find out who he is. Can you think of a way?"

"We simply need to keep an eye on the cathedral and see who comes out after you or goes in before you. Have you thought of asking the man by the river bank to keep an eye?"

"I've done that, but he has failed to see anyone. He does not keep to as simple a pattern and, of course, he could come out of the back door or the main door. He is a very clever and careful person."

"Can't we keep an eye on the place? Perhaps we could see him and even if we were not to recognise him we would, at least, know what he looks like."

"I'm willing to try it again, because I would like to know who I am dealing with," he said. "I must tell you I have tried that before, but have not seen anything. Having two people who can trust each other watching the doors would help of course."

"Let's try it next time. I'll come early and meet you before you go in, if it's possible for you."

"I'll try my best," he said.

They finished eating and left the cottage. She observed that he closed the door firmly but did not lock it.

They were soon back by the tavern and separating to go their different ways. She noticed that the man was back sitting by the river and so, as soon as Hywel was out of sight, she circulated around the tavern and could see that Hywel was making his way back towards their house. She assumed that the man was again checking to see if he was being followed.

She liked Hywel – he meant a lot to her. If she followed him now he would know because the man would signal him with the white cloth and that would be it. There was only one thing for it and that was to go back to Garth Celyn.

She wished that instead of having to do all this in a clandestine way, she had asked him directly if he was married or living with some other woman or, better still, that he would have told her without her asking.

She returned with her escort in good time to talk to Eleanor and Llywelyn.

CHAPTER 15
Late September 1281

IN THE DAYS leading up to the late September visit to Bangor, Beth convinced Tudor to leave even earlier than usual if it was a fine morning. She wanted to observe the cathedral from daybreak if possible. Tudor willingly agreed.

It was a dry morning with a clear sky and the full moon was still in the sky. They started a good half hour before dawn and travelled in the shadow of the mountains for a while; but that morning the moon served as their lantern before it faded away with the coming of daylight as they approached the ford on the river Ogwen.

They crossed the river Ogwen with little more difficulty than the last time, but with the river level higher and the water flowing faster, it looked more threatening. Beth, when halfway across, did have a fright when her horse slipped on a loose stone and for a second or two she regretted setting out on the journey, but Tudor was at hand to encourage her forward to the other bank and she was grateful to him for that.

Safely on the west bank she was relieved but it was tinged by a pang of guilt at what she was doing to Tudor.

They rode quietly on and forded the river Cegin without incident. It was cold but they were both well wrapped up and the early morning sun was now warming their backs and encouraging them on towards the cathedral. They arrived above the cathedral just as people were stirring to their many tasks. Beth left her horse with Tudor giving him the responsibility of keeping an eye on the main entrance. He was to note all those who entered and to study their faces until it was time for him to go in to meet the black monk himself.

Beth went around the bell tower which was on the north side, looking up at the belfry as she did and wishing she could hide up there to see exactly what was going on. She walked slowly towards an old yew tree just below the church, thinking that she could observe the path leading to the back entrance from there without being seen. She decided to stay there for a while.

There were very few people about. She believed that the monk would not appear for a while yet.

Her feet were getting cold while she stood still and she began to walk about a little, yet kept herself hidden under the tree. Looking down at her feet placement was essential because she feared falling over the protruding roots which, she imagined, were entwined around the skeletons of the many buried there. Occasionally, she would lift her head and study the empty path leading up to the cathedral.

It was very quiet but the sound of what she thought was a door closing reached her ears and she looked quickly up the path, squinting through the branches towards the cathedral's north door, annoyed with herself that she might have missed someone entering.

Then she heard footsteps approaching. Peering through the thick branches she saw that it was someone dressed in black walking the path leading to the north door. The man was moving quickly up the path and, suddenly, when he was adjacent to her tree, stepped from the path and to her horror came towards her tree and the two were face to face before she could do anything.

The man, shocked to see another person there, lifted his arm to defend himself assuming he was to be attacked. Beth, however, after the split-second rush of fear, recognised her intruder as Hywel.

"Hywel. It's me. It's Beth."

The tension dissolved from his body and he put his arms around her and kissed her.

"Are we doing the same thing," he asked her.

"I think so," she replied. "But why are you dressed in black?"

"I thought I would be less visible under the tree here while observing the cathedral," he said.

"I've been here a while and I've seen nothing but I did hear the door close a moment before you appeared," she said.

"I thought I saw someone dressed in black entering the door," he said. "I was too far away to see clearly, but whoever it was must have walked along the north wall to approach the door because I did not see anyone on the path ahead of me."

She had seen nothing but she knew that her concentration had drifted at the wrong time.

Beneath the yew tree was a strange place to ask him questions, but she did. "Why are you doing this? I came here from curiosity, and now I'm involved because I love you." She shocked herself even with her last words, but did not regret what she had said and knew that it might well be an admission as well as an inducement for him to tell her why he was involved.

"Why are you doing this?" she asked again.

He became very agitated. "Beth, I can't tell you all the details now. It's very sensitive and raw. I suppose I thought I was doing the right thing for myself, Gwynedd and Wales."

He hesitated for a second or two and then, seeing her hurt and puzzled look, he mellowed and continued with his confession. "I guess that you know some things about me. I'm sure Llywelyn, or others at Garth Celyn, will have told you. You know that I was married and that my wife died."

Beth nodded her head.

"During the last war, four years ago, I paid homage secretly to the king in order to keep my lands in Anglesey which the king had occupied during the war. Llywelyn does not know that I paid homage to the king and abandoned him. I suppose it was greed. I simply did not wish to lose my estates."

Beth again nodded her head to show that she had understood.

"I thought that Llywelyn was going to be defeated and ousted from Gwynedd and that the king would take control. However, it did not happen because my uncle, Tudor ap Ednyfed, who was Llywelyn's chancellor at the time, and his deputy, Goronwy ap Heilyn managed, against all odds, to negotiate a peace that allowed Llywelyn to rule Gwynedd including Anglesey. I did not dream for an instant that he would allow Llywelyn to rule in Anglesey, but I was wrong and that was my mistake."

"So?" she questioned.

"Well, my homage to the king became known to a high-ranking and unscrupulous person. I don't know who he is but I have, in effect, been blackmailed by him ever since."

Beth was still puzzled and looked it.

"You see Beth, I hold my lands now from Llywelyn and I paid homage to him and therefore loyalty to him. I have never admitted to Llywelyn that I had also paid homage to the king."

She was still puzzled by his answer and it continued to show on her face. "How can you be blackmailed for that."

"The man is threatening to inform Llywelyn."

"I'm sure Llywelyn would forgive you like he has forgiven his brother, Dafydd."

"He might well forgive me but he could also take my estate away from me. Don't be disappointed, I will tell you everything in time," he said cuddling and kissing her.

She didn't raise the question again under the yew tree and it was only later when he had left her to go to his meeting with the black monk and she was on her own, that she was worried by the fact that he had not responded to her declaration of love for him.

She had thought of getting her horse and going up to the cottage to have a good look around to see who was there and return to meet Hywel at the end of his meeting. But she was too deflated in spirit to do anything. Instead, she pondered on what Hywel thought of her. He couldn't possibly feel much for her, otherwise he would have responded to her declaration of love. On the other hand, whenever he was with her he behaved as though he loved her, and he did have a lot on his mind.

The two met later outside the tavern and his first words to her were, "You told me earlier that you loved me. I feel exactly the same towards you. I hate parting from you and when I'm with you I feel so happy. I love you too, Beth."

Her spirits lifted immediately as she took her horse and mounted it. He had made her happy to her very soul.

CHAPTER 16

Later the same day...

THE ELDERLY MAN sat in his usual place by the river as they rode leisurely away, content in each other's company.

The clear sky was clouding over fast and they could see a mist moving slowly but surely into the mountains from the direction of Criccieth – a sure sign of rain to come. They were happy together as though they were going on a long journey.

The sea was beginning to lose its blue colour of the morning as the clouds took over the sky. The cottage had not changed since she was there last, but there was a thin carpet of orange and brown oak leaves blown off the trees by the late September winds. Fewer leaves on the trees allowed more light to fall on the little cottage, making it look fresher and bigger.

Hywel tied the horses to a tree and nodded for her to go in. She knocked as she entered because she did not have his confidence. It was dark and she stepped hesitantly for the first yard or so and then more confidently until she collided with something soft yet solid and giving, but which pressed back at her.

She touched it as her eyes got accustomed to the darkness. She let out an ear-piercing scream and ran out into Hywel's arms in the doorway. She could not speak, but pointed into the house.

Hywel went in while she retreated towards the horses with her hands covering her face and her head bent forward. Her whole body shook violently.

The next thing she remembered was Hywel at her side with his arm around her. He didn't say anything; he didn't need to say anything. She knew exactly what she had touched in the cottage. It was the body of a woman hanging from the rafters.

"Is she dead?" she asked.

"Yes, but she has only just died. Her body's still warm. I'll go back to cut her down once you have recovered enough for me to leave you."

"How horrible?" she said through her tears. "How did she do it?"

"There is a fallen stool on the floor behind her. So, I assume she used it to hang herself."

"You must know her. Is she the one who's prepared the cottage for us? She is isn't she?" she said still crying and looking up at him.

He nodded to confirm that she was. "I can't bear to think of her hanging there. I'm going to cut her down Beth."

He went back into the cottage but was soon out again to tell her that he couldn't do it without her help. He asked her if he took the weight of the body, could she cut the rope. She agreed and he gave her his dagger. She took the fallen stool, placed it upright and stood on it just like the dead woman had earlier. The dagger was sharp and went through the rope quickly.

Beth could see that the woman was elderly. She was now unrecognisable because of the distortion to her face caused by the tight rope. Hywel lowered her gently and carried her outside, placing her on the ground surrounded by the fallen leaves.

Beth, still in shock, leant heavily on Hywel. He was looking at the tight knot around the dead woman's neck.

He helped Beth back towards the cottage and stood her to lean against the frame of the door while he went inside. He wasn't inside for long.

"It's odd," he said. "I have known her for a long time and

she and her husband have been with my family since I can remember. I could trust her with my life. She didn't seem to me the type to kill herself, but I suppose no-one ever knows."

Beth could not respond even if she wanted to. All she could do was listen. She knew that some people did kill themselves. She had, with the rest of society, regarded it as an act against God and of an insane person. This was the first time she had encountered such an act in the flesh.

"I'm surprised that she laid the table for us, prepared the bed, arranged our food on the table and then killed herself."

Beth was barely listening. "What are we going to do?"

"The man that checks if I'm followed is her husband. You know the one sitting by the tavern. They live here."

"Oh my God," was all she could say. She then asked, "What's her name?"

"Meg."

He used his dagger to remove the rope from around her neck. It was a task he found very difficult but eventually managed it. He then picked the body up, took it back into the cottage and placed it on the bed. It was then that he felt a wet patch in her hair; it was blood coming from an injury to the back of her head. He examined the wound and commented loudly, "I don't understand how she could have had this wound, unless it happened before she hung herself."

Then he added, "Of course, she could have tried to hang herself and fallen hitting her head against the stool then tried again and succeeded."

He was, to all intents and purposes, talking to himself. Beth was hardly listening.

When he came out of the cottage he held Beth tight and talking mainly to himself said, 'This is very strange. I don't understand it.'

"I wonder if she has been murdered and it has been made to

look like a suicide. Could it be a warning to me or to us?" Beth asked worriedly.

Hywel made no reply.

Beth asked, "Is that possible?"

"It would require two people, one to hold her up while the other tied the rope around the beam. Unlikely, I would think. Also, I can't think of a reason why anyone would want to murder her. But there are desperate people about Beth. There is a lot of money and power at stake these days and people can do evil things. I had better go and tell her husband. I've no idea what to say to him. He will be devastated."

Beth hesitated, and her clear incisive mind, was again working fast. "Why would someone murder her? Clearly she was not killed for her wealth. It doesn't make sense to me," she said shaking her head in disbelief.

She started looking around for any signs of intruders and walked around the cottage, followed by Hywel. There was no sign of a struggle anywhere. All she could see were the marks of squirrels and birds scratching for food here and there. Then she noticed scratch marks on the daub wall at the back of the cottage. The walls were flimsy enough anyway, but there were distinct attempts made to remove some of the daub at about eye level.

"What are those marks there?" she asked, pointing them out to Hywel. He was only vaguely interested but went to have a closer look.

"It's nothing much," he said. "Probably a woodpecker or one of the smaller birds looking for worms."

Beth had moved to the far side of the cottage and called out, "Come and look at this."

Hywel went around to the side where Beth pointed out another similar mark again at about eye level. "Do you think this was also made by birds? This one looks older than the other."

He was still a little sceptical. "What are you suggesting Beth?"

"It's possible that someone wanted to know what we were doing in there," she said looking puzzled at him as she was trying to make sense of it all. Then her eyes lit up and he could see that she had found an answer.

"Both these holes are at eye level," she said, though to reach them she had to stand on her tiptoes to look in and it was so dark in the cottage that she couldn't see anything anyway. "But they are also at ear level. I think someone has been trying to hear what we have been saying in there. This small hole here is near where the head of the bed is located."

Hywel managed a ponderous, "Yes."

She had moved to the back again and Hywel, who was still studying the hole at the side, could hear her say, "This is slightly to the right of the door as you walk in. It's in line with where we sit to eat."

He joined her at the back and was told, "I think we've worked it out," she said, not wishing to take all the praise. "Someone has been here listening to us. He had a hole made to listen to our conversation, but must have been disappointed by our pillow talk and wanted to hear what we said while eating."

Hywel, gradually coming round to her idea said, "Do you think so?"

With her imagination at full speed she said, "He arrived here earlier, thought that Meg had left and was probably working on the hole in the back when she came out to see what the noise was and caught him making the hole. She might have recognised him, but even if she didn't, he could not explain what he was doing and killed her with a blow to the head. Then he made it look like she had committed suicide."

"It's possible," he agreed now.

"I'll go and talk inside and you listen by the hole."

Beth did just that and Hywel, in reply, spoke into the hole to say he could hear every word because the wall was so thin anyway and the hole penetrated through the wall.

She came out with a worried look on her face and asked quietly, "Do you think he is watching us now?"

"It's possible," he said again. "Let's pretend that we are just looking around the house. If we are being watched, then whoever it is will be well hidden and could be anywhere in these trees. It's best to get out of here as soon as possible. Come on, Beth."

She made no comment but followed him as he went to close the cottage door. She was only a few steps behind him but, as she turned the corner, she saw he had his sword drawn. He was now concerned for their safety.

They returned to the tavern without incident. Beth left Hywel before he approached Meg's husband and she made her way to the cathedral to meet Tudor.

She was concerned and shocked by the events of the day and was glad of Tudor's calm, though slightly inebriated presence, on the way home. She and Hywel had agreed that he would return to the cottage with Meg's husband and get help for him to bury his wife. Her death looked like suicide and they were agreed that it was best for it to remain that way.

More important to Beth now was that she and Hywel had agreed that they could not meet at the cottage any more but that, in two days time, Hywel would go to Bangor and ride across the Ogwen river and meet Beth near a large stone on the coastline a little over a mile to the west of Garth Celyn.

Beth spoke to Llywelyn and told him everything. While he was interested and worried by the account he heard, his mind was occupied by more important matters, including negotiations on an agreement with Roger Mortimer and a vexatious case concerning Arwystli, in mid Wales.

CHAPTER 17

30 September 1281

LYWELYN AND HIS court left Garth Celyn for Montgomery on the last day of September leaving Eleanor and Beth at the royal court. He was going to attend the king's court on the second of October to present his case concerning Arwystli.

Later the same day Beth left the court with Eleanor and her servants to walk down to the beach. Eleanor was keen to act on the advice that she was getting from others at the court. They were telling her that light exercise, like walking, and sea air would help her get pregnant. She and Beth had agreed the night before that they would go down together to the shore and Beth would then walk along the beach towards the Ogwen estuary, hopefully to meet Hywel.

The plan went well and Beth separated from the others, lifted her shawl over her head and followed the shoreline westwards. The tide was in but the sea was calm and still, with hardly a ripple on the surface and only small waves gently lapping the land. The birds, waders of various types, sandpipers and gulls were very noisy and obviously enjoying their feeding time. The cockle gatherers would not appear for another few hours, so the shoreline was deserted.

Eleanor and her servant were to check to see if anyone followed Beth.

Beth had walked about a mile, reaching the agreed stone, but Hywel was not there. She decided that she would continue westwards, turning around occasionally to check that she was not followed and that there was no-one on the shoreline behind her. Most travellers used the track a little distance from the shore and away from the lower flood plain next to the sea.

She walked along with a purpose, now assuming that no-one was watching her and confident that Hywel would be in the trees on the banks of the Ogwen waiting for her.

The ford was some distance from the mouth of the river and the area was covered in trees and tall reeds inhabited by countless moorhens and wild ducks. She deduced that the area around the stone was too exposed for them to meet and that Hywel had instead decided to meet in the trees and reeds.

She now hoped that Hywel would be watching her approach and would come to meet her.

As she approached the trees she could see him waiting for her at the edge of the reeds. She was nervous, particularly recalling what she had witnessed at the cottage, but seeing him put her at ease. She also knew now that they were both meeting simply to be together and not from the need to find out some secret or other about their respective masters' enemies.

He had watched her approaching for some time and, when she was close, he called her name softly and beckoned her to come towards him at the edge of the reeds.

She went to him and into his arms.

"Were you followed?"

"I don't think so," she said.

"I suppose you could have been seen from the track above. Someone could have watched you from there but they can't come down here without us hearing them."

They went into the reeds and he put a blanket down under them.

They were just two lovers now, meeting because they wanted to meet. Beth was deeply in love with him and she believed he was with her; he was mindful of all her needs and she responded likewise. She may have mentioned the Arwystli case and Roger

Mortimer, but only incidentally and not as a bait for him to divulge any information. She loved him.

Even recollecting Meg's death two days earlier, about which Hywel had learnt nothing new, did not distract from their time together that day.

The moorhens and ducks ignored them and they could hear the rustling of the reeds as the birds walked stealthily through the vegetation; there was also the occasional splash as a duck took to the water.

Beth and Hywel were secure in their own nest in the reeds. The tranquillity was occasionally broken by a heavier than usual bird or a clumsier than average duck or heron, but there was nothing to alarm them.

They were sad to part to go their separate ways.

Eleanor and her servants had left the shore as agreed and Beth made her way back up to Garth Celyn alone.

Llywelyn and his court returned during the second week in October. He had some successes to report and some significant disappointments, as Eleanor told Beth.

The court had travelled diagonally across Wales to Montgomery, passing under his old castle of Dolforwyn destroyed since 1277 and crossing the Severn at the very ford where Llywelyn had negotiated his supremacy in Wales with Henry III in 1267. After presenting his case to the court in Montgomery, arguing that Welsh law should be applied to the case, he had left to meet Roger Mortimer, his cousin and his old adversary, at Radnor Castle on the ninth of October.

Roger's health was failing and he knew it, and he was keen that his sons Edmund, his heir, and Roger would take over from him without facing too much opposition.

The presence of these young men made the weakness in Llywelyn's political position to be more obvious, particularly since Eleanor was still not showing any signs of being pregnant.

The agreement they arrived at was most unexpected and consisted of a loyalty pact towards each other, but to show also their respective loyalty to the king.

While with Roger, Llywelyn was informed that he had lost the Arwystli case. He was disappointed but did not allow it to dampen his spirit. He was aware of the increasing unease among the Welsh nobility regarding the oppression imposed by Edward and he knew that there was unrest mounting.

Eleanor was also worried and confided in Beth how concerned she was about the future, her own inability to conceive and the possibility that Llywelyn would be forced into another war.

CHAPTER 18

October 1281

THE DISAPPOINTMENT OF Montgomery was fading as the end of October approached, when Beth had agreed to meet with Hywel at the Ogwen estuary.

Tudor had left for Bangor early and Beth had asked him to purchase some goods for her and had encouraged him to meet his friends for a drink after. This she hoped would keep him out of her way for the day.

She followed the same route as last time and met Hywel at the edge of the reeds, which were now yellow and dying back. They did not give such good a cover as they had a month earlier but both considered themselves adequately hidden as they lay on Hywel's blanket.

They were happy in each other's arms, expressing their love for one another and, afterwards, he wanted to talk about the gossip at the royal court and she was happy to indulge him.

She noticed that he was a little quieter than his usual self and she put it down to his concerns about the state of the country and, in particular, the unrest amongst the Welsh nobility. He clearly wished that a rebellion could be avoided and that the country would settle into a peaceful period, but did not know how the demands for the use of Welsh law in the courts could be satisfied.

He expressed his concerns to her; she listened and gave Llywelyn's viewpoint on the issues of state, confident that she was divulging information to a friend as well as a lover.

They both agreed that Llywelyn's position was weakened by

the fact that Eleanor was still not pregnant and he had no heir. They discussed everything now since love for each other had taken over.

Hence their meeting was sweet and happy until a clumsy bird or perhaps an otter stumbled into the water nearby. It caused them both to startle and then smile at their own reaction.

"An otter I'm sure," said Hywel. "I saw one earlier at the ford."

Beth agreed.

They were about to continue talking when there followed a different noise, not unlike the suction noise of a shoe or foot being drawn out of thick mud. This alarmed them both.

Hywel placed his finger over his mouth signalling to her not to make a sound as he peered into the reeds behind him. There was silence, but neither of them wished to carry on with their conversation and Hywel signalled that he would go in the direction of the sound and that she should stay where she was.

He moved slowly into the reeds, sword drawn.

He could not have gone more than about ten yards, Beth reckoned, though she could not see him after he had moved three yards because the reeds, though dead, were still very thick, before she could hear voices.

She could not hear what was being said but she didn't have to wait long before Hywel appeared from the direction in which he had gone.

"It was a man who claimed he was trying to catch a duck for supper and his foot got stuck in the mud just as he was about to jump on one. I pretended to believe his story but I don't. He told me he is one of the servants at Garth Celyn."

"I've told him to walk back via the shoreline so that I can make sure he went back safely, but really I wanted you to see him. There he goes, look. He's too far for you to recognise isn't he?"

"Yes, I think so," she replied. "He could be anybody from Garth Celyn. I'm sorry, he is too far away and his face is turned away as well. But his walk is somehow familiar."

"I noticed when I helped him out of the mud that he had six fingers on his right hand. Definitely six – two index fingers I think."

"Oh my God," she exclaimed. "There's a servant they call Dan six fingers."

Looking at Hywel and then at the man rapidly disappearing in the distance, she said, "Yes, it could be him. Do you think he was watching us?"

"I'm afraid so. He was lying when he said he was trying to catch a duck. Yes, he was definitely lying."

"I suppose he was."

"We'll wait till he has gone out of sight and then you can return. I'll follow you some of the way to make sure you are safe."

They waited about half an hour before they set off and Hywel escorted her more than half way, keeping some distance behind her, before turning back.

Beth arrived back safely at Garth Celyn and made her way immediately to see Llywelyn and reported it all to him. He seemed to be in a particularly good mood.

He had Dan discreetly arrested and questioned immediately, while Beth stayed with Eleanor. Dan, being of weak resolve, confessed instantly that he was watching Beth and that Tudor had paid him to do it because he wanted to know if his wife was being unfaithful to him. Dan had assured Llywelyn that he had never done it before and that he had been caught on his first mission.

Dan had begged for his life to be saved because he had children to feed and that's why he had agreed to spy on Beth. Llywelyn, being in a very good frame of mind and a sympathetic leader, spared his life and instead had him taken to Dolbadarn Castle where he would be detained.

Beth was relieved that Dan's life had been spared.

It was agreed that Tudor would not be informed about Dan's capture nor the sentence meted out to him.

Beth returned to the accommodation she shared with Tudor to wait for his return while the story was circulated that Dan had gone to Dolbadarn because a trusted servant was required there. Beth was to reinforce this tale when Tudor returned from Bangor that evening.

Later that night, as she was preparing to go to bed, Eleanor sent her a message asking Beth to visit her in her room.

Eleanor was alone in her room, beaming from ear to ear when Beth arrived. She apologised for asking her out so late saying she could not go to bed without seeing her. "I am almost certain that I am pregnant. Though it's only early days, I am happier than I've ever been in my life."

"When did you tell Llywelyn?"

"This morning," she replied. "I had agreed not to tell anyone else for at least a week, but I had to tell you."

"I am so happy for you Eleanor."

Beth was jealous of her friend but she was also overwhelmingly happy for her and Llywelyn, as she was for Gwynedd and Wales.

CHAPTER 19
Late November 1281 to January 1282

BETH AND HYWEL met frequently in the reeds at the mouth of the river Ogwen in the period from late November and throughout December. They would have liked to have met on Christmas day but this proved impossible.

They wanted to be together and every day that they were apart seemed an eternity to Beth.

She told him about Eleanor's pregnancy at the first meeting they had after she'd found out and had kept him informed of Dan's plight and his detention at Dolbadarn.

While she was delighted by Eleanor's condition, Hywel was concerned about the threat an heir would pose to Dafydd and the king, and wondered what their response would be.

Every time Hywel met his contact in the cathedral, he and Beth would arrange to meet in the reeds at Aberogwen. There was no Dan to follow her and she was becoming more at ease with their arrangements as the weeks went by.

She was confident now that their love for each other was cemented by their meetings and that love was becoming almost the only reason for their trysts.

During this wonderful period of great happiness in her life there was only one thought that niggled her. She was sceptical about Dan's explanation and wished that she'd had an opportunity to question him. She wanted to raise these concerns with Hywel when they were due to meet at Aberogwen after Christmas.

When that day arrived, it was a clear, cold, typical January day, with a thick layer of frost covering the hills and meadows down to the shore. Tudor had left early for the cathedral. From her open window, she could see a thin layer of mist floating a yard or two above the sea and stretching east and west and across to the far shore. But the sun, even in the early morning, was powerful enough to penetrate the thin layer and give a bluish hue to the water below, making it an unusual scene but one she had seen before at that time of year. It gave a mystical look to the bay opening out below the royal court.

Tudor was not usually expected back until the late afternoon or evening, which gave her ample time to get some chores done and talk to Eleanor before going to meet Hywel.

Her walk to the reeds was uneventful and he was there waiting for her. Once with Hywel, she divulged her concerns about Dan.

"Do you think that Tudor paid Dan to follow me just to find out if I was faithful to him?" she queried him.

"Why? Do you doubt Dan's explanation?"

"Yes, to some degree."

"I am surprised that Tudor would be interested if I were faithful or not," she said knowing Tudor's lack of interest in her since they were married which she had not fully revealed to Hywel mainly because she was too embarrassed by it.

"Every man wishes to know what his wife is up to and I suspect the same applies to women."

"Yes, I know. But you don't know Tudor as well as I do."

"That's certainly true," he laughed.

"I just don't see him paying Dan for that. It's more likely that he wanted to know what we were talking about and what secrets we kept."

"Perhaps," Hywel said, not giving it much serious consideration.

"Perhaps he was hoping to find out something about you."

"But what?"

"I don't know… but it's possible."

"Yes, it's possible I suppose, but why would Dan lie to Llywelyn?"

She was quick with her reply because she had turned it over in her mind for some time, "He may have lied to cover a bigger crime."

He turned and looked at her puzzled.

"Yes, Meg's murder," she announced triumphantly. "Dan could have followed us to the cottage. He could have been caught there by Meg and murdered her."

Hywel went quiet, taking her argument more seriously now.

"Well! What do you think of that?"

"That's impossible," he pronounced. "It needed two people to take Meg's body down and it would have taken two to hang it up also."

She was slightly deflated because she had not considered the difficulty they had in cutting the rope. However, she continued with her theory by saying, "Dan may have been one of the two involved."

"Possibly," was as far as he would commit himself to her theory, but it had made him think.

She did not pursue the matter further, deciding to leave it for another day as she had been looking forward to far better things than boring talk about Dan anyway.

She had a wonderful time and they shared the food and drink she had brought with her. She returned to Garth Celyn rejuvenated as she always was after meeting him, and was already looking forward to their next meeting.

The sun was beginning to descend over Anglesey by the time Beth had ambled back to her room to wait for Tudor to return from Bangor.

She sat in her chair getting ready for Tudor's arrival, wishing that she was actually waiting for Hywel.

She opened the shutter on the window again and could see the sun setting slowly over the far horizon as a bright red ball lighting the land below the court and the sea in front of her, with Anglesey as a long dark shadow separating the sea from the sky.

It was a cold evening but she stayed at the window until the sun had gone out of sight and darkness had settled over the royal court. She could hear people talking somewhere and there were lights by the gates, but no sign of Tudor as she closed her shutter on the world.

The fact that he had not returned did not unduly concern her. She assumed that he had stayed in Bangor and gone drinking with friends.

The next day dawned just as the previous had, with a thick frost and a thin layer of mist over the sea. Beth, after opening the shutters, enjoyed breathing in the cold morning air through her window bars and knew that Tudor would be back later that morning having slept off the drink he would have consumed.

At mid-morning, after a visit to Eleanor, she decided to go to ask the guards at the gate if Tudor had returned during the night.

As she approached the gate there was a cart arriving with baskets of fish from Bangor.

The driver, a scruffy and hard-looking man, shouted at the guard at the gate, "Look what I've got for you here."

The guard replied, "I know exactly what you've got; barrels full of stinking fish not fit to eat."

Drawing the cart to a stop at the gate the driver laughed knowing that there was truth in the guard's comment but said, "No, I've a large, sweet-smelling fish for you here with the baskets. Come and have a look."

The guard went to peer into the cart, followed by a curious Beth.

Wedged between the baskets they could see a body lying quite still. "A drunk? Sleeping by the side of the track was he?"

"Yes, he's dead drunk," laughed the driver.

Beth recognised the occupier of the cart. She recognised his clothes. She knew it was Tudor and assumed he had been found drunk as the guard had suggested. "I'm afraid he's my husband. Can one of you get him on his feet please?"

"That's going to be difficult lady because he is long dead," was the unfeeling reply.

She looked at the driver in disbelief and almost said to him, 'Don't be as stupid as you look.'

She looked again into the cart at the body which lay there face down next to the heavy baskets.

The commotion had by now attracted somewhat of an audience. Beth stood looking at the body in disbelief but it was others around her who noticed the arrow protruding from Tudor's back.

The driver was still trying to communicate with her, "Are you sure it's your husband?" He had jumped into the cart and grabbing Tudor's head by the hair, he unceremoniously tried to turn it so that she could see his face. After a struggle with the stiffened body and a tighter grip on the hair he managed and called to Beth, "Well?"

She looked at the expressionless purple blotchy face and managed, after closing her eyes and turning her head away in horror, to say yes.

Then the guard shouted, "Yes. It's him. I recognised your husband immediately lady."

"I've done a good job then haven't I?" said the driver as though he expected some sort of reward for his find.

Other workers arrived at the gate, all confirming that the dead man was indeed Tudor. Beth didn't have to be told repeatedly that it was Tudor, she knew who the dead man was.

She felt faint as she touched Tudor's boots which she also recognised.

The cart driver wanted to tell her what he had seen. "I was walking along the track leading this old beast, just as dawn was breaking. We had just forded the Ogwen when I happened to stop at a bush on the side of the track and there I noticed your husband's body partly concealed by the bush. Whoever killed him tried to hide his body and, but for the call of nature at that very place, I wouldn't have seen him. He was covered by frost see, so he must have been killed yesterday. He was like a block of ice."

Hearing the commotion by the gate many more people were coming out and some from the main hall – among them was Llywelyn.

"What's happened?" he asked.

The driver was quick to explain, repeating the story he had just told Beth.

"Take care of Beth," Llywelyn ordered. "Take her to the hall to Eleanor."

Eleanor was already on her way to the gate and soon had her arm around her friend.

Through the haze in her head Beth could hear Llywelyn questioning the driver.

"He was killed with an arrow from behind, this side of the Ogwen ford," said the driver.

"Take him down," ordered Llywelyn. The driver and the guard obeyed instantly and were helped by others. They placed the body on its side until Llywelyn ordered them to pull out the arrow.

The guard bent down and pulled at the arrow, which slid slowly out. Very little blood came out and they could see that the blood had congealed. The body had remained face downwards overnight and the blood had drained into the face and the chest discolouring the front of the body giving it that purple blotchy appearance.

"That was deeply embedded in his back," said Llywelyn and all around were in agreement. "He had no chance of surviving that shot; it must have gone very near his heart. He would have died quickly."

Llywelyn was given the blood-covered arrow. He looked at it as did others around, including Goronwy ap Heilyn, the chancellor.

"It's was used in a crossbow at close range," the guard at the gate declared.

Then someone in the crowd said what the others had been thinking, "It's a well-made arrow."

However, someone else added, "You can get those types in many places these days."

Llywelyn delivered the final word on the matter saying, "It may be a well-made arrow, but it has been used for a very bad purpose."

There was silence.

The driver had more to say. "The guard said that he was on a horse. There was no sign of the horse when I saw him, so whoever killed him took his horse."

Beth, still believing that it was all a dream, could hear Llywelyn ordering that the body be searched.

"I've searched him already," said the driver as though he had done a good service. Realising his error under Llywelyn's glare he added quickly, "I had to check him over for other wounds."

One of Llywelyn's servants then bent down and searched the body thoroughly but found nothing other than a silver St Benedict cross hanging around his neck. There were no other wounds. The single arrow had done its work.

Tudor's body was taken and prepared for burial. Eleanor had taken Beth into the hall when they were soon joined by Llywelyn.

"Who did it?" Beth asked.

"He may have been killed for his horse," said Llywelyn. "But a common robber would have searched the body more thoroughly and would probably have taken the silver cross. So, it's possible that he may have been assassinated for some reason."

It was clear that Llywelyn did not believe that Tudor's killing was the work of common robbers.

CHAPTER 20

January 1282

Following Llywelyn's suggestion, Beth agreed to rely on the courtiers at Garth Celyn to make arrangements for Tudor's funeral and burial. She showed what signs of grief that were appropriate for the loss of a husband and, indeed, did not find it difficult because the shock was raw and her reaction to that covered her lack of genuine grief for Tudor.

He had become someone she relied on. He was dependable. She was not alone when he was about. As for loving him, she didn't and hadn't for a long time, if she ever had. She had never had the same feelings for him that she had for Llywelyn and definitely not those she felt for Hywel now.

Beth was lonely without Tudor. They had been together as brother and sister for a long time and she missed his company naturally. But she wished that Hywel was there with her now.

Llywelyn promised her that he would hunt the outlaws and bring the killer or killers to justice and that his soldiers were already out searching the surrounding area for the culprit or culprits and making enquires with local people to see if they had seen any strangers in the area recently.

With regard her husband's funeral he told her, "I sent a message to the cathedral to tell them what has happened to their envoy here and I've had a message back insisting that their hardworking and loyal servant be buried in Bangor in two days' time."

"I don't know what I want," she said. "And I have no idea what Tudor would have wanted."

Llywelyn was also unsure what was best and said, "We could say that he has already been buried, but I see no point aggravating the bishop any more than is necessary. If you do not object then I am of a mind to hand his body over to the bishop."

"I have no objections. It's the best solution and we can hold the funeral in Bangor. I would like to attend, of course, since he was my husband. What will you do? It might give you an opportunity to meet with the bishop... if you want to, that is," she added quickly.

"I'll have to think about it, but we are agreed that the body should be taken to Bangor?"

"Yes."

"We will go on the morning of the funeral then," he said. "It's very cold and the body will be preserved well enough for another day or two. You can accompany it and I will think about what I shall do. Once I have decided I will send a message to Bishop Anian to let him know."

"Thank you," she said with feeling, then added hesitantly, "Llywelyn, for what it's worth, I think you should attend. If you don't, it will give Bishop Anian a chance to criticise you."

"You're probably right. It's just that Tudor didn't do me any favours and was dishonest to you and me. But if you can forgive him, then so should I."

Of course, there were other worries going through Beth's mind, not least the fact that she had walked to Aberogwen on her own on the day that Tudor had been killed. The same man or men could have attacked her; she would have to be more careful in the future.

On the morning of the funeral, Tudor's body was taken to Bangor, accompanied by Llywelyn, Eleanor, Beth, the chancellor and Llywelyn's personal armed guard.

The cortege stopped at the place where Tudor was killed at Beth's request.

She looked around the area and was shown the bushes behind which her husband's body had been found.

Through her tears she pointed out that the trees either side of the track had been cleared for some distance some years earlier to ensure that the risk of a surprise attack was reduced. She noticed that there was no obvious place for the attacker or attackers to hide in preparation for an ambush, other than a dead oak tree trunk with a few withered branches.

"It's very difficult to imagine what exactly happened here," she said to the others.

They agreed and Llywelyn told her, "It's possible that Tudor came across a man or a group of men on the road here and was attacked by them as they passed him. The arrow was fired from close range for it to have penetrated so far into his body."

Beth absorbed the atmosphere of the place, which was now so peaceful with its view of the mountains above the trees and of the Anglesey shore in the distance to the north and, as she knew well, Aberogwen and her reeds only half a mile away. All seemed perfect and very different from when her husband had been killed at this very place.

"Could the attacker have hidden behind that old oak tree?"

"Anything is possible, Beth."

"Which way do you think they escaped after the attack?" she asked.

While there were many different opinions, the general consensus was that they probably followed the river up into the mountains, but the possibility that they crossed on a boat to Anglesey could not be ruled out. However, all were agreed that it was very unlikely that they went towards Garth Celyn or back to Bangor.

Llywelyn made the telling point, "If there were more than one man involved then it's very surprising the no-one saw anything at the time and we've not been told of any men seen escaping into the mountains."

Beth took her time to look at everything before she agreed to continue the journey to Bangor.

They arrived in good time at the cathedral to be greeted by Bishop Anian himself, with Archdeacon Madog and a group of priests waiting for them at the main doorway.

Beth glanced quickly at the priests, half-hoping to see one in a black gown and hood, but there was none. However, when she looked to the right of the entrance she was taken aback to see Hywel standing there looking straight at her, smiling and mouthing some message to her which she could not understand and, since there were so many eyes on her, she did not wish to be seen staring at him for too long, though with her husband now dead she would soon have more freedom.

She was convinced that her heart missed a beat when she saw him and it was now racing with excitement at the possibility of meeting him at her husband's funeral.

Overcoming her desire to go to him, she approached the entrance where the bishop and the other priests stood. Tudor's body, covered in a shroud, was in front of her and, as she came up to the bishop, she bowed to him and he nodded his head in response, displaying an appropriately sad face.

Beth was familiar with the building and could not but think of the number of times Tudor had passed through the entrance for malevolent purposes.

About a yard from the doorway she stopped and glanced back at Llywelyn and Eleanor who were with the bishop. She noticed that Llywelyn hardly nodded his respect to the bishop, while Eleanor bowed deeply in front of him.

Eleanor stepped forward quickly to Beth and whispered, "He

didn't show the required deference. That's certain to annoy the bishop." And indeed it did.

As Llywelyn was stepping slowly past him, the bishop looking directly at the prince and said, "I see you attend our church so infrequently that you have forgotten our customs."

"What exactly have I forgotten," asked Llywelyn. He was not willing to show much respect to a man who had deserted him and his people in their hour of need.

"If you attended regularly you would not need to ask," was the terse reply.

The archdeacon stepped in with a smile and said, "Llywelyn, I am so pleased that you have taken time to attend our friend's funeral. We know how hard pressed you are. Yes, indeed. Thank you for giving your time to bury such a trusted and loyal servant of yours and ours."

"My goodness," whispered Beth to Eleanor. "He's a smooth talker!"

The bishop took up the theme with yet more poisonous words, "There would be better law and order in Gwynedd if you were to take more heed of the church and the Lord."

Beth and Eleanor gasped in disbelief at the bishop's comments and the clear criticism of Llywelyn's rule in Gwynedd. They were concerned that Llywelyn would hit him and Eleanor stepped back to be near his side to calm him or even restrain him if it became necessary.

It wasn't necessary, as Madog was talking again, "This was a very unfortunate incident. Poor, innocent Tudor on his way home, sober as a saint, and not a treacherous thought in his mind. Poor man, attacked by vagabonds from the Isle of Man I understand. Poor man. My deep sympathies Llywelyn. It's a very sad occasion indeed. Such a trusting and kind young man. Yes. Very sad."

Llywelyn mumbled his thanks to him while glowering at Anian.

No sooner had that conflict been resolved at the cathedral's entrance than Anian began again with, "You need to find a compromise with the king over the use of Welsh law. You need to see the king's point of view as well as your own. You need to learn to bend."

Clearly the bishop was determined to score a few points or advise as he saw fit, even before the funeral.

Llywelyn was quicker off the mark this time and told him, "I am quite prepared to compromise on that issue as I have on numerous occasions in the past. The king also needs to see our point of view. The Welsh nobles are not happy with his stand."

The bishop opened his mouth with, no doubt, the intention of delivering another vitriolic remark but, yet again, Madog was at hand. "Tudor was such a good man and so talented at finding a compromise in all difficulties. He will be so sorely missed by us all." He was now beckoning Llywelyn to move on and join his wife. He obviously knew that there was to be little compromise on the cathedral steps.

The group moved forward and followed the coffin into the body of the church and away from the difficult bishop.

The funeral oration was delivered by Anian and to everyone's relief it was over quickly. There were a few snide remarks by the bishop, as was to be expected, but he was no great orator hence the brevity of the sermon. The burial followed without delay in the graveyard outside, where Llywelyn and the bishop were successfully kept apart.

As they were leaving the graveyard, Hywel worked his way to Beth's side.

"Can we meet next Wednesday in Aberogwen in the early afternoon?" he asked.

"I really do want to meet you as soon as possible," she

pleaded. "But next Wednesday will do. We can't talk much more here, there are too many about and I will have to return with the others soon."

"Let's meet next Wednesday then," he said.

"Why did you attend the funeral?"

"I heard about Tudor's death and came to Bangor this morning thinking I would travel on to Garth Celyn to give my condolences at the court, but heard that the funeral was to be here in the cathedral and so I waited here for your arrival."

"Thank you." And turning her head towards him and leaning forward slightly she whispered, "I love you."

They then parted and went their different ways.

CHAPTER 21
January to Easter 1282

AS AGREED BETWEEN them at Tudor's funeral, Beth set out on her walk along the shore to meet Hywel at Aberogwen.

It was a damp afternoon. It had rained heavily all morning and she was glad that they had agreed to meet at their usual time in the early afternoon after his morning meeting with the dressed in black monk.

All she had to face now was the wet ground and slight drizzle. Anglesey was out of sight, with the clouds hanging low over the dark grey sandbanks. To brighten her journey there were signs of better times, as a small patch of blue showed in the western sky.

The sea was out and the cockle pickers were there somewhere on the sands and she knew that, as long as she did not dither, she would be back before them. They knew her and she would recognise many of them too. They were known to be a tough breed and not to be tangled with too frequently, so she preferred not to approach them.

In the estuary, the winter weather with its strong winds and heavy falls of snow in late December had flattened most of the vegetation, and the reeds were in a sorry state.

She walked slowly away from the shore along the edge of the reeds and water pools until she saw movement on her right. There he was beckoning her to come to him. He stood by the side of a willow tree, whose tangled mass of bare branches gave him some cover.

She approached him and heard him say quietly, "I have not

seen anyone. The weather is in our favour. Let's sit here." He lowered himself down on a blanket under the tree, resting his back on its trunk.

"Come down here and rest your back on my shoulder," he said, helping her down.

She relaxed immediately and kissed him affectionately but she needed to talk first as Tudor's death was still on her mind.

He suspected as much and asked her, "Do you miss Tudor?"

"Only as a companion," she said. "He and I were never like husband and wife, so my loss is not as great as many people imagine."

He did not question her further and she did not volunteer any additional information and the two sat quietly in each other's company for a while, both content with the normal noises made in the reeds.

After a while she turned their attention to Meg's death and asked him, "Do you think that Dan killed Meg?"

"I've thought a lot about what you said the other day and I can only conclude, like you, that it's a possibility."

"I don't suppose we will ever know will we?" she sighed.

Hywel made no effort to reply and she took, from his silence, that he agreed.

She saw Hywel as the perfect man for her. She did wish that he were more loyal to Llywelyn and showed less allegiance to his enemies. She knew the reasons for it, having heard his explanation, and she knew that she could not change that part of his life.

Whenever he raised issues involving Llywelyn or criticised her prince she would, instead of suffering his critical argument and her own disappointment, turn her face towards him and kiss him and she found that the power of her lips connecting with his brought his treasonable talk to an end. This was how she had power over him.

It was his desire for her that she used to bring to an end his concern for the political future of Gwynedd and Llywelyn's leadership.

As they parted company he said to her, "You are a free woman now Beth."

"Yes," she replied. It was the first time she had thought about her new position in that way and it did bring a sense of excitement with it.

"Will Llywelyn have another envoy from Anian at Garth Celyn?" he asked, laughing.

"Not likely, I should imagine," she replied also smiling.

They were both standing and he kissed her and said, "I'll stand a chance then, will I?"

She looked up at him, still smiling happily, and he put his hands on her waist and said gently, "We had better go. Shall I see you in two weeks' time?" He kissed her again and released her like he would a bird, to be on her way.

"Yes, please," she whispered as she left his grip.

She left reluctantly, looking back at him standing there under the bare willow tree. She was smiling happily as she trekked back along the shore, with the cockle pickers still out on the sands.

As the weeks went by, it became apparent that no-one was to be apprehended for the death of Tudor.

Beth grew to accept this fact but felt sure that it was likely that Tudor had been assassinated for what he knew, and not murdered for what material wealth he possessed.

She accepted the facts as reported to her and accepted her fate gracefully, but was reluctant to become resigned to a life as a childless widow and so rested her hope on her true lover, Hywel, marrying her soon.

* * *

Life at court continued with the stresses and strains of the relationship with an aggressive King of England dominating politics and discussion.

Beth met with Hywel regularly every two weeks. It was a very happy period in her life and she could see that it was set to continue and get even better. They kept their relationship secret as they had when Tudor was alive but, in reality, the secrecy was no longer necessary for her, though it was only decent to allow a reasonable time to pass before being seen with another man in public.

Hywel, as far as she knew, continued to meet the black monk at the cathedral before meeting her at Aberogwen. They never spoke about it anymore; it was taken as fact by both and, by Beth, as an evil that had to be endured.

She did dream frequently that he would soon ask her to marry him; indeed it was her greatest wish and felt confident that it would happen.

Inevitably she imagined herself living with him and if there was going to be a choice she would encourage him to make their home on his estate in Anglesey where the weather was better and had wonderful views of the mainland's mountains. Yes, Anglesey would be her choice.

During one of their meetings in February Hywel had asked her, "What are your plans now that Tudor is dead? I hope you don't intend to leave Gwynedd."

"It will depend on my prospects here. If Eleanor is delivered of a baby successfully, then I will surely stay."

"I wish we could be together more and do more things together. Do you think that time will come soon?" he asked.

These were golden words for her and she desperately wanted to say to him, "Please let's start today," but she knew of the restrictions they had placed on themselves for the sake of decency and answered him accordingly with, "I hope so Hywel."

"How long do you think it will be?"

She turned her face away from him so that he would not see her blushing and said, "I would like it to be as soon as possible."

"Shall we talk about it after Easter," he asked. "It will then be three months after Tudor's death."

She wished it sooner but, not wishing to show haste, she replied, "Let's see what Easter brings and then we can decide."

"If you think Easter is too soon that's fine by me; after all it's your husband who's died."

Still facing away from him she reiterated, "We can talk about it after Easter."

She wanted to marry him and worried that she had been too hesitant in her response.

She faced him and pecked him on his lips a few times and told him, "I love you Hywel." He responded by kissing her back and the moment passed, but she knew that it would return and she would be better prepared.

After returning to Garth Celyn, she discussed what had been said between her and Hywel with Eleanor. It was a conversation they both enjoyed and Eleanor was pleased to see her friend so happy. Eleanor felt sure that Hywel was going to ask Beth to marry him soon.

But Eleanor also expressed her concern to Beth that the pressures on Llywelyn were increasing as his nobles demanded that he took some kind of action to regain some of the powers lost at Aberconwy. Llywelyn himself was pondering on what was the best action to take, yet avoiding anything that would lead to another war.

Beth knew that he was also absorbed by Eleanor's pregnancy and that he was hoping for a boy, as was Eleanor. A boy born to Eleanor would change the whole balance of power between him and Dafydd and between him and the king. He would be in a much more powerful position.

Chapter 22
Easter 1282

B ETH, IN THE weeks leading up to Easter, was in a good frame of mind. Her personal life had taken a turn that pleased her and she was looking forward to spending much more time with Hywel. But then, like a thunderbolt out of a clear blue sky, on Palm Sunday 1282, Dafydd started a war in the North East.

He attacked Penarlâg Castle in the early hours of the morning with shocking, violent and decisive consequences. But, his was not the only instance of rebellion, as a number of castles were also attacked across a wide area of west Wales.

The news of the attack on Penarlâg was brought to Garth Celyn by a messenger in the late afternoon of the same day. Llywelyn was with his chancellor when the rider was brought into the hall but, within minutes, they were all outside ordering that the court be placed on full alert and sending messages to Llywelyn's military commanders to inform them of the attack and to instruct them to gather their armed forces ready for any eventuality.

There was great activity and Beth became part of that, going to comfort and reassure her Eleanor that there was nothing to worry about – a difficult task with Eleanor seven months pregnant and all the while wondering if this pregnancy was at least partly the cause of the new war.

Men and women were furiously preparing for an imminent attack on Garth Celyn; who was likely to do this was not altogether clear, but the dogs of war had been let loose and that was enough.

However, in the middle of this mêlée, groups managed to gathered to gossip and speculate. Some thought there had been coordinated attacks but most were of the opinion that there had been no advanced planning and that it had been spontaneous actions, resulting from the general discontent of the Welsh nobility with the king's rule across Wales and, of course, Llywelyn's inaction over many months.

Feelings had been running high for some time and Llywelyn himself had experienced the king's contempt for Welsh law in the Arwystli case. Many others had similar and some even worse experiences and a few nobles were of the opinion that the king wanted another war and the oppression was his way of igniting the flame. It became apparent that it was King Edward who had put Dafydd up to the attacks, to drag Llywelyn into a war.

Whether there had been planning or not, all at the court knew that Llywelyn had been taken by surprise. This was also Beth's view, based on her discussions with Eleanor. Beth was not really surprised; she knew he was an honest man not given to intrigue and was, in the main, a very trusting person and hence his intelligence gathering network had again proved to be woefully inadequate for the time.

Because of this unexpected turn of events, Beth and Hywel failed to meet. She did go to their meeting place but Hywel did not turn up. He had never missed an arranged meeting before, but she understood that there were meetings all across Gwynedd with many of the nobles concerned about their estates.

There was unease and uncertainty everywhere in Gwynedd. Some wanted to support Llywelyn but did not wish to bring the king's wrath on themselves and possibly lose their lands if Llywelyn were defeated. Others believed that the war should intensify immediately and started to prepare for it seriously, arguing that if Llywelyn kept Gwynedd out of the conflict, there was a risk that his brother would take on the leadership of the disgruntled Welsh nobles.

Beth imagined that Hywel was struggling with these conflicting views at this time.

Llywelyn's hesitation at the beginning of the war was not surprising, as he not only had this discord to resolve but also he had Eleanor expecting their first baby. His councillors were also divided on the issue, with some for supporting Dafydd, others distrusting him and stating quite openly that it would be disastrous to take on Edward's might at that time.

April passed, with Llywelyn making no definite move except planning and opening lines of communication with the king. The king, on the other hand, knew what he wanted to achieve and started to gather a massive force to attack Wales.

Numerous imaginary sightings of the English fleet approaching the coast were reported and even acted upon until it was realised that it was all a fiction generated by the panicked population.

It was late May before it was realised that the king's preparation would take time and it was only then that the country became calm again, with fewer soldiers manoeuvred from place to place and the movement of people from place to place becoming closer to normal. People started to live normally again, and to be relatively happy again.

With this calmer atmosphere prevailing Hywel rode boldly into the royal court one mid morning in late May. He had an audience with Llywelyn and the chancellor and then visited Beth who, having heard from Eleanor that Hywel was in the hall, went to sit in a prominent place outside hoping to see him to arrange another meeting.

It wasn't long before he strode out, appearing a little concerned but casting his eyes around obviously looking for someone specific, and soon he spotted Beth and went to her immediately.

"Are you going to invite me to your room?" he asked.

Blushing deeply, she managed to say, "Follow me." She turned towards her room and indicated that she expected him to follow her.

Once in her room and holding her tight he said with great feeling, "I've missed you Beth."

"And I've missed you, too."

"I'm sorry I was couldn't meet you last month. There was chaos everywhere and I could not get away from my estate in Anglesey. It was a very difficult time for everyone. But now everything is quiet again, as if nothing had happened and, what is almost worse, as if nothing will happen."

"I understand."

"Also, I'm not required to visit the monk at the cathedral any longer. Things have changed and I feel freer."

She looked deeply into his eyes and saw that there was concern there as well as love for her. "Do you think we are all in danger?"

"There is great danger ahead for us all Beth, including you and me. The king will attack – it's just a matter of time. He will invade Gwynedd and Garth Celyn will not escape his fury."

She kept her eyes fixed on his.

"I have tried to warn Llywelyn about what is to come but he is only concerned about the baby Eleanor is expecting. I have tried to warn him not to join his brother and lead this rebellion. I have told him that it will lead to disaster for Gwynedd and Wales. If you get a chance, try to tell him the same thing. Perhaps Eleanor will listen to you and she might influence him."

"If you think I should, then I will try my best with Eleanor but, as you would expect, her mind is entirely focused on the baby."

"Yes, that's understandable. But if you can please have a word with her – she has a strong influence over him."

"I will try," she assured him.

"Let's drink to it," he said. "Can you get some fresh mead from the hall."

"Yes, of course," she said delighted at the prospect of having a drink with him.

When she returned with the mead, Hywel was on his knees by the bed. He raised his head as she entered and said, "Come and sit on the bed I've got something to ask you."

He signalled her to sit on the edge of the bed and she obeyed. She was not in the mood to discuss affairs of state anyway. She had missed him too much and leant forward to him kissing him playfully. There was little talk of politics after.

Before he left her, he raised the fact that they had agreed that after Easter they would talk about their future together: "Easter has come and gone and we've not had an opportunity to talk about us."

"I know and I so much want us to."

"This war has delayed everything. It's made it more difficult to meet but my coming openly to Garth Celyn to see you today, is progress. It's a small step but it's a start."

"I know," she said hiding her disappointment.

"I hope that the war will end as quickly as it started and if Llywelyn condemns his brother's action and sides with the king it will be over soon. Do your best to convince him Beth so that we can start our lives together. I would be so happy with you."

"I will talk to Eleanor." She felt disheartened that the message she was getting from him was that they would have to wait until the war was over before they could marry.

However, Hywel left her in a good mood because she was sure that she would marry the man she loved – not immediately but as soon as the conflict with Edward was over – and this time she knew that this man would give her everything she wanted.

A short while after Hywel had left her, Beth went to talk with Eleanor, who had heard of Hywel's views from Llywelyn. She assured Beth that she was of the same opinion as Hywel and would try to keep Llywelyn and Gwynedd out of the war.

It was not difficult to realise that the last thing Eleanor wanted was for a war to break out while she was at an advanced stage of pregnancy.

About three weeks after Hywel's visit, Eleanor gave birth to a healthy baby girl, whom they named Gwenllian.

However, though the prince had the best physicians available attending on the princess, they could not stop the bleeding that followed the birth and gradually Eleanor became weakened by the loss of blood.

Llywelyn and Beth could see the life draining from her until she became too weak to speak.

He frequently asked Beth for advice and for her opinion. "What can I do Beth? I feel she is slipping away from me."

Beth reassured him as best she could by saying, "She did eat a little about an hour ago. That will help her."

"But we need to stop the bleeding. I am beside myself with worry for her."

Beth had no answer for that and could only pray that the bleeding would stop. However, more experienced observers knew that the chances of that happening were very small.

There was little hope for Eleanor and it was not long before Beth, while sitting at her friend's bedside, heard what sounded like a rattle in Eleanor's throat. It was as though Eleanor was struggling to overcome a restriction in her windpipe, but it was, in fact, a result of her declining strength even to breathe normally.

Eleanor died in the early hours of the morning of the

ninteenth of June after she had been so weakened. Her soul was able to slip quietly and effortlessly into the darkness.

Great sadness fell over the royal court. The court had lost a princess, a fine woman who had been at their prince's side, given him and her adopted country hope for the future and given her own life in the process.

Llywelyn, though aware of Eleanor's imminent death, was distraught at the moment of her actual departure from this world and stayed on his own with her body until daybreak.

When he eventually emerged he was drained of all energy and composure. Beth was there, waiting for him to come out of the chamber and embraced him gently, crying on his shoulder. He was also angry and could neither be consoled nor calmed, even in the presence of his baby, Gwenllian. In those early days he felt that fate had been cruel to him and he railed against it all.

Beth had lost a true friend and her grief at losing Eleanor was far greater than following Tudor's death.

The news of her death spread fast and many of the local nobles called to express their sympathy to Llywelyn and the royal court. Beth did expect Hywel to arrive at any time, but he didn't appear. However, though she was disappointed, she felt sure that he would attend the funeral.

Bishop Anian was among the first to arrive to grieve with the prince. Llywelyn did not wish to meet him but was convinced by Beth and others that he needed to receive his blessing and that the bishop would have to be the one conducting the funeral.

Beth and others, including the chancellor, agreed to be present at the meeting as support for the grieving prince.

Anian entered the hall and walked to where Llywelyn sat, with his hands held out to the grief stricken man. "Bless you my son," he said with great sympathy and feeling.

"May God help you at this, your hour of need."

Llywelyn with tears in his eyes, yet displaying signs of great anger, stood and showed deference to the bishop.

"You have suffered a great loss Llywelyn and you have my deepest sympathy. Kneel and we will pray together for her soul and for God's strength to overcome this loss of yours."

He dutifully knelt and the bishop prayed for strength and forgiveness. Beth and the chancellor knelt instinctively with their prince.

Beth was impressed by the bishop's ability to empathise with Llywelyn. He was a totally different person to the one she had seen at Tudor's funeral. Anian seemed to be, at that moment at Garth Celyn, a man of substance and a sympathetic person.

They agreed that the funeral would follow the same pattern as that of Joan, Llywelyn Fawr's wife half a century earlier, and Eleanor would be buried at the priory in Llanfaes just across the sea from the royal court.

The day of the funeral was a clear blue June day with a pale sliver of a waning moon in the northern sky high above Anglesey.

The prince, his family, his chancellor and the great men of Gwynedd were gathered in the hall in the presence of Eleanor's body which was laid on an oak bier. The bishop and his assistants were arrayed behind a long table ready to take the funeral mass. The Croes Naid, reputedly containing pieces of the true cross from Jerusalem embedded in an oak cross decorated with jewels of different colours – a magnificent and the most holy relic of the princes stood on the table.

The cross, with its keeper, had arrived from Cymer Abbey two days earlier in preparation for the funeral. Llywelyn's personal silver chalice and platen, to be used in the mass and arranged on the table in front of the bishop, had also been brought from Cymer Abbey at the same time.

Bishop Anian, assisted by Archdeacon Madog conducted the

mass for the dead, while Llywelyn's head remained bowed and tears flowed down Beth's cheeks.

With the mass over, Eleanor's body on the bier was carried out and placed on a four-wheeled cart to be drawn by two immaculately groomed sturdy black horses, waiting patiently outside the hall's main door.

Her body was dressed in white, with a silver tiara on her head. The cart was adorned by bundles of white hemlock, foxgloves and yellow marigolds, picked at dawn that day in the meadows surrounding the court.

The mourners, now surrounding the cart, could see the frail yet elegant body even in death, strapped firmly to the cart ready for its final journey.

Then as the horses were about to take their first steps, a slight breeze arrived from the sea and dislodged a few loose wisps of her long brown hair, waving them across her face causing Beth to expect Eleanor to lift her hand to push the irritating strands aside. Realising that Eleanor would not lift her hand, she wanted to step forward and do it for her as she had on many occasions, but this time she recognised that it would be to no avail as another breeze would dislodge it again during the journey across the open sands.

The entire court's population followed the cortege out through the gates. The black horses were led by a member of the royal court guards and immediately behind the cortege came the lone figure of Llywelyn wearing a black ermine cloak and his state crown.

Then, behind Llywelyn, came the chancellor followed by the Groes Naid, carried high by its keeper, and then Bishop Anian in his full ceremonial regalia. Anian was followed closely by Archdeacon Madog and behind them came the great men of Gwynedd, including the prince's brother, Dafydd.

The funeral cortege moved slowly over the marshy ground

below the court and on to the beach. The body on its bier was lifted on the shoulders of four strong men and taken onto the landing stage and lowered carefully and gently onto the waiting boat. Llywelyn joined Eleanor on the first boat.

Looking at the sad scene from the beach Beth, like the others around her, was in tears as the boat left its moorings to cross the sea carrying Eleanor de Montfort's young body to Llanfaes.

The main mourners entered the other waiting boats and followed the lead boat across the calm sea.

Beth went further down the beach for a few yards as if to try to follow the boats then, with others, stopped to watch the fleet of boats continue their journey in line across the sea. She knew that at a service in the priory, Eleanor's body would be placed in a stone sarcophagus and a temporary wooden lid placed on it till a stone cover would be carved.

The boat became no more than a speck on the distant Anglesey shore and out of sight of the spectators at the Garth Celyn beach. Beth hoped that her Hywel would attend the service at Llanfaes and was disappointed that he had not been able to pay his respects to Llywelyn at the court prior to the funeral.

It was some hours before Llywelyn and the mourners returned to the court and, as much as Beth wanted to ask him if Hywel was at the service in Llanfaes, she didn't – she didn't think it was appropriate to do so at this time.

The death of the princess left a sad atmosphere at Garth Celyn for weeks after the funeral. Her empty chair at the table was eventually removed but there remained an empty space at the table for a long time.

CHAPTER 23
July 1282

WITH NO ELEANOR to occupy her time, Beth spent long periods at her window keeping an eye on the gate and all those who entered, hoping that she would see Hywel visiting.

Early one day in July she was rewarded and was delighted to see him approach from a distance along the track from Bangor. She recognised him and his horse immediately and was thrilled to see him dismount below the gate.

The sadness that she had been suffering since the death of Eleanor was lifted by the sight of Hywel looking up at her window smiling and waving at her. She thought that he would wait for an audience with Llywelyn before coming to see her, but was surprised when she heard a knock at her door.

She was delighted to see him and they kissed. He looked around the room taking in every detail. He looked out of the window – admiring the view – then returned his attention to the room. He examined the few pieces of furniture and remarked on their workmanship, and then came towards the bed.

"This is a fine bed, with a large space under it. I suppose you keep all your secrets under there? I hope you've not hidden anyone there now."

She laughed and said cheekily, "No. I don't keep anything under the bed – mice can hide in things under beds. In any case, I would have thought you would be more interested in what's on the bed."

They were so happy to be together again and immediately set

about fondling and kissing each other with a passion reflecting their long separation.

"I did not expect you to come here immediately; I thought you would see Llywelyn first," she said enquiringly.

"There you are, I have come to see you first. I hope you are not disappointed," he said, laughing.

"Llywelyn won't be offended, will he?"

"His men told me that it would be better to leave him alone for a while because he is at his lowest state in the morning, and his spirits improve as the day progresses. They promised that they would inform him that I had called and that I would like to see him this afternoon."

"He has not been out hunting since Eleanor's death and they are right, he can be very dejected in the mornings. He needs time to heal his wounds but it will happen soon, I hope."

Hywel made no reply and did not seem convinced that the healing process would be a quick one. Of course, had Beth not been so engrossed in her own happiness of being with him, she might have remembered that Hywel had experienced the same grief as Llywelyn.

Beth did not reproach him for not attending the funeral at Garth Celyn – she was just delighted to see him and be with him.

"Let's go for a walk in the woods," he said. "We have lots of things to talk about and I prefer the open air when I have a lot of things on my mind."

She agreed and he added much to her delight, "It's nice to go out in the open together and be seen as a couple. Come on, I'm looking forward to it."

They went out of the court's perimeter wall and up towards the woods above. It was steep but they were healthy and fit and, buoyed by their mutual excitement, they were soon out of hearing of the guards on the walls.

"There didn't used to be so many guards here from what I can remember. Is this normal now?"

"It is," she replied. "And there are more on guard at the top of this hill also. I think they are afraid that Edward will attack Garth Celyn soon."

"I think that's unlikely. They are far more likely to attack Anglesey and that could happen any day now. Most of my land is in Anglesey and I could find myself losing it all. That's what I want to see Llywelyn about." Looking around to ensure that there was no-one about he said in a lower voice, "I want to try to influence him not to enter a war with the king and to try to arrive at a compromise with him. The king is very powerful and, barring a miracle, Llywelyn will be defeated again and this time he will not be allowed to hold on to Gwynedd."

She could see the anger building in him and asked, "Why are you so angry? Are you angry with me?"

"No! No! I suppose I'm angry with Llywelyn for not declaring his brother a rebel and siding with the king."

"Oh!" was all she could say.

"I intend to tell him today."

"Be careful Hywel. He is at a very low ebb and may not take advice like that very well. There are some here at the court and in Gwynedd who are advocating war and for him to move across the Conwy and join his brother in an all-out attack on the king before he is properly established in the east."

"I have to tell him that there is another opinion held by many, that he should condemn the attacks by his brother. He needs to do it immediately otherwise his silence will be taken as a sign that he is condoning his brother's rebellion and it could be too late soon."

"I see."

"So I must tell him today."

"Do it carefully. Don't show any anger. Remember he has

just lost Eleanor. He has also lost her calming influence. Please be careful how you try to advise him. It's all very raw with him at present."

"I will."

She then led him towards a tree trunk which had fallen years ago where she and Tudor had often sat. It had not brought her much luck in the past she thought but it was the only convenient place to sit and it did provide an excellent view of the sea and the shoreline. The trunk itself, a stump of a tree brought down by a storm, had weathered greatly since she sat there with Tudor. The woodland insects had eaten into it; moss and lichens had penetrated the bark darkening its colour and softening the fibre of the wood.

Pointing at the distant priory she said sadly, "Isn't it good that we know so little about the future. There is Eleanor who was healthy and laughing just a few weeks ago now buried over the water there in Llanfaes. Who would have thought it possible?"

"Yes."

"And now we are talking about a war that will result in many being killed. All I know is that life is cruel enough without wars. Why does the king want to conquer our land? Why can't he just leave us alone to our own way of life, our own laws and our own customs? Who gives him the authority to molest us here?"

He was not able to answer her probably because he was more concerned about his estates in Anglesey. He gave her a sideways glance and saw that she was still fixed on Llanfaes in the distance.

She looked wonderful with the light casting shadows on her face. Her beauty was unsurpassed and unchallenged at the royal court. It was easy to see why she had been chosen by a prince to live at his court.

She found this talk about war and its consequences too

depressing and decided to raise a matter that was much closer to her heart.

She kissed him and placed her arms around his neck.

He responded but he also laughed saying, "There's talk that Llywelyn wants you for himself now. How can I compete with a prince?"

"How can he compete with my Hywel?"

Their conversation in the woodland above Garth Celyn ended there and, a while later, they went back down to the court.

They parted delighted to have spent time together and Hywel, after meeting Llywelyn, left the court to go back to his own lands, which he still held by Llywelyn's grace.

CHAPTER 24
July to October 1282

TOWARDS THE END of July 1282 Llywelyn was spending more time with Beth. In fact when he was not involved with the court and attending to threats brought about by his brother's act of war against Edward, he was to be seen with her as though she was a replacement for Eleanor. She was more than just pleasant to look at, she was interesting to be with, and she had been Eleanor's friend.

Gradually Beth re-entered Llywelyn's life as he started gathering and preparing his forces while, at the same time, engaging in diplomatic communication with the king. It was, nevertheless, openly accepted that Llywelyn would inevitably be drawn into war.

Beth felt their relationship was back to where it was before Eleanor was released by Edward. Llywelyn frequently turned their conversation to talk about Eleanor and Beth did not mind this as it gave her an opportunity to console him and guide him through his grief.

They spent hours together talking about Eleanor and what it would have been like if she had lived. Had she had another child, perhaps, it would have been a boy. After a few weeks she was able to get him to reflect on the good times that he and Eleanor had spent together. It was thus that they spent their time together and their friendship grew stronger.

His advisers again encouraged Llywelyn's attachment to Beth, seeing her as a new possible source for a male heir.

However, whatever the wishes of the court and the advisers, Beth was committed to Hywel and she looked forward to being his wife and living with him, so this time, there was only the wish for Llywelyn as a friend.

Llywelyn and Beth spent hours talking together – sometimes reflecting on their time with Eleanor and at other times they shared their worries about politics and the military position. She also, whenever it was prudent to do so, encouraged him to improve his intelligence gathering so as to be, if possible, one step ahead of the enemy. He would agree but, for one reason or another, little progress was made on the matter.

Of course it was natural that she wanted to know more about Tudor's death and would on occasions turn the conversation with Llywelyn in that direction. In late July she ventured to ask him, "Have you had any more thought about Tudor's death."

She did not wait for a reply but typically expressed her viewpoint, "I would like to know if he was assassinated. I think it unlikely to be the person he was meeting in Bangor, unless Tudor had somehow become a liability and the monk wanted him out of the way. Perhaps he knew too much about their organisation or about some individual in that organisation."

"As you know Beth, I made extensive enquires at the time and did not find anyone who had seen or heard anything about his death. No strangers were seen in the area."

"I know," she said.

"So, I can only assume that it was a planned assassination by someone who knew exactly what he was doing – one of the Edward's agents working in the area may have had him killed, though I can't think why?"

"I don't see that he would be enough of a threat to anyone to warrant killing him," Beth opined.

"I suppose that one of the Marcher barons could have had him murdered. The most obvious one being Roger Mortimer, though he and I had arrived at an agreement months before Tudor was killed."

"But why would Mortimer want him killed?"

"He might have been killed simply to destabilise the situation here at Garth Celyn and in Gwynedd by causing more bad blood between me and Anian for example. You can remember what the bishop was like at Tudor's funeral. Perhaps they think that you have a great influence on the affairs of the state through your position and your access to me. And that by murdering your husband they could cause you to leave Garth Celyn and move to a more vulnerable place, say back to Aberedw, where they could abduct you and question you about the court and its views."

"That's a little far-fetched isn't it?"

"This conflict has been a long time in the making, Beth. Some have been planning it for years."

"If it wasn't the king or Mortimer, then who else could it be? Could it have been your brother, Dafydd?" she ventured to ask him.

"Well," said Llywelyn. "It would not be beyond my brother. Though I can't see what benefit it would be to him to kill Tudor."

"Who else could it be?" she asked again.

"It could be anyone Beth, including someone here at the court."

"I am puzzled by it all and wonder if it had any political or military ramifications that we don't know about. So, I would like it solved for all kinds of reasons."

After a pause he said, "Perhaps it was a crime of passion. It could be that someone had fallen in love with you and wanted Tudor out of the way."

This surprised her and he followed up by asking her, "Has anyone shown special interest in you recently…?" Then he added quickly, "More than usual I mean."

She was dumbfounded by this suggestion and could only think of Llywelyn himself.

Eventually she said, "No. I don't think that's a possibility."

"Beth, I'm not sure that you are aware of how beautiful you are and how many men long to have your company."

She blushed and her mind raced, trying to think of other possible suitors but, other than Hywel, none came immediately to her mind and decided that it was something best considered when in her own company.

That night, Llywelyn's suggestion that Tudor's murder was a crime of passion would not leave her mind. She knew her own feelings towards Llywelyn but his feelings towards her were a mystery to her. He had appeared, from the time they met at Aberedw many years ago, to like her company. No, she thought, *like* was not a strong enough word; she could honestly say he *enjoyed* her company. He was in her company far more frequently than any other woman she knew.

Before he married Eleanor she could have loved him in the same way that she loved Hywel but, now that she had given herself to Hywel, Llywelyn could only be a very good friend.

Llywelyn spent much time with her and they were happy together. She was sure that he was not involved in Tudor's death because, at the time, he had a pregnant wife to whom he was devoted. She knew him as an honest and honourable man.

Throughout the rest of July and into August, Llywelyn's suggestion that Tudor's death could be a crime of passion stayed with her and each man who gave her more than one glance – and there were many – became a potential suspect in her mind.

August at Garth Celyn was hot and dry, the very weather that Llywelyn did not want. It was ideal for the king to make his war preparations and the possibility of a deep penetration into Gwynedd became a distinct possibility. The ground was hard, making it perfect for an army to move from Rhyddlan to at least the east bank of the river Conwy.

The fear of waking one day to see an armada of ships and boats heading for the shore at Garth Celyn was becoming the normal state of affairs at the royal court, and it was not pleasant.

Llywelyn was not willing to surrender or give an inch to the king's demands and was now taking the lead in what could only be described as a war. It was becoming increasingly obvious that Dafydd had acted in haste and had no long-term plan.

Dafydd had given the king good reason to invade, and Edward's objectives were simple and clear – he intended to conquer Gwynedd and Wales.

Llywelyn and his advisers knew that their forces would be no match to Edward's. His were greater in number and better equipped and, barring a lucky break, the conflict would be very one-sided and Edward would win.

Some at the court advocated coming to some kind of an arrangement with Edward through negotiation. Others were equally strongly of the belief that God was on their side and that theirs was the just cause as Edward had no right to invade a foreign country.

Llywelyn was very cautious but, by August, he had decided that some tentative negotiations would be necessary and these were set in motion through the services of the church and, in particular, the Bishop of Bangor.

Then shock news arrived at the court in August: Edward's forces had taken Anglesey and his main force was camped at Llanfaes. Messengers and refugees had arrived during the night bringing the dreaded news.

The possibility of an invasion of the Garth Celyn shore increased and the daily threat was now much greater.

This made everybody very anxious, but it gave a spur to the

negotiations. Anian, the bishop, was not regarded as a reliable negotiator because he had shown favouritism too often in the past and there was nothing to suggest that he would be different this time. Things looked grim.

Beth was also very concerned about the turn of events. She did not know where Hywel was and she had not heard from him for weeks. She wondered if he was at his estates in Anglesey when the invasion took place and, if so, she wondered if he had been captured by the king's troops.

Inhabitants of the court could see the king's forces gathering at Llanfaes. There was considerable coming and going by sea, with the king obviously preparing for an invasion of the mainland.

Speculation was rife that they would attack across the Lafan sands and Llywelyn ordered guards to be posted along the coast facing Anglesey and that the shoreline facing Lafan sands be prepared to counter an invasion, particularly below Garth Celyn, which was vulnerable.

Beth neither received a visit nor a message from Hywel throughout the early autumn.

She spent many hours walking the shore looking wistfully at the Anglesey coast, hoping that she would see a small boat being rowed across bringing her lover to her. She wanted him to tell her that all would be well. They could walk in the wood again. They could lie in the reeds again.

No boat appeared and she was told that it wasn't possible to cross in daylight anymore and, if he were to come to her, it would be at night. So, every night she listened for sounds of her lover coming to her, but in vain. The sounds were of the winds whistling around the hills and through the trees. She would get up to the window in the early hours of the morning and stare across the sea, but could not see his shadow crossing the Lafan sands.

She had even been to the reeds, just to remind herself of what had happened there and that Hywel did exist.

She spoke to Llywelyn about her concerns more than once, but he had told her the truth – he did not know what had happened to Hywel and that he was not receiving information about what was going on on the island. The king's forces were guarding the shores very carefully and had placed lookout posts around the island, turning it into a fortress. He assured her that as soon as he heard anything about Hywel, she would be the first to know about it.

This was a very frustrating and worrying time for Beth, not knowing whether Hywel was alive or dead. She wished that Llywelyn had built a wider network for gathering information.

During the months of September and November, Beth and Llywelyn became closer friends, despite the fact that he was often away from the royal court in various parts of his principality generating support for a resistance to Edward's invasion.

The king was still at Rhyddlan with the bulk of his army, consolidating his position in the North East and in Anglesey, while his allies enhanced the king's cause in the South West.

CHAPTER 25

End of October to 5 November 1282

TOWARDS THE END of October hopes were raised when it became known that the Archbishop of Canterbury, John Peckham had obtained permission from the king to conduct direct negotiations with Llywelyn at Garth Celyn.

However, there was uncertainty with the news that Roger Mortimer had died on the thirtieth of October and that his sons were likely to take over his estates. However, the King was not in a hurry to confirm their inheritance, probably because he wanted to ensure their loyalty first.

Archbishop Peckham, accompanied by the Bishop of Bangor and Archdeacon Madog, arrived at the royal court on the first day of November, having been given safe conduct by the king's forces on Anglesey and by Llywelyn on mainland Gwynedd.

He was welcomed at the court's main gate by Llywelyn, dressed in full regalia including his crown, the chancellor, and other Gwynedd nobles.

They walked together into the hall where a feast had been laid on for the guests. Once they had finished eating, the discussions began without delay.

The attempt at negotiations continued intermittently for a few days but made little progress and the hope that everyone had placed on Peckham's visit did not materialise. The negotiating team left for a day and returned to continue with their effort, but hope of a successful outcome was fading fast and the possibility of an all-out war becoming more of a reality.

Beth was despondent with the national situation, as well as

with her personal plight having had no message from Hywel, who she thought might have come to at least pay tribute to Archbishop Peckham's efforts to reach a peaceful solution. She was getting more fearful for her lover's well-being by the day.

Then on the morning of the fifth of November, her heart started to pound uncontrollably in her breast as she looked out through her window and saw a rider approach the gates.

It was the rider's horse, with its distinctive white patch on its neck, which she recognised first. The similarities were close enough to send her bounding out of her room and down the stairs into the courtyard and towards the gate. As she approached the gate she did manage to control herself better, but when she was about twenty yards from the entrance, she could see clearly that the rider was Hywel and that he was riding his horse towards her. He greeted her with a broad smile and she was overjoyed to see him again.

She stood where she was and he brought his horse towards her. "Am I pleased to see you?" he asked. "You look as beautiful as ever."

"Oh! Hywel. You are all right. I've missed you and I have been so worried about you. I thought you had been killed when the king invaded Anglesey."

"I'm fine. I must pay my respects to Llywelyn and the archbishop and then can we meet in your room?"

"Yes, of course," came the delighted reply.

They parted. Hywel stabled his horse and Beth returned to her room. She was beside herself with happiness and ran back upstairs even quicker than she had come down earlier.

She expected Hywel to be some time in the hall, meeting the others and discussing strategy and the archbishop's proposals. But, indeed, it was not very long before she could hear his footsteps at her door and his soft knock.

He walked in, confident that she would be waiting and ready for him.

She ran into his arms almost knocking him over. He steadied himself and they kissed passionately as lovers do when they have not seen each other for a long time.

"Remember it's the middle of the day and things are very busy here at the court and have been for the last few days," she said restraining him with her hands. "The servants are in and out of here frequently at this time of day."

He surprised her by saying, "Good."

She looked puzzled at him.

"Let's go for a ride along the shore. Let's get our horses. Come on," he insisted, this time dragging her towards the door.

"People will think it's odd that we are leaving the court while the archbishop is still here."

"No, they won't," he said emphatically. "They are too interested in the archbishop and how he is going to prevent a war."

She was convinced. "Let me change into my riding clothes and while I'm doing that you can get both horses."

He left her and she called one of the servants to help her dress. She wanted something loose, but colourful and warm, and she was in a hurry and excited. She'd been waiting for him a long time and she wanted to be with him for every available second. She dressed quickly but smartly.

"How do I look?" she asked her helper.

"You look beautiful, my lady, but you must wear a headdress remember it's November and it's cold. You don't want to catch a cold at the beginning of winter. Look, put this on," and she reached for a white scarf, which she proceeded to wrap around Beth's head covering her hair.

"I look like one of the cockle pickers dressed in this," Beth announced, trying to imagine what she looked like to others.

"Only from a distance. Everyone can see that your face is too pleasant and delicate to be a cockle picker. It'll keep you warm."

Beth had no time to argue with her and left, thinking she would remove it once she was outside.

Hywel was waiting for her with the two horses.

"Look at this silly scarf," she said.

"It looks good on you," he told her as he was mounting his horse, a much taller beast than hers. "You will need it once we are down by the shore. There is quite a breeze down there and no shelter. I had to put my hood up when I was coming here earlier."

She was helped onto her horse and they left at a slow pace through the gates, nodding respectfully to the gatekeepers.

The horses were ridden gently down to the shore and then the two had a gallop along the sands with the breeze in their faces. Hywel allowed her to keep up with him and she appreciated that. She also appreciated the scarf around her head because she would have been cold without it.

They galloped in the direction of Aberogwen. She knew where they were going and she was happy.

Having dismounted, they approached the reeds, with Hywel lending her a helping hand. They led the horses into the reeds and out of sight.

"Beth, I think of this place as belonging to us. It's our place. It's our magical place. We are away from the world and its problems. Let's leave the horses here."

He tied the horses to a willow and went further into the reeds, slightly ahead of her.

He found their place. It had changed but it was still their place. He took his cloak off and placed it carefully on the ground.

"I love you Beth. Will you marry me immediately after this war is over?"

"Yes, you know I will. There may not be a war; tell me a war is not inevitable. The archbishop may be able to find a way around the difficulties – after all he is a man of God and a clever man."

"Hmm!" he murmured noncommittally.

"I'm sure there's hope," she persisted. "Llywelyn has disbanded his army for a few days and he wouldn't do that unless he was fairly sure that there will be no attack for a few days at least. They have been on alert for weeks and he wanted to give them a rest. I don't see an attack coming while the archbishop is here anyway."

"What about Dafydd's forces on the Conwy? Does he expect an attack?"

"I don't know about the Conwy front. I overheard the order given for the forces facing Anglesey, and they dispatched riders with the messages yesterday. One was to go along the shore as far as Clynnog giving the message to the frontline troops and the other was to go inland where the reserves are waiting, ready to be called."

Hywel's expression did not change while he reassured her, "I'm sure Llywelyn knows exactly what he is doing and the archbishop may work a miracle."

"I'm so glad you agree, Hywel. I love you so much."

They lay on the cloak in each other's arms for a long time, happy and contended, thinking just of each other and their future lives together. Beth was convinced that a war could be avoided but aware that Hywel was not so certain. She just knew that a woman's intuition was often better than a man's.

There came the time for them to part go their different ways. She didn't want to leave him but he assured her that he would return to see her as soon as he could.

She wanted him to depart first because she could not bear the thought of leaving him. He eventually agreed when she told him that it was her intention to walk her horse back to Garth Celyn. She wanted to savour every second they had spent together in the reeds and taking her time to go back would give her the feeling that she had extended their rendezvous.

"You go," she said. "I will stay here for a while and dream of our lives together."

She stood after he placed his cloak around his shoulders. She left her head scarf where it was and would put it on later as she left, because once out of the reeds she knew that she would feel the cold.

"Go," she said. "I love you."

"I love you Beth," he said with his head bowed and looking dejected. "I don't want to leave you."

"Go now. Go before I start to cry."

He left. She could see him further away through the dead reeds mounting his horse, and slowly the sound of him departing faded.

Beth stood there staring at him as he departed. She decided that she did want to wave to him as he might not turn around to wave back at her.

She grabbed her white scarf from the ground, and turned quickly to follow him but unbalanced herself and extended her arms out to soften her fall. However, she recovered before she landed on the ground saw Hywel's purse pressed into the soft soil where her scarf had been.

On picking it up she could feel that there was something rattling inside it. Though she was fairly sure they were only coins, to make sure that there was nothing of importance in it, she opened it slightly, just enough to peer inside, and saw that there were indeed a few coins, a key and a small seal in it. She took the seal out and saw that it was Hywel's personal seal.

Shouting his name, she ran after him, though suspecting that it was too late. She reached her horse and led it out of the reeds but Hywel had long gone out of sight.

Running alongside her horse in the direction he had gone,

she continued to call his name, but knew it was probably pointless. She found a fallen tree nearby and managed with difficulty to climb from it into the saddle.

She decided that she would try to catch him at the ford on the Ogwen and urged her horse to gallop in that direction. She reached the ford but Hywel had crossed and she could see him in the distance near the top of the hill about half a mile away, but too far away for him to hear her calling his name.

Closing the gap between them was possible she decided, and continued to follow him. Feeling cold she wrapped the scarf around her head and entered the river slowly and carefully.

She reached the top of the hill in a short time and could again see him in the distance having just crossed the river Cegin. She felt sure that she was catching up with him a little and carried on after him. By the time she crossed the Cegin, he was again out of her sight and it was only when she came to the brow of the hill before turning towards the cathedral that she saw him again. She had definitely gained ground on him but was still too far away for him to hear her calling.

She was surprised when she realised that he was not going towards the cathedral but across the Hirael Bay on the shore side of the friary. She spurred her horse forward. Hywel, however, was already almost in the trees and starting to ascend the hill.

She hesitated again wondering where he was going but, by now, she was driven forward by her own curiosity as well as the need to give him the purse.

He was following a track that she suspected would lead to Meg's cottage, or at least in that general direction.

She followed, wrapping the scarf tighter around her head and was now pleased that she resembled a cockle picker on her way home.

The further up the hill she went the more she became convinced that she would catch up with him at the cottage. He was surely going there to visit Meg's husband to see if he was all right. She knew Hywel was a kind man and she would also have the joy of seeing him again.

She was right; about a hundred yards from the cottage she could see that Hywel's horse had been tied to a small tree outside.

She stopped her horse and looked straight ahead towards the cottage. About halfway between where she had stopped and the cottage, and just above the track, there was a large pile of broken branches of all shapes and sizes ready for burning.

Though the sun was directly behind the cottage and shining into her eyes, the trees sheltered them enough for her to have a fairly clear view. From being a dull day, it had turned to be a fine evening over Anglesey and it bore well for the next day she thought.

The cottage brought memories back to her of Meg's body hanging from the beam in the dark – a shiver passed through her body. She overcame her momentary fear and thought of Hywel's live and vigorous body, and slipped off her horse, landing gently on both feet.

The death of Meg, like that of Tudor, remained a mystery to her and she decided at that moment that on her return to Garth Celyn she would ask Llywelyn to question Dan again.

She wanted to shock and surprise her lover and walking quietly towards the dwelling, avoiding the crunchy, noisy leaves, she arrived at the back wall and the spot where months earlier she believed someone had listened to Hywel and her conversing. She was laughing to herself at how she was going to surprise him by calling his name through the hole.

She was still smiling as she put her face to the hole.

She could hear two voices. One she recognised as Hywel and the other was an older man whom she thought had to be Meg's husband.

They were talking quite loudly and she could hear every word. If only she had heard the start it might have made sense to her. She heard Hywel saying, "No don't worry. I am almost certain it will be tomorrow at Moel y Don. The tide will be favourable and Llywelyn's soldiers, I know, have been dispersed. I've already found enough out to say that with confidence but we have to be certain that there are no soldiers in key areas."

"What areas are they?"

"That's where you are important to us. We wish to have a good foothold on the mainland before Llywelyn attacks. To arrive quickly at Moel y Don, he will bring his troops through Bangor. So, if an hour before daybreak tomorrow there are no soldiers entering Bangor on their way westward, light that beacon. That's all you've got to do. Once the beacon is burning well, leave the area and don't return for a few days."

"Yes."

"That's it then. Let's drink to it."

She could hear the sound of viscous mead being poured and then she heard Hywel saying, "To the king and to a successful crossing."

She moved away from the wall, dazed. Had she misunderstood? Surely, she thought, she had misheard. Hywel, wishing the king well? She had heard him being critical of Llywelyn more than once as many others were, but when it came to the crunch they were loyal to him. It was surprising to hear him drinking to the king's success.

Also, what did he mean by saying, 'To a successful crossing,' and why was Meg's husband to light the beacon? While these thoughts were rushing through her mind she was moving away from the cottage as fast and as quietly as she could. After what seemed a very long time she reached her horse and led it away down the track as quickly as she could, looking back through tears to see if she was being followed.

There was no-one following her but that did not stop her looking backwards every ten yards or so which naturally slowed her retreat. Tears were flowing down her face as she reached the shore of Hirael Bay where she stopped to gather her thoughts. She rearranged her scarf to resemble the attire of a cockle picker and was able to mount her horse and continue her journey.

She was now relieved that she resembled a cockle picker and not the young noblewoman that she was. She felt safer in her disguise travelling along the track in the evening, knowing that she would have to pass the place where Tudor was murdered.

Her thoughts about what she had heard at the cottage were rolling wildly in her mind. She looked for new meanings to things and doubted her own sense of judgement, particularly her judgement of men.

She had told Hywel innocently about Llywelyn having dispersed his forces in recent days. She knew she should not have said that, but what did Hywel mean when he said, 'I've already found enough out to say that.' She was ashamed of herself.

The man she loved so deeply had let her down, had betrayed her trust in him and could not possibly love her. She was sobbing quietly as her horse walked slowly along the track in the direction of the royal court. The most devastating discovery had been that he did not love her and had merely used her for his own pleasure while at the same time getting valuable information from her that would be of great use to her prince's enemies.

She realised on that journey that she had to somehow think of Hywel as having died. She would impose upon herself a process of grief to wash him out of her mind, but she knew it was not going to be easy.

She crossed the Cegin without much difficulty, which was a relief to her as the sun now setting fast in the red western sky. As she was climbing up the slight slope from the Ogwen, her horse slipped and her heart sank, but the reliable animal recovered its step and she continued to the top of the rise, only to be faced by two men walking towards her in the gloom.

Garth Celyn was still some distance away and she was apprehensive, faced with the two men while in such low spirits. However, she gathered courage, played her cockle picker role and addressed them confidently with a "Good night" in as deep a voice as she could manage.

The men's responses were nervously delivered. Cockle pickers were well known for their toughness and meeting one in the gloom was not a welcome experience.

She came to the place where Tudor had been killed and, as always, urged her horse to move faster – the old oak tree trunk was getting to look more like a crouching man every month. It unsettled her every time she passed it, even in daylight, but in the gloom she found it scared her and made her wonder what exactly had happened there.

She arrived back at the royal court safely to be told by the guards that the archbishop, the bishop and Madog the Archdeacon and their supporting clerks had left and that there had been no progress towards peace.

She knew exactly what she had to do; she had to find Llywelyn immediately to tell him everything.

CHAPTER 26

5 November 1282

BETH DISMOUNTED HER horse and ran towards the hall, praying that Llywelyn would be there. The guards, who knew her well, stepped forward to slow her down but when faced by the determined look on her face stepped aside and allowed her in.

Llywelyn was sitting with his brother Dafydd at the table at the far end of the hall. The commotion she caused entering the room made them both look up. Llywelyn sensed immediately that there must be something wrong and rose, but he was hardly standing before Beth was suddenly leaning across the table with tears running down her face and fright in her eyes. Through her sobbing she managed to say, "I think the king's army will invade from Anglesey at Moel y Don tomorrow morning."

Everyone sat at the high table heard what she had said and fell silent – not a sound to be heard anywhere in the great hall.

"Come with me," Llywelyn said, and he led her to an adjacent room.

Beth told him what she had seen and heard, and admitted that she had told Hywel that Llywelyn had stood down his troops for a rest.

He reacted immediately. Returning to the hall he called his main councillors together, including Dafydd. The two had been cooperating well since August.

Llywelyn announced that Beth had brought him information that suggested that the king's forces on Anglesey would invade the mainland from Moel y Don the next day. They all knew that the troops on Anglesey had been building boats at Llanfaes for some time, and it had been assumed that they were going to be used to cross the Menai. The only thing in doubt was whether they would row the boats across or tie them together to act as a bridge across the narrow straits when the tide was out.

Someone said, "It will be low tide at about eleven tomorrow morning."

Someone else said, "They've chosen Moel y Don because it is the shortest crossing and out of our sight here."

Another added, "It's the furthest short crossing from here. They hope to get a good foothold before we attack them."

The chancellor then responded, "I did not think they would invade across the Lafan sands. I always thought it would be too exposed to our scouts on the hills and too far across to supply their soldiers after the initial landings."

"We must get our soldiers there by low tide," Llywelyn announced. "Send messages out immediately to gather our men at St Cedol's Church in Pentir, below Moel Lleucu. Don't send them through Bangor. Keep clear of that cathedral."

Dafydd said, "I will send for my men in the Conwy valley."

"No, keep them there, the king's main force may try to cross there at the same time. It would make sense if they did and split our forces."

"Go to them as soon as you can Dafydd. Go now with your men. I need to know that the Conwy is well defended. It's a dark night, so go carefully. Lead your horse; I need you to arrive there safely."

Dafydd nodded obediently and left with his four men.

Llywelyn organised his trusted friends to carry messages to various parts of the hinterland to bring soldiers together at Pentir. He was hoping to gather about five hundred there by the morning.

He started to prepare himself for the battle he felt sure was ahead of him. He knew Beth was reliable and could be depended upon to have brought him accurate information.

Garth Celyn was placed on full alert, but everyone was told not to use any more torches than usual so as not to alert the enemy across the water. Then, the soldiers at the court, mainly Llywelyn's special guards, were told to have a few hours' sleep and that the war horn would be sounded to wake everyone up at the appropriate time.

They left the court as an army unit at about five in the morning and, marching in the dark, set off for Pentir. They crossed the Ogwen at the ford on the Bangor track, and then followed the east bank of the river Cegin to Pentir where they were joined by the other soldiers coming from Clynnog Fawr, Llanllyfni and the Gwyrfai valley, Dolbadarn and the Seiont valley and Dyffryn Ogwen.

Llywelyn's troops, infantry and cavalry, did not have to travel far, nor did they have to carry heavy loads of food – so they travelled light and fast. Even so, they had supply wagons at the rear moving at a much slower pace. These were carrying people to take care of the wounded and to carry heavier weapons.

While his main force was still gathering at Pentir, Llywelyn dispatched observers to watch the coast opposite Anglesey and to report anything unusual to him.

He had to bear in mind that the attack could come anywhere and that there was no absolute certainty that they would cross at Moel y Don. The attack at Moel y Don could be a diversion to draw his troops westwards, while the main assault could still be on the coast near the royal court. By placing his main force at Pentir, he was well positioned to counterattack any invasion from Anglesey onto the opposite mainland coast.

Many women accompanied the force that left Garth Celyn and Beth had asked if she could go with them, but was told by Llywelyn that she would be needed at the court to help with the communications between the army and the court and to receive and send messages to the Conwy valley.

The soldiers left in good spirits, many happy that, at last, there would be an end to the phoney war and looking forward to the fight. Others were apprehensive and fearful for their futures.

Sometime after the troops had left and shortly before dawn, Beth also left the royal court dressed as a cockle picking woman, and this time she had a cockle picker's basket with her on the horse. She was too involved to just remain sitting in her room, waiting for events that would affect her life. She hadn't slept all night, with her hatred of Hywel mixed with what she had heard at the cottage churning in her mind.

She arrived at the ford on the Ogwen as dawn was breaking. There was enough light for her to see her way across easily and safely. When she came to the Cegin she did not follow the troops up the river but crossed it and made her way towards Bangor.

Directing her horse across Hirael beach, she could see that the sea was already ebbing and had left the high tide mark a while earlier.

She climbed the hill towards the cottage and, as she approached, her nose alerted her to the faintly sweet and pleasant smell of burning timber. She thought it could be coming from the houses below but, as she progressed up the path, the smell got stronger until she could see that the pile of branches she had seen the previous night was burnt and all that remained were glowing embers. It must have been quite a blaze, she thought.

She stopped her horse and peered through the trees.

There was still a column of smoke from the embers rising high into the sky, and she turned to look towards the opposite coastline and the area beyond it. It was too far for her to see any movement in the trees and vegetation, but she guessed that the fire had been seen on the island and that someone across the water had been waiting for the signal that all was clear for the invasion to take place.

She guessed that a blaze made of branches and leaves would not last long and so whoever lit the fire was not that far away. She knew what his instructions were, but she did not know where he was to go after setting the fire alight.

Since he had not walked down the way she came up she knew he must have followed the path along the hilltop towards the *ffriddoedd* (sheep walks) above the coastline or one of the two paths leading down towards Bangor. She had no wish to meet Meg's husband and led her horse carefully down the steeper, more treacherous but much shorter path towards the cathedral. At the bottom she remounted her horse and turned right and followed the track up the river Tarannon westward, up the small shallow valley towards Caernarfon.

There were very few travellers on the road, giving the appearance of a normal and peaceful morning. As she approached the headwaters of the river, she turned slightly southwards climbing the hill that she knew would give her a view of Moel y Don.

She guessed that if there was anything happening at Moel y Don she would surely see it from the top of the hill. While she did not wish there to be an invasion, she was concerned that she might have sent Llywelyn and his troops on a wild goose chase.

Her horse made steady progress up the slope and was not far from the summit when a strong-looking man, who had been hiding in the bushes by the track, held a spear inches away from her. Though she and her mount were startled, she heard the man ordering her to stop.

She did so and heard the man asking, "Where are you going?"

She remembered who she was and told him in no uncertain

terms, "There's better cockle picking in Caernarfon than in the Lafan sands so I'm going there you fool. Now get out of my way."

He was taken aback by her reply and manner but managed to say, "You can't go this way – there's going to be a battle here – cockle picking or not."

"Who's fighting whom?"

"The king's troops are crossing from Anglesey to conquer Gwynedd and Llywelyn is going to stop them."

"Well! Let me at them." Pointing to her basket she said, "The very smell of these cockles will turn their stomachs and then you can slay them while their faces are down puking." She even impressed herself by her imitation of a typical cockle picker, but she had seen so many at Garth Celyn that it was easy for her to imitate them.

"Let me through," she demanded.

"I don't dare. Llywelyn would kill me. If you want to see what's happening come off your horse and lead him into the gorse that way. But stay out of sight. There are about two thousand English soldiers and a cavalry of two hundred just starting to cross the bridge."

"Is Llywelyn here?"

"Yes. We've only got about five hundred soldiers."

Though disappointed to be told of the imbalance of numbers, she said nothing more and quietly did as the guard suggested and entered the gorse. She tied her horse, with difficulty, to a large gorse bush and stepped closer to the edge to see the Menai below.

CHAPTER 27

6 November 1282

FROM HER POSITION above the Menai, Beth could see that the bridge of boats the enemy had taken hours to construct extended from the small peninsula of Moel y Don across the straits. It had been built as the sea retreated to its furthest point, reducing the distance across to its minimum. The boats were linked together by ropes and were rocked gently to and fro by the waves.

Looking at this bridge she guessed that it had just been completed, as Edward's soldiers and their leaders were beginning to fill most of the boats on the Anglesey side and advancing towards the ones attached to the mainland.

She could also see hundreds of soldiers, some with lances, others with swords drawn, archers and horses, waiting to be led across the bridge. It shocked her to see the strength of the invading force and her heart sank at the thought of what was to follow.

The Welsh soldiers were hiding in the gorse and bushes on a slope to her left and immediately below her position, but above the intended landing area.

Then the leader of the invading force, seeing that the bridge was complete, gave the order to attack and the soldiers charged across. They flowed over like a wave, a mixture of men and horses, their polished metal armour, swords and spears giving it a mercurial glow in the morning sun.

Once on the mainland they fanned out and were organised quickly into groups and directed towards an old fort located slightly above the Menai. That would provide them with a foothold in Gwynedd and an easily defendable position. This was a well-planned invasion and the weather was perfect for them – clear, dry and still.

When they were about halfway to the old fort and climbing slightly uphill, the order came loud and clear from the Welsh horn to attack. It was clear to Beth that the Welsh commander wanted to prevent the invaders reaching the old fort and establishing themselves in a defendable position.

The Welsh descended on Edward's men with brutal force, hitting them side-on as they ascended the low hill, while the bridge across the Menai continued to disgorge its lethal content onto the beach, spreading like oil on a wet surface, and covering the mud, sand and gravel.

A second wave of Welsh soldiers was released by another horn signal and it appeared to Beth to be a much larger force than the first and struck at the middle of the incursion on the beach.

From her viewing point Beth could see Llywelyn leading this charge and it was obvious that his intention was to reach the end of the bridge and disconnect it from its moorings.

The battle on the beach was furious with swords waved in all directions. She could see that there were men falling on both sides and lying still on the ground in the midst of the fighting. The Welsh pressed hard and gained ground in the middle where their greatest effort was concentrated. It was a vicious battle, but with the invaders' access to the beach restricted by the width of their bridge, and the Welsh arriving in greater numbers, they began to overwhelm the invaders.

To her great relief she saw that the defenders of the bridge were slowly losing ground on the western side of the moorings and that the Welsh were able to use their swords to hack at the ropes.

The invaders' resolve on the eastern side of the moorings began to weaken and Beth could well imagine that they would be concerned about being cut off from the bridge. Their role had changed from being an invading force to becoming defenders of the bridge for their comrades to retreat across. The tide of battle was swinging against them as was the tide in the straits.

She could imagine that others on the beach would be concerned that their escape route was being cut off and, indeed, within a few minutes the whole battle scene had changed from a well-organised attack by an invading force to one of panic and confusion.

The soldiers on the bridge didn't realise that their comrades on the beach were in retreat and kept pressing forward, causing chaos on the bridge. Matters got much worse for them when the Welsh managed to break moorings on the mainland end of the bridge and then the tide began to swing the line of boats like a pendulum away from the mainland shore. It was all happening so quickly that Beth had difficulty in observing everything.

The invading troops making their way to the old fort were in disarray. Hit hard by the first wave of attackers and seeing the disaster on the beach behind them, they knew that they had to retreat to the beach to reach the bridge as soon as possible. It was a calamity for them and Beth could see they would not reach the bridge in time. Many were cut down by the pursuing Welsh soldiers, others ran into the advancing sea where they were joined by the soldiers and cavalry who had been fighting on the beach.

The line of boats was now about ten yards from dry land and the strain on the ropes and planks was beginning to tell. The structure soon started to disintegrate before their eyes, with men and horses unbalanced and dislodged into the water.

She could see that the invasion was an unmitigated disaster for Edward. Llywelyn and his forces had been ready for them and she believed that she had played her part in the success. Hundreds of the invaders were dead, either killed in battle or drowned in the sea.

It was over and, from her position above the Menai, Beth had seen it all; the invading dead were lying where they had fallen on the beach. Many of the bodies were slowly been swallowed by the incoming sea and she knew that, within an hour, those perished on the beach would also be covered by the cold, grey water.

Those who had retreated into the sea and had failed to get to a boat were already drowned, and their bodies were being pushed to and fro by the waves like small tree trunks, lifeless and unresisting. Some faced the sky, others had their faces in the sand. Some had their feet wedged in the stones, and their bodies behaved like small boats at anchor. It was a scene that Beth knew she would never forget.

She raised her gaze to the bridge of boats that was a broken line of tangled mess. Those firmly hooked to the Anglesey shore were still tied together, but were at the mercy of the tide throwing them on the Anglesey beach in a disorganised heap. These boats also contained dead and severely wounded soldiers, with their comrades on shore still too dazed to organise their rescue or, perhaps, aware that they were already beyond being saved.

Other boats had been scattered onto the mainland's beach and were now being examined by Llywelyn's soldiers for any threats or booty.

Compared with the chaos at the height of the battle half an hour earlier, the scene below her was now very calm. The Welsh soldiers, having celebrated on the beach, were in the main going back up the hill to examine their gains. It was also a surprisingly peaceful sight, but for the splashes of red which Beth could see from her vantage point, soiling the grass, gravel and sand wherever a body lay, revealing the reality of what had happened. The water around the floating or marooned bodies was of a brown appearance to her, but she knew it had acquired that colour from the blood of the killed soldiers.

All the dead that she could now see were invaders, because she had watched the Welsh carry away their perished and wounded comrades. Many of the dead, killed or lost to the sea, were members of the English nobility and Llywelyn would ensure that their bodies would be respected and returned to Anglesey through the services of local priests.

Beth decided that she would go down to the beach and follow the track back to Bangor along the bank of the river Heilyn that flowed from the east into the Menai, almost opposite Moel y Don.

She led her horse down slowly and reached the western edge of the battlefield, where bodies strewn across the land sloping down to the beach. There was no pattern to the carnage; it was as though the corpses had been dropped from above by some gigantic bird. The details of the injuries were now obvious to her and she averted her eyes from the severed limbs and gouged bodies.

She was not alone leading her horse towards the shoreline. People from the local hamlets and women and children had gathered there on the shore, in both directions. People, young and old, were taking the opportunity to thank God for the victory, to praise the action of the men who had fought, while others were there to look for what valuables were to be found or likely to be washed ashore.

Many had their eyes on the boats – even if they were unable to salvage them whole, the boats were made of solid wood which could be put to good use.

Sadly, she could also see that they were also taking boots and clothes off the corpses. She wanted to dissociate herself from this group of people and turned in the direction of Bangor for her journey home.

But, on the beach she couldn't stop herself from looking at the dead faces. She didn't recognise any of them, but still she wondered who they were, whose father, brother or son lay dead. Some were scarred beyond recognition, others looked as though they were peacefully asleep.

As she walked along the beach she heard a man shouting after her, "Going to fill your baskets with what you can find are you? More valuable than the cockles, I bet."

She turned around to see a small, thin middle-aged man and three women standing near her. She reminded herself that to them she was a cockle picker and, glaring at the man, she said, "Didn't fight, did you? I've picked many a stronger-looking cockle than you."

The man's jaw dropped and the women giggled as Beth turned and went on her way.

She passed some priests and monks arriving with the intention of giving the last rights to the mortally wounded. She knew they were far too late for the men she had seen strewn on the battlefield, but doubtless they would search among the dead for those they could still offer comfort to before they died.

Stepping carefully and leading her horse down towards the water's edge, she noticed marks on the sand suggesting that something had been dragged from the water up to the beach. She thought perhaps that someone had picked up a piece of a boat to use as firewood and dragged it out of sight to come back later with a friend to take it home.

But while looking towards the sea and settling her mind to say a prayer for all those killed, she heard a rustling noise in the grass behind her higher up the beach. She turned and saw a body lying there, partly hidden by dead brambles with its feet resting on the larger rounded stones at the edge of the beach.

Instinctively she stepped backwards, and was about to move away when it dawned on her that the sound she heard must have been the body moving. So, though the soldier lay very still, he was still alive. She stood her ground and, after a short pause, stepped towards it taking her horse with her.

As she got closer, she could see that it was a body of a man dressed in heavy armour with a sword belt. He might have had a helmet, but that had long gone and was by then probably worn by one of Llywelyn's soldiers as a trophy.

She slowly and carefully approached the body and when within a yard or two of its feet, she heard what she thought was a quiet groan. This stopped her in her tracks, and she peered at the soldier who was soaked from his hair to his boots. He lay face downwards surrounded by blood-stained grass and brambles. She realised he must have dragged himself up the beach and had fallen into the dead brambles and was hidden from the view of those who had searched the beach for anything of value.

She moved closer to the body and again heard the weak groans and also obtained a better view of her discovery. She could not see his face though and his wet hair was making it difficult to even judge his age.

She could see that his right arm was partly severed just below the shoulder and he had lost a lot of blood from the wound. For all she knew he might well have other injuries on the front of his body, though the chest-armour would have protected the upper part of his torso.

She was in two minds whether to call for help or not, but when she remembered the group who had tried to laugh at her earlier, she knew she had to try to do something on her own. She bent down again, with the intention of lifting him out of the brambles by taking a firm hold of his uninjured left arm. He was too heavy for her but, as a result of her effort, the man's body turned on its back.

At the same time her legs gave way under her from the effort she had exerted, and she fell onto her bottom next to the injured soldier and looked at him. But without having to move any of the matted hair, she recognised the man as Hywel, her Hywel.

Chapter 28

Later on – 6 November 1282

S HE WAS SHOCKED, frightened, confused and bent over him in the brambles unaware of the cuts to her own hands and the discomfort of the rough ground under her. She loved him and the fact that he had betrayed her and Llywelyn was not relevant to her at this moment. He had tricked her and she had been angry with him, but she had also been very happy with him. They had shared so much; they'd had moments of great joy together and that's what mattered to her.

They had cared for each other, they had worried about each other, they had been happy and sad together and they had loved each other. They had trusted each other and for some time he had been her best friend and confidant. How could she cope without him anyway?

She was so pleased that she had found him alive. She was determined that she would nurse him back to health and forgive him for what he had done to her and her prince. He was exciting to be with and she was always excited to be there with him. She had told him everything and so many things had happened to her since she had last seen him which she desperately wanted to tell him about.

She tried to talk to him. "Hywel, can you hear me?"

Hywel did not even groan in response.

"Please talk to me," she pleaded, repeatedly kissing him on his head.

He did groan this time. She put her ear near his mouth and

appealed to him again. This time she heard him whisper with great effort what she thought was, "Last rights."

She was panic-stricken because she was determined to get Hywel back to health and his attitude was not going to help her if he was asking to have the last rights given to him.

"Come on Hywel. It's Beth. I'm here to help you and make you better."

But he repeated the same words very faintly again and there was no mistaking them this time. He was asking for his last rights to be given him.

"Hywel you are not going to die. You're injured but you are a strong man and will get better in a short time. Come on, let's get up. I'll help you to sit up."

He made no reply.

She tried to turn him on his side, but he was too heavy for her and he was entangled in the brambles.

She realised that she needed help and started looking around. She did not want to reveal his position to the people gathered on the battle site but needed assistance urgently. She wondered if she should try somehow to bandage his arm to stop the bleeding, which would be very difficult for her on her own, or should she go immediately to search for reliable help.

She decided to go for help. Leaving Hywel and her horse, she ran back along the beach to find the monks she had seen earlier.

Then, about thirty yards ahead of her, there appeared a monk in a black habit coming towards her with his hood up and deep in thought. He was a young man and was shocked to see a female cockle picker running towards him. Before she could say anything, he clearly assumed the worst, made a sign of the cross, turned his back on her and walked away from her.

Beth called after him, "Brother, I wonder if you can help me."

He quickened his pace as he tried to flee from her. Beth called again for his help but he turned this time to glance at her and, judging that he had a good start on her, started running away from her.

She followed and called out to him, "I thought you had a duty to help. My friend has been injured in the battle and he is asking for your help. Please help us."

He slowed down, looked backwards again and realised that she had stopped following him. "Please help us," she said again. "My friend is lying in the grass just over there."

The monk was calmed by her words and nervously followed her to where Hywel lay.

When they arrived, she could not hear any further groans or moans and said, "Hywel I've brought some help."

The monk bent down over Hywel's head and wiped his face gently. "I've come to help you," he said calmly. The monk's manner pleased her and she moved closer to hear what was being said.

Then she heard Hywel say in a faint voice, "Can you give me my last rights please?"

"I've only recently qualified to take people's last rights," the monk said, turning to Beth.

"But surely he is going to live," said Beth through her tears. During the search for help she had been able to hold back the tears, but now that someone else was taking the strain of the occasion, she could no longer restrain her feelings.

The monk looked her straight in the eyes and, as inexperienced as he was, knew that Hywel was dying and said to her, "I'm afraid your friend is close to death. You must prepare yourself for the worst; that is what he is doing."

"But how can we mend his wounds?" she asked, as if she had not heard what the monk had said.

He did not repeat what he had just said but proceeded to listen to Hywel's confession.

Taking in his hand a cross that hung around his middle, he said, "I will listen to the confession of your sins. Then, if I believe you are truly repentant, you will be absolved of your sins."

Turning to Beth the young monk said, "We have not much time, I'm afraid. I hope I will get this right." Then to Hywel he said in a clear but low voice, "What have you to confess my son?"

"I have sinned against God and wish forgiveness. I wish for forgiveness for all whom I have killed and maimed in battle…" He hesitated and added, "… all my violent actions and all whom I have been cruel to during my time on earth."

"Are you truly contrite?"

"Yes."

"Then you are absolved," he said and held the cross near Hywel's mouth for him to kiss.

"You have shown contrition and you are forgiven, my son. Go on your journey with the Lord's blessing. Amen."

Beth heard it all. Hywel had made an enormous effort to speak so that the monk could hear him.

The monk turned to her and asked, "Did I get it right, do you think? Did he say the right words?"

She was in shock and did not answer. She still believed that her Hywel would recover and said to the monk, "He will feel better now and his injuries will heal."

The monk put a different interpretation on Beth's words, rather than the meaning she intended and replied, "Yes, he will be relieved of all his pain and will depart this world soon. I will stay with you until he is gone."

"Is he going to die?"

"Yes, soon I think. Though I am young I have seen many as they approach death. I can say from his breathing that he is near the end. He has lost too much blood. Look at his arm and I think he has some wounds at the front of his body which we can't see,

195

but look at the blood here," he said, pointing to a pool of blood seeping from under his body.

Hywel was talking faintly again, "Will you hear my last wish?"

The monk glanced at Beth and then looked back at Hywel and said holding his hand, "Yes, I will my son."

With an immense effort, Hywel was able to say, "I wish my estate in Anglesey to pass to my son by my first wife, and I wish my estate in Arfon to pass for the benefit of Margaret, my new wife and the woman I truly love, for her life and then to my son after her death."

Beth couldn't believe what she had heard; she couldn't believe this man was Hywel. She was angry and grabbed Hywel's shoulder and, with the extra strength rising from her anger, she pulled so that she could see his face clearly. At that moment relief came over the injured soldier's face as he was dying, and she recognised him as Hywel, leaving no doubt in her mind.

Beth sat still, as life drained away from the still body next to her and as her love for Hywel drained from her soul.

The monk remained with her for a while, but eventually checked Hywel's breathing and then his pulse and announced, "There, your friend has now left this world completely."

Beth was weeping and could not come to terms with what had happened. The monk eventually said that he would have to leave her to administer to others on the beach.

She did not wish to be left on her own with Hywel's body and, as the monk was leaving, she appealed to him to stay and told him that the dead man was a close relative of the prior of the Dominican friary in Hirael. She appealed to him to inform the prior and asked if he could arrange a decent burial for him. She did not wish to leave him there on the beach to the mercy of the people scavenging the corpses.

The monk immediately told her not to worry. He would

inform the prior and ensure that with his fellow monks, Hywel's body would have a decent burial in the friary. He went to fetch other monks from the beach to help carry Hywel's body and left Beth alone with Hywel's body.

She checked his breathing again but could hear no movement at all, nor could she feel his pulse and had to accept that he was dead.

She had loved him but, clearly from what he had confessed, he had not loved her. He had deceived her in love and had been disloyal to her, Llywelyn and Wales. Of all these, by far the cruellest blow was the fact he didn't love her and had used her.

Though she knew that she would grieve for him, the events of the last twenty-four hours were dramatically changing her feelings towards him.

Her horse was still standing nearby, occasionally stamping its hooves on the mixture of gravel and sand, indicating that it wanted to be on its way. However, it was a while before the monk returned with his four colleagues. Only then did she start to worry about the long journey back to the royal court.

They picked up Hywel's body and placed it on a cart on top of other bodies. By touching Hywel's hand she bid a tearful farewell to him and led her horse to the track leading towards Bangor.

On her return journey she met many who were jubilant at the result of the battle, but she could not share their joy because she had lost everything, apart from her own life, in the battle.

Bangor was bustling with celebrating soldiers, so she progressed slowly and, turning right, away from Hirael and the Cegin estuary, she looked down to the sea and where the Anglesey shore should be. She could see very little because a thick mist had descended over the area, rendering everything damp, gloomy and darker.

She forded the two rivers without incident and, as she

approached the place where Tudor had been murdered, as was her usual practice she urged her horse to move faster. The horse obliged but the track was slippery in the mist and the horse was cautious. She decided to let him go at his own pace rather than risk a fall in that dreadful place.

It came to her mind again that on the day that Tudor had been murdered, she had met Hywel in the reeds not more than half a mile away from where she was now. The tinted veil that had covered her eyes when it came to Hywel had slipped – she remembered how she and Hywel had separated and gone their different ways in the afternoon. Tudor and Hywel could well have met that afternoon.

The fading sun had just enough warmth to pierce through the mist just at that moment, and it might have been aided by the slightest of breezes from the mountains. Whatever it was, something shifted the mist momentarily. The sun's rays brightened the Ogwen estuary; she could see the reeds bathed in golden sunset light and for a brief moment it shone on her, warming her depressed soul. Then it was gone again and the mist reoccupied the space. She looked around with an uneasy feeling and saw the old tree trunk – it looked exactly like a man crouching, waiting for someone or something. What was left of the old tree looked like Hywel's face on the beach, drained of its lifeblood.

She shivered and wondered if Hywel had, for some reason, killed Tudor. Was it a crime of passion after all? Did he want to have her for himself only? No. If he had killed him, one thing she was sure of, he wouldn't have done it to have full possession of her.

These thoughts alarmed her and this time, when she urged her horse forward, she meant it and the horse responded likewise.

When she arrived at Garth Celyn a party was in full swing. There were people celebrating everywhere. The royal court had not seen anything like it for years. Gwynedd had not seen such victory for a long time.

Beth decided to wait till the following morning before sharing her experiences with Llywelyn. She missed Eleanor that night and knew she would cry herself to sleep.

CHAPTER 29
10 November at Garth Celyn

WHAT BETH HAD heard on the beach had turned her life around. She had lost the man she loved even if his love was false, even if he had deceived her.

It was in this dreadful state of mind that she lay crying on her bed when there was a knock on the door. It was a messenger from Llywelyn wondering where she was and requesting her presence in the hall on such an important night. She was pleased that he was thinking about her and, of course, she would go to him, but she could not possibly join in the celebrations because of Hywel's death and what she had heard him say as he died.

She dressed and went out into the chilly night; the mist had cleared but the sky was rapidly clouding over and a cold easterly wind was blowing. She looked towards the mountains towering above the court and wondered if the mild autumn that they had experienced was ending. She looked to the east and thought that there might be some snow on the way.

There were celebrations outside as well as inside the hall, but she was beckoned in immediately by the guard and, once inside, mingled her way through the gathering towards the top table where Llywelyn sat. She could see that he was not as drunk as those around him, which was typical of him she thought – he rarely let his guard down.

"Thank you for your message Llywelyn. I did not want to go to bed without seeing you and hearing about the victory from your mouth," she said leaning over the table. "But I did not want to burden you with my sadness on such a night as this."

"What? Why are you sad? I don't understand."

"Hywel was a part of the invasion force at Moel y Don and he was killed on the beach." She stopped to give herself a chance to control her tears. "I was with him when he made his confessions to a monk."

"I'm so sorry Beth. You must be feeling awful. I'm so sorry," he said, rising and walking around the table to put his arm around her.

"Hywel is dead," she sobbed. "But that is not the worst thing. The worst thing is that he loved the woman he lived with, some woman called Margaret," and so, Beth told him everything she had seen and heard on the beach.

He insisted that she drink some warm mead to help her overcome the shock.

"I did not like to try to see you earlier because I knew you would be celebrating. It was a fantastic victory; it will make Edward think twice about attacking us here."

"I am not so sure Beth. He is a strange man; it could make him angrier and he could attack immediately. He has a very powerful army and, as the battle today confirms, his army is much larger than ours, but our soldiers were outstandingly brave and determined and that's why we were able to defeat them. They lost about three hundred soldiers, almost twenty knights and their leader Luke de Tany was also killed."

"Yes," she said, sipping her mead, only to be told by Llywelyn to take a proper mouthful of it.

Her head was spinning but she could hear him encouraging her to drink more mead.

"Drink that mead. My brother Dafydd may be coming to join us soon and he will entertain you."

"Is he leaving his troops on the Conwy?"

"Yes, the weather is changing tonight and real winter weather is coming from the east. We may well have snow tonight. So, the king can't move far for a day or two at least."

She felt better having spoken to Llywelyn, as was always the case. He was able to lift her spirit. She stayed for a while in the hall, but left before Dafydd arrived.

The mead helped but she did not sleep well. Grief and confusion filled her heart and mind. She tried numerous times in the night to think of other things and other people: her parents and Aberedw, but she kept returning to Hywel's death and his last wish, then Tudor's death and Meg's death.

She resolved that in the morning she would ask Llywelyn to question Dan again, for her to get at least one thing out of her mind.

Late morning she went to see Llywelyn who was recovering from the previous night's entertainment and took the opportunity to ask him to question Dan again.

Llywelyn was sensitive to her experience the previous day. "It must have shocked and upset you to learn the truth about Hywel."

"Yes it did. I was angry and disappointed at how deceitful a person he was and yet he was so loving and nice towards me. It was all pretence. It was as though he had two sides to him."

"He certainly did. It will take you a while to recover from the shock."

"Yes. I may never recover. But I am determined to try and it would help if I understood why Tudor was killed and why Meg was killed."

"I can understand your feelings, Beth," he said, while taking her into his arms. She rested her tearful face on his shoulder.

It took her a while to recover, and then through the sobs he could hear her saying, "I think Dan knows more than he is admitting and I would like you to question him again."

"I will see to it that Dan is returned here and we will question him again. I agree with you and I need to find out exactly what Dan knows."

During the day the enthusiasm for celebrating the victory at Moel y Don waned as it dawned on everyone that Edward was not going to abandon the war and return home to England.

The following day, Llywelyn called to see Beth. "We have brought Dan back from Dolbadarn. We are about to start questioning him. Do you wish to witness the questioning?"

"Yes, as long as he won't be tortured."

"We will be very kind to him. Come on," he said, laughing.

They left for the hall where Dan was standing in irons, with fear clearly showing on his face. The chancellor and two soldiers were present also.

"Well, Dan. This is Beth, who you were following when you were caught at Aberogwen. You've told us that Tudor, her husband, paid you to watch her because he suspected her of being unfaithful to him."

Dan nodded his head in agreement while glancing at Beth.

"We don't think you told us the whole truth when we questioned you last time, and we want you to tell us everything this time. As you know Tudor is dead and so is Hywel, so you can tell us the truth. If your story does not match what we know already, we will know that you are not telling the truth."

"Yes."

"When did you start following Beth? Last time you told me that the occasion you were caught at Aberogwen was the first time. We don't think that was the truth, Dan."

"But it is the truth," he protested.

"No it isn't. Don't make life difficult for yourself. You followed her to Bangor didn't you?" he asked quickly with conviction.

Then Beth asked him directly, "Did you kill Meg?"

"Who's Meg?"

"An old woman who lived in a cottage on the hill above the Menai near Bangor."

"No, the old woman fell."

"So you were there when she was killed," stated the chancellor. After that it was not as difficult to break Dan's resistance. His time at Dolbadarn had also weakened his resolve.

Llywelyn looked him in the eye and said, "The truth Dan. Meg was one of our enemies and she was working against us at Garth Celyn, so you did your prince a favour by killing her. So tell the truth – we won't punish you for killing a traitor."

Dan's eyes brightened as he said, "Are you sure that she was a traitor?"

"Yes, she and her husband. So, there is nothing for you to lose by telling us the truth. You did your country a favour."

"This is what happened. I wanted to tell you this when I was here last, but I thought you would hang me for murder."

"If you killed her you did well. Tell us what happened," encouraged the chancellor.

"On Tudor's instructions I had to follow you to the cathedral and wherever you went from there, while Tudor was in the cathedral," looking directly at Beth. "I followed you to the cottage. When I told Tudor where you were going, he told me to listen to what you were saying, and so I dug small holes in the wall. I dug the first on the side where the bed was, but you were talking by the table. So I made a small hole at the back of the cottage. But I could not hear you speaking clearly."

"Carry on," said Llywelyn. Beth was embarrassed but wanted to know the truth.

"On the day that the old woman died I knew you would probably be going to the cottage. So I went there to make the holes bigger to hear everything clearly. I thought the old woman had left but she hadn't and, while I was there, she must have heard the noise I made and came out. She was very strong and grabbed me by the throat. I panicked and pushed her hard and she fell and hit her head on a stone. I did not know if she was dead but I could not hear her breathing."

"So what did you do next?" asked Llywelyn.

"Tudor had told me that if anything went very wrong, that I could go to him in the cathedral and that I would find him in the belfry. He had said that as soon as he would see me there, he would stop his work and come and talk to me. He told me I was not to go there unless it was an absolute necessity."

"Yes, so what happened?"

"Well, I thought that the old woman dying was an emergency and ran down the steep path to the cathedral to find Tudor. I rushed upstairs to the belfry so quickly that no-one tried to stop me. I was surprised to see your man, Hywel, there talking to a monk through a screen, as though he was making a confession. The monk, on seeing me enter the room, stood up suddenly. But as he stood up quickly, his hood slipped slightly off his head and I think your Hywel might have seen his face and might have recognised him – I'm not sure but I think he did because I saw surprise on his face."

"Well, who was he?" asked Beth.

Dan was not to be rushed. "The monk lifted his hood back over his head and brought the meeting to an end immediately and said goodbye to Hywel, who then went down the stairs."

"Who was the monk, Dan?"

"He crossed the floor towards me and, lowering his hood, I was relieved to find that it was Tudor."

However shocked Dan had been at the time, his audience was now far more shocked and Llywelyn asked him, "Are you telling the truth, Dan?"

"Yes. The absolute truth."

"So what happened after that?" asked Beth.

"I told him what had happened. He took off his black habit, placed it in a coffer and took out a spare bell rope. We then went down the stairs together and out of the cathedral and up the hill to the cottage by the steep path as quickly as we could. Between us we managed to hang the old woman's body onto the beam to make it look as if she had committed suicide."

"Oh my God!" exclaimed Beth.

"We were hardly out of the cottage before you arrived with Hywel," said Dan, looking at her.

Beth could not help but continue the story herself, "So, Tudor was the monk dressed in black in the belfry and he was meeting Hywel there, but told me that he was meeting a monk there, while it was Hywel who was really meeting a monk in the belfry. Hywel and Tudor's stories matched, of course, but Tudor was describing the meeting to me as if he were Hywel and so I was getting the same well-matched story from both."

"Tudor was the black monk. Well! Well!" said Llywelyn.

Beth was astounded.

They decided that Dan should be returned to his wife and children because he was deemed to be neither guilty of treason nor murder.

"Are you happier now Beth?" Llywelyn asked her. "You now know that the mysterious black monk was none other than your husband and that Dan killed Meg."

"Yes. I'm much happier. But I don't think that Tudor was the brains behind it all. There must be someone more important pulling the strings."

"Definitely, and we need to identify him or them."

Then she declared, "I think that Hywel killed Tudor. He was in the area at the time. I know because I met him near there. From what Dan said, he knew the black monk was Tudor and that he was the one collecting information about you, your forces and what the Gwynedd nobles were thinking and planning."

"It's very possible."

"Tudor was gathering intelligence about you from me and from Hywel. Who was he collecting it for? It has to be someone who is plotting against you Llywelyn."

"These are difficult times and there are spies and traitors everywhere," Llywelyn said calmly. "I agree with you there is someone in an important position controlling the operation. I think it's Anian and there is not much I can do about that cleric. The king wants to know everything about us so that he can destroy us."

He then told her how he was also receiving information that Edward would attack again across the Conway with his full army, and that his likely target was the royal court. There were negotiations going on, and the archbishop was involved, but not directly. The terms offered by Edward were not acceptable to him and that he would have to reject them because it would mean the end of independence for Wales.

Beth spent the next few days considering whether to stay at the royal court or to return to her parents at Aberedw. Things were not looking favourable for Llywelyn, despite the success at Moel y Don.

If Llywelyn wanted her to stay at Garth Celyn then, of course, she would, but she was now uncertain as to what her role could be. Gwenllian, his baby daughter, was cared for by her nurse and a nun. Beth, although she saw her daily, had no part in her upbringing.

She whiled away the early winter days walking to the seashore, remembering the dreams that she had had earlier in the month of a life shared with Hywel. All her dreams had been shattered and the future looked bleak.

The weather did not help as it became cold and grey. With the summits of even the low hills near the sea covered in snow, and the mountains behind them all wearing a thick blanket of snow, the locals predicted that it would last a long time. This added to Beth's gloomy outlook on life.

She knew that she would have to make some difficult decisions in the days or weeks to come. There were political and military issues that were limiting her options and her own life would have to take a new course.

CHAPTER 30
4 December 1282

O N THE FOURTH day of December, Llywelyn received a visit from two friars of the Dominican order, claiming to be messengers from Wigmore Castle, the home of the Mortimer brothers.

They brought Llywelyn a letter signed and sealed by Edmund Mortimer, his younger brother Roger and other Marcher lords. The signatories expressed their support for Llywelyn in his opposition to the king's oppressive rule and wanted to join forces with Llywelyn to oppose the king.

The letter also suggested that Llywelyn should go south to meet them and join forces with them in the Builth area on the eleventh of the month, and stated that Gruffudd ap Owain of Aberedw, Beth's father, would act as an intermediary between the signatories and Llywelyn.

Llywelyn received the brethren cordially and in the dark days of early December it was welcome news for him. Since Beth's father was to act as an intermediary in any negotiations, he naturally spoke openly to Beth about the contents of the letter, as well as discussing it with his inner circle of advisers.

Many saw the possibilities presented by the letter and thought it worth serious consideration. They argued that the king could no longer attack from Anglesey and the weather had turned against any attack across the Conwy, and so Gwynedd was secure for a while, at least.

Dafydd was called to the court, and the contents of the letter divulged to him. He was overjoyed and could see that the war he started could turn to a victory against the king. He was the most enthusiastic supporter of Llywelyn going to meet the conspirators at Builth.

The more cautious, however, were convinced that it was a trap organised by the king. The magnets named were guilty of treason and, if Llywelyn were to take the letter to the king, the king, unless he was part of the plot, would have to bring charges of treason against all named, including the Mortimer brothers.

The monks who delivered the letter had been instructed to get a reply within two days to reduce the risk of the king discovering the plot. This time limit, though reasonable enough, added pressure on Llywelyn and his advisers to arrive at a decision.

Llywelyn decided that he would sleep on the matter and would give them a reply in the morning.

That evening he spent some time with Beth and told her that he would send a positive response to the letter and would agree to a meeting at Builth. However, he was not totally convinced, and wanted her to go ahead of him and his army to see her father, and find out what he knew of the plan. He would take his army south a day or two later and meet her at Aberedw the day before he was to meet with the Mortimer brothers, to see if her father was involved and what were his private views.

She agreed immediately believing that it was a good idea and so started her preparation for the journey to Aberedw where she'd meet Llywelyn on the tenth of December.

As she started to collect her possessions for her journey, among her private things she came across Hywel's purse. She held it in her hand, studied it through her tears, opened it and emptied its contents on the table. Hywel's seal was there, a few coins and a key. She was unsure what to do with the purse and its contents and, while contemplating this, she looked at the key again and it crossed her mind that it looked like a key that Tudor used to carry with him.

She examined it again and decided to try it in the lock of Tudor's personal box which she had left undisturbed under the bed. It had been pushed back against the wall after Tudor's death.

She went on her hands and knees to try to reach the box, but it was hidden and wedged at the very back by some old bags. But for the fact that she knew it was there, she would have abandoned her search. She would have to move the bed. While still on her knees, she remembered the day when Hywel had visited her in her room and she had found him on his knees by the bed. On a previous visit, she recalled he had jokingly asked if she had anything under the bed.

The memory of those two visits filled her with annoyance but also with determination. She got up and, with some difficulty, managed to pull the bed away from the wall far enough for her to reach the small box and lift it onto the bed.

She placed Hywel's key in the lock of Tudor's box and turned it. It was a perfect fit – the lock opened and she lifted the lid revealing a neatly folded black habit of a Dominican friar. She took out the top folded piece and placed it carefully on the bed. Clearly Tudor kept a spare black habit in his box in case of emergency.

She was emotional and tearful. It was all getting too much for her and, as she lifted the corner of the next layer of garments and though she could see that there were some documents at the bottom of the box, she decided that she would return everything to the box and take it with her to Aberedw and examine it all again when she felt stronger.

She locked the box and returned the key to the purse, confident that Hywel must have taken Tudor's key from his body after he killed him and kept it in his own purse until he had an opportunity to search her room for a lock that could be opened by that key.

This brought even more tears as she placed the purse among the things to take with her on her journey. She was staggered by her own naivety and how she had allowed herself to be deceived so badly by Hywel.

She believed now that she had proof that it was Hywel who killed Tudor and had taken the key.

The two monks left early the next day, the sixth of December, with Llywelyn's reply that he would meet the plotters on the eleventh day of December at Builth. The monks were well provided with provisions for their journey. They had refused any guards to accompany them on the journey claiming that they did not wish to attract attention and they felt safer just walking on their own.

When the time came for Beth to leave on the seventh of December, Llywelyn wished her farewell and a good journey with a kiss on her cheek. There were six guards accompanying her and her servant on the journey. It was important for her to find out the truth from her father as soon as possible.

Llywelyn reminded her that he would meet with her and her father on the tenth day of December the day before he was to meet with Edward Mortimer and the other Marcher lords.

They travelled west along the track towards the Ogwen river and on towards Pentir where Llywelyn's troops had gathered before the battle of Moel y Don. They continued their journey through valley to the east of Bwlch Mawr and over the watershed that separated the rivers feeding Caernarfon and Cardigan bays. She well remembered coming over this point years earlier and experiencing her first view of Anglesey stretching into the distance. Now she had to look backwards to see that same view and she did so many times.

She was sad to leave Garth Celyn; she was worried about Llywelyn's future and concerned about what was to become of her country. She had grown to like the royal court even though it was associated with very sad episodes in her life. It had been difficult to say goodbye to Llywelyn and his five-month-old baby daughter, Gwenllian, but she hoped that she would see her again.

The soldiers with her were still high on their victory at Moel y Don. Most had been present and were enthusiastically explaining the crucial role they had played in winning the battle, but it was Hywel's death and guilt that was foremost in Beth's mind.

She occasionally felt sickened by the whole performance and could not help but think of the soldier she had found on the beach who had died after making his peace with God. Hywel, however much he had betrayed her, was still dear to her and she grieved for him deeply now that she was leaving Gwynedd. She also could picture the numerous other soldiers killed fighting for or against the aggressor Edward – she could see their faces again.

The rivers they crossed were full but not flooded, because in recent days the weather had been very cold and cloudy but on the whole dry. They travelled quickly and for many long hours, and only spent two nights on the road, staying in a farmstead south of Maentwrog on the first night, and they reached Prysgduon, a little north of Cwm Hir on the second night.

The Prysgduon family was known to be strongly supportive of Llywelyn. They had stuck with him through the good and bad times. They were hard-working, reliable, trustworthy and honest people. Four children had been brought up at the homestead; three girls and a boy, the youngest of the brood. The girls had married and left their parents but the boy, now a young man, lived at home with his parents. Llywelyn knew this family and had recommended them to Beth and her escorts as a place they were sure of a warm welcome.

Beth was tired as they crossed the Severn and climbed

onto the Radnor hills, but they continued until the Prysgduon farmstead came into sight tucked in below bulky Domen-ddu hill. Daylight was fading as they approached this elegant old house with its well-kept thatch roof above a wooden structure.

Rhys, the son, was in the yard waiting for them, having been warned of their approach by the barking dogs. He was suspicious of them initially until they identified themselves, but then the welcome flowed and when he saw Beth his enthusiasm became even greater. It was not often that a beautiful woman like Beth visited Prysgduon.

After spending a few hours with him and the others by the fire while eating and drinking, she assessed Rhys as being exactly what he was – a person of no guile, no pretence but happy, contented in his life and happy in his work on the farmstead. How refreshing, she thought. In the few hours they were together she grew to like him and would have loved to have had him as a brother when she grew up at Aberedw.

She was sad to leave this happy homestead, but they had to be on their way early. They passed close to the abbey at Cwm Hir on the third day and arrived at Aberedw in the late afternoon of the ninth day of December.

CHAPTER 31
9 and 10 December 1282

O N THE LAST stage of the journey, Beth took time to think about her mission to Aberedw and the political and military conflict she and her father were being drawn into.

Llywelyn's negotiations with Edward had failed, with the king only offering him terms on which to surrender. But, though possessing the necessary military power to attack Llywelyn's stronghold in Gwynedd, Edward was afraid to do so, particularly in winter. The letter from the Mortimer brothers, on the other hand, was suggesting a plan that could lead to success and while she could see why Llywelyn was tempted by it, she was very suspicious of it.

She knew that Llywelyn would have set out on his journey south only a short while after her, in order to meet her at Aberedw on the tenth of the month.

Beth and her escorts travelled to the east of Builth and the Wye river for a few miles before her father's castle, her home, came into sight high above the river plane, with its superb view of the confluence of the rivers Wye and the Edw and with a large flat-topped hill forming a dark background.

The countryside here was very different from the high, snow-covered mountains of Gwynedd. She experienced joy arriving home, seeing the familiar hills with the grey, layered rocks on the east side and the red sandstone to the west of the Wye and the tree-covered slopes either side of the river.

They had been seen from a distance and were met by soldiers who, when they realised who the visitor was, extended her a warm welcome and led her up the steep hill towards the castle, passing St Cewydd's Church on their left, and announcing her return joyously as they progressed.

Her father met her just inside the main entrance, and was delighted to see his daughter again. Beth thought he looked well and marvelled at the fact that he had managed to keep loyal to Llywelyn without attracting the wrath of the Mortimer family.

The rest of the ninth of December was spent celebrating Beth's return. She related to them her experiences of the past seven years but omitted to mention her relationship with Hywel.

Then, after the excitement surrounding her return had subdued and people were making their way to their beds, sitting alone with her father she approached the subject of the letter sent to Llywelyn.

She started by asking, "You managed to live well with old Roger Mortimer, but how do you get on with his sons?"

"As you know, it's never easy to deal with the Mortimers. It's like walking on eggs; you have to think of them as a nasty bunch and watch your back at all times. Old Roger had improved towards the end, only because his health was beginning to fail and he wanted to ensure that his boys could take over from him without too much difficulty."

"I suppose that is why he came to that agreement with Llywelyn a year ago."

"I'm sure it was," he replied. "It was not like him to agree to anything much. His one constant thread was that he was loyal to the king and that always kept him out of deep trouble. You know don't you that the king has not given the boys the estate yet, and people around here believe that is because he does not trust the younger generation. I don't know what to think. Who knows what the king has in mind for any of us."

"Have you met Roger's two boys?" she asked.

"Only when they were very young. Of course, I know them

by their reputations. Edmund intended to become a priest but changed his mind when his elder brother died. That's English law for you – there is nothing fair and right about it. It's all to do with preserving the estate and the wealth of one member of the family. It's all very unchristian. That's one reason why we prefer our Welsh law and hope that Llywelyn can keep our laws and the Christian principles of equality on which they are based on."

"What do you know about Edmund? You will have to co-exist with him in the future."

"I don't like someone who says one day he is to become a priest and then, when he suddenly becomes wealthy, has a change of heart. I would say he is not to be trusted. The general feeling is that he will do anything that will push his ambitions forward, so he will do anything and everything that will please the king."

Beth knew that her father was a wise man and had forgotten how incisive a mind he had or was it that she had been too young and too inexperienced in life to appreciate his wisdom in the past. He would be ideal to advise Llywelyn at this his hour of need. Her father had already given her enough information to make her suspect the veracity of the letter sent to Llywelyn.

"As for the young Roger, Edmund's younger brother," her father continued. "He is not to be trusted in any way. He has a weakness for women to such an extent that they are not safe in his company, whether they are married or not. He has the most awful reputation and most people, even the nobility, dislike him. He is ruthless in all ways."

The more Beth heard, the more she thought that it would be a great error for Llywelyn to place his trust in the contents of the letter from these Marcher barons. They were for enhancing their own estates it seemed.

"Llywelyn has received a letter from the Mortimer brothers

inviting him to join them at Builth, and to take that castle and establish a league against the king. The letter is signed by the Mortimer brothers and some of the local nobility. Llywelyn is unsure as to how much faith to place in the letter. What do you think?" she asked.

"I would not trust it," he said with conviction and without any hesitation.

"The letter also suggests that you are in agreement with the plan and would act as an intermediary between them and Llywelyn. This has given it more credibility in Llywelyn's mind and the minds of those on his council."

"I know nothing about it," he said. "No-one has asked me for my opinion. It has to be a trap to capture Llywelyn."

"The situation is difficult for him in Gwynedd. His wife is dead and Gwenllian is only a baby. He has beaten off an attack from Anglesey but he has not defeated the main force to the east of the Conwy. The king can attack across the river at any time and is going to as soon as the weather improves in the spring. So Llywelyn has been tempted out of Gwynedd by the letter and should be here tomorrow."

"We need to warn him not to come here," said her father.

"How can we? He must be more than halfway here by now. He was preparing for the journey when I left Garth Celyn."

"Why can't he leave it until the new year? Why is he in such a rush?"

"Those who wrote the letter suggested they should meet at Builth on the eleventh of December and Llywelyn intends to meet us here the day before to check that it's not a trap. It's the tenth tomorrow, so he is likely to be here tomorrow afternoon," she explained. "What can we do to stop him?"

"We could try to inform the king of the treason expressed in the letter by his noblemen in the Marches, but if the king is already in on the plo, then it would be useless."

"Do you think the king is involved in on the plot?" Beth asked.

"Yes, I do," her father said. "It is very unlikely that these barons would send such a letter unless the king knows about it. If that letter fell to the wrong hands and was taken to the king, then he would immediately have to use the full power of his army to destroy them first. The Marcher lords are a greater threat to him than Llywelyn at the moment. The king must know about this plot."

"So, all we can do is to try to stop him from coming to Builth?" she asked.

"Yes," he said emphatically. "Which way do you think he'll come, Beth?"

"He is likely to call at Cwm Hir Abbey, I think."

"We must send messengers out as soon as we can in the morning."

Beth retired to her old room at Aberedw Castle soon after this conversation and was deeply anxious about Llywelyn.

Before dawn on the morning of the tenth day of December, Beth and her father were together on the castle ramparts. They felt they'd like to shout at their leader to warn him to go back to Gwynedd.

The sky, instead of lightening, was darkening fast and the mild breeze of the previous evening had been replaced by a cold wind from the east which was already bringing a few flakes of fine snow with it.

"Snow," her father pronounced.

"It's only fine snow and it won't come to much," she said.

"I'm not so sure," he said. "The saying is that fine snow produces a heavy snow fall. It may prevent us sending messages out, but it may also send Llywelyn back north or at least keep him wherever he is."

Beth hoped he was right.

Her father had obviously considered the dilemma they were in and said, "I think the best thing to do, is to do nothing, and wait for Llywelyn to arrive here today and warn him then that it's a plot and send him back north before he meets the plotters tomorrow."

They stood there for a while on the ramparts watching the fine snow settling on the land, the trees and the roofs of the buildings below them, and even at their own feet.

The snow was soon covering everything except the area outside the blacksmith's forge, where some normality remained with the snow kept at bay to the rim of the hot hearth.

It stopped snowing for a while, giving the two of them a view down the valley and across to the opposite slope where trees could be seen clearer now that the snow highlighted all the individual branches, tracks and boulders. Everything was clean, clear and distinct. But it did not last for long, and the fine snow began falling again.

It was time for the occupants of the castle to prepare for a heavy fall of snow and Beth knew that it was unlikely that Llywelyn would reach Aberedw that day, as he had planned.

Later, Beth and her father were out on the ramparts again and were about to go in from the cold when he remarked, "Was that a herd of deer I saw then? There on the opposite side," he said pointing to the opposite slope.

But Beth could see nothing as the snow thickened and a gust of wind blew it like a cloud off the castle roof.

She turned, going in from the cold, when she heard her father calling, "The snow is clearing again, perhaps you can see better than me."

She returned to the rampart to find that the snow was stopping again and the visibility improving. Her father was pointing in the same direction again. She focused on the opposite side of the valley and could see a group of horsemen riding in a line along the side of the hill. They were clearly visible through the trees.

"There are at least ten horsemen there. They've stopped now," she said. "Are they your soldiers?"

"No," he said. "But they are definitely soldiers and, look, there are about ten foot soldiers behind them. What are they up to I wonder?"

"Why have they stopped?"

"Strange. If the snow hadn't cleared at that moment I would not have noticed them. Indeed, if there had been no snow on the ground I would probably not have noticed them," he said deep in thought.

"Do you think they are going to the castle at Builth because they have heard that Llywelyn is on his way?"

"I hope not," replied her father.

Then the snow moved in across the valley again, obliterating their view slowly and it did not clear for a while. The snow was there to stay this time and, despite frequent visits by Beth to the rampart, the snow was falling too thickly for her to be able to see the other side of the valley.

She had to suffer the frustration of not being able to move from her father's castle and could do nothing to warn Llywelyn.

Imprisoned by the snow, Beth remembered Tudor's box and took the key and opened it again as she had done at Garth Celyn. She took the clothes out and removed three parchments from the bottom.

Two had nothing written on them, but the other was a letter which she saw was written in Tudor's hand, and apart from the fact that it was not addressed to anyone, it was complete and she read it.

The first sentence praised the holiness of the intended receiver and continued to request more payment for the dangerous work he was doing at great risk to his life. He reminded the receiver that he had married Beth on his instructions, and that with tensions between Llywelyn and the king increasing, his tasks were becoming more difficult and very dangerous. For these reasons he was asking if he could receive additional payment or be removed from the position he was in. He ended the letter with praise for the intended receiver and signed his name at the bottom.

From the praise at the start and end of the letter, she gathered that the intended receiver was a senior holy man and she concluded that it was probably Bishop Anian of Bangor. She also felt that whoever the letter was intended for was the person controlling Tudor's espionage.

When she went out to get some fresh air following her discovery, she could see that there was a thick layer of snow and the children of the castle workers were already playing in it, throwing snowballs and sliding down the slope towards the church.

The snow kept falling till the middle of the afternoon, giving a covering of about four inches in thickness and when the sky cleared there were no horsemen or soldiers to be seen in the distance and their tracks were covered.

Beth knew that there was very little daylight left and that neither she nor anyone else at Aberedw could do anything to warn Llywelyn. She realised that the snow might well have delayed Llywelyn's movement south and it was becoming clearer to her that he would not meet her as planned that day. She decided that she would leave the next day with the soldiers who had come south with her from Gwynedd, and try to see if there were any indication around Builth that the army from the north was camped nearby or on its way. She would make her way, the best she could, to Llechryd the ford on the Wye just north of Builth, and she was happier having made her mind up to leave things until the following day.

She stayed out in the snow for about half an hour and her feet were frozen, forcing her to go inside to warm herself by the fire. She turned to leave but, at the last moment, decided to go down to the blacksmith to warm herself there just as she used to do when a child.

She walked down carefully and, as she approached the blacksmith's workshop, she could feel the heat from his hearth. The glow from the white hot furnace lit up the numerous faces standing near the fire. There was a mixture of men and children there, the children were there to warm up before going out again to play in the snow. Nothing changes she thought; the children were doing exactly what she used to do when she was a child.

Some of the men were there because they had been too disorganised to collect wood for a fire of their own, but some were there to gossip and to get the latest news.

Even the village's stray dogs and cats were there at the edges of the workshop keeping warm.

The noise of the bellows, worked by a young man, was deafening. The blacksmith was hammering on a horseshoe, which he had almost completed, but there were still red hot sparks coming from it as he struck it.

She was disappointed that she did not recognise the blacksmith until she remembered the accident to the one she was so friendly with. She had expected to see her old friend there, hammering away on the anvil, but this blacksmith was new to her.

They all nodded at her as she approached the open, wide entrance. She recognised some of the faces and smiled back at them. She knew her presence was not wanted in this male-dominated place, but she didn't care. She had as much right as the others to be there and stepped a little closer to the fire.

Though confident in her right to be there, it was rather

nervously that she spoke having waited for a lull in the movement of the bellows, "It's very cold out there."

There were numerous nods, with some hoping no doubt that once she was warm she would leave them to their manly thoughts and words.

Again having waited for her chance, she asked, "Is that for the horse outside?"

One of the men, whom she thought she knew, laughingly said, "Yes, but with a woman here it may well be fitted on his hoof the wrong way around." All the others joined in the laughter.

They were cheeky but meant no harm and she smiled, but ignored the comment, as did the blacksmith who continued working on the horseshoe preparing to hammer nail holes in it. She assumed that the horse's old shoe had been lost, possibly in the snow.

Addressing the blacksmith, one of the men asked him, "Are we likely to get more snow?"

The blacksmith grunted that he didn't think there was more snow on the way.

The joker then added, "It will be a fine day tomorrow, you mark my words."

The blacksmith then said, "It might be a fine day, but there's talk that Llywelyn is only a day's march away with his army. They were seen near Rhayader before the snow came."

Beth was struck dumb by this comment. She was concerned that it was general knowledge that Llywelyn was coming to Builth.

She did not stay long thereafter and left to go back to the castle. In any case she didn't like to be present when the blacksmith placed the hot shoe onto the horse's hoof; she did not like the smell or the thought of the hot metal burning its way into the hoof.

She told her father what she had heard, but neither of them could think of a way to alert Llywelyn to the possible dangers for him in the Builth area.

Builth Castle was occupied by John Giffard and his wife, Maud Langspee, Llywelyn's cousin. Beth's father, who knew them fairly well, was convinced that Giffard wouldn't surrender the castle to Llywelyn without a fight. It made no sense to him.

Llywelyn, however, did not arrive at Aberedw on the tenth of December, as had been agreed.

CHAPTER 32

11 December 1282

THE FOLLOWING DAY, the eleventh of the month, Beth was again on the ramparts looking into the distance hoping to see her prince leading his men through the snow to meet her. He was now a day late for his meeting at Aberedw and she was getting very concerned for him.

Later, her father joined her on the ramparts and told her that he had heard from the blacksmith that Llywelyn had taken his army across the Wye at Llechrhyd north of Builth, and camped near Cilmeri, with the river Wye protecting it to the east and the river Irfon to the south.

It was also reported that he had gone to the castle at Builth half expecting the occupants to surrender, but Constable Giffard had refused and Llywelyn had gone away to organise a siege of the castle.

As soon as she heard this news, Beth knew that Llywelyn had been deceived in being persuaded to leave his stronghold in Gwynedd and that he was in peril. Events were moving fast and a bad dream was becoming reality.

She wanted to search for him but knew it was an impossible task in the rapidly thawing snow. So she stayed on the castle ramparts staring towards Builth for any sign of movement. She expected and hoped to see him leading his full army along the banks of the Wye towards Aberedw.

But there was very little movement in the valley below, where the tracks were now mostly free of snow. The ground under the trees, sheltered from the sun, was still white, but there was nothing much to be seen there other than crows and buzzards, which she could hear making their cat-like noises while desperately looking for carrion.

Then, from the castle ramparts, she could see a group of about twenty riders approaching along the track by the side of the Wye. They were too far away for her to recognise anyone, but her heart missed a beat when she thought that she recognised one of Llywelyn horses carrying the leader of the group.

They were proceeding slowly towards her father's castle. She hoped it was Llywelyn so that she could warn him that the letter bringing him to Builth was a trap about which her father knew nothing and that his name had been used simply to entice Llywelyn out of Gwynedd. As they slowly came closer, she felt sure that these were men from the north and that they were led by Llywelyn himself.

They came close enough for her to see that there was a monk wearing a black habit walking just behind the lead horses. She had a perfect view of the group from above and she counted eighteen men in all, including the monk.

She turned around to her father and shouted, "Look, it's Llywelyn." She was full of excitement and all the anxiety of the last few hours had disappeared.

"I'm sure it's Llywelyn," she shouted at him. "Thank God he is safe and we can warn him of the trap set for him."

Her father standing next to her could see the group clearly, but his eyes were diverted by movement on the opposite side of the Edw valley where a large group of men were moving down quickly towards the people approaching the castle. The trees were hiding them from the approaching group but there was something menacing about them.

"Look," he called to Beth, but her hands were already up to her face covering most of it in horror. She could see that it was an ambush. There was malice in their approach. There was stealth. There was viciousness. She could see and sense it all.

The enemy was approaching fast and soon the riders with swords and spears at the ready were breaking into a gallop down the gentle slope towards the eighteen. These men heard them; therefore their leader, realising that they were being attacked, directed his men to face the onslaught despite not being aware of the number of attackers. Beth and her father, perched above the ensuing battle, knew that the eighteen were outnumbered by at least three to one, with the attackers having the advantage of surprise and the higher ground.

The attackers hit the group with force, scattering them in all directions and slaughtering them with ease.

Beth kept her eyes fixed on the one she believed to be Llywelyn and was in agony when she saw him taken from his horse with a lance. This, she now knew, was the trap set for Llywelyn and she had been part of the bait to lure him. The letter delivered by the monks to Garth Celyn had been horribly false.

She kept her eyes on the figure, whom she felt sure was Llywelyn. He lay motionless on the ground. She was too far away to see if he was bleeding, but could see that his horse had returned to him.

The attackers circled around the wounded making sure that they were dead – they pierced the defenceless bodies with swords and spears.

Then, through her tears and with her father's arm around her, she saw a monk approach Llywelyn. This was the monk that was in the group led by Llywelyn earlier and would have travelled with him from the north to assist in any agreements that he would come to with the Mortimer brothers.

The monk bent over Llywelyn and looked as though he might be giving him his last rights and listening to his confessions. The monk remained with Llywelyn for some time. Beth wanted to go out of the castle and down to where the slaughter had taken place, but she was restrained by her father.

She stayed where she was and watched the scene below with great sadness and growing grief.

One of the attackers moved to where Llywelyn lay with the monk. The monk left and, to her absolute horror, the newly-arrived soldier grabbed the injured man by the hair and swung his sword, decapitating him and lifting the cut head high for the others to see and cheer loudly.

Beth did not see any more because she had fainted into her father's arms, and it was just as well because another attacker approached the monk and pierced his body with his sword. The others looked on in silence, but there were no cheers this time – more of an acceptance that it was something that had to be done.

The group who had attacked the eighteen departed in the direction they had come from and disappeared up the valley towards Rhulen.

Beth's father sent two men to follow the attackers but he did not wish to get involved because he knew he couldn't match the forces available to the Marcher lords.

Once they had gone out of sight, a group of men gathered quickly to go down to where the eighteen bodies lay scattered in the snow. Beth, by now recovered, insisted that she went with them and was accompanied by the men who had escorted her from Garth Celyn. She went straight to the headless body and even with the head cut off she knew it was Llywelyn.

She could see that his body had been searched and whatever he had on him had been taken. She felt sure that the presence of the monk indicated his intention to agree to some written agreement, but she also wanted to believe that he had come to see her.

It was not difficult to work out that the attackers had taken the treacherous letter they had sent to Llywelyn and any seals he would have had in his possession or were held by the monk.

After seeing Llywelyn's body and weeping over it, she bent down and kissed his right hand which was already cold in the snow.

She went to the monk, and one of the men who had accompanied her from Gwynedd said to her quietly, "He's not quite dead yet. I've heard him saying something. Who would sink so low as to kill a monk?"

Beth bent down near the monk and the soldier told her, "They have taken all his vestments. Why would they do that?"

"Can you hear me?" she asked him quietly as she glanced down his torso. There was blood flowing out of what was clearly a deep wound in his abdomen.

The soldier said to her in her ear, "He won't last long."

"Can you hear me?" she asked again, this time louder.

"Yes," he said and she was so pleased to hear it.

"Who did this to you?"

By now the men had checked all the bodies around and confirmed that they were all dead and were now gathering around the dying monk and Beth.

"Who did this to you?" she asked again.

"It was one of Edmund Mortimer's men but he was told to do it by Le Strange himself," he said with surprising strength.

"Were they mostly Mortimer's men?"

"Yes."

She turned to the men around and, finding her father there, she asked him, "Can you send for your priest please?"

"He's on his way, Beth."

"Why did they do this to you?" she enquired of the dying monk.

"They ambushed Llywelyn and they didn't want any witnesses."

The priest arrived and Beth moved to make room for him. He knelt by the monk and asked, "Are you ready to make your confessions, my son?"

As the priest gave the monk absolution, she returned to the dying monk and asked, "Did you hear Llywelyn's confessions?"

The monk replied in a low voice, but quite clearly, "Yes, and I gave him absolution and he kissed my cross, which they've taken from me."

Beth was relieved.

"He will be taken out of his pain soon," said the priest holding the monk's hand and soon after the monk died.

They all stood around, sad and dejected.

Then Beth said, "Llywelyn must be taken to the castle and given a Christian burial. They must all be given a decent Christian burial."

Her father agreed with her and they started to discuss the arrangements they would make, but the possibility that the soldiers might return made everyone anxious and caused them to move with greater purpose and haste.

"Let's move Llywelyn's body to the castle," Beth urged them. At that moment they heard the men who had followed the attackers return announcing that there was a great army on the march down the valley of the Edw towards them.

"What if they are coming for Llywelyn's body?" asked someone.

Beth's father suggested that she should go back to the castle and prepare a place for Llywelyn's body. She agreed and left the men to bring the headless body back with them and it was not long before they followed her with Llywelyn's body.

"I hope they will not be looking for Llywelyn," Beth said to her father, clearly afraid that the coming army would attack the castle.

"Don't worry," he said. "They will find him with the others where they slew him."

She looked at him in surprise and he enlightened her, "This is Llywelyn's body," he said. "But we had to cut off another soldier's head and dress him in Llywelyn's tunic and place him where Llywelyn lay. I just hope they don't make a head count."

Llywelyn's body was placed in a wagon and covered with straw while Beth and her father went to the ramparts. Before long they could see the army that they had been warned about marching down the valley as dusk was falling. There were many hundreds of soldiers and a substantial number of cavalry. They were marching quietly, but purposefully, keeping close, to the base of the hill where the ambush had taken place earlier. They then turned to the right in the direction of Builth.

Their leaders had no interest in Aberedw Castle or its occupiers. They had bigger fish to fry, but doubtless they would be back.

A small detachment of troops separated from the main body and went down to where the seventeen dead lay. They picked up the body that had been placed where Llywelyn had fallen and proceeded back up the valley with the headless body.

Beth's father sent soldiers out to follow the main body of the army and another pair to follow the group carrying the body.

Beth, her father and the others debated what to do with Llywelyn's body. There was a general consensus that the body should be buried at Cwm Hir Abbey, and it was agreed that they would set out on the journey the following morning.

The soldiers sent to follow the main army were soon back reporting that the army had set up camp for the night about three miles from Aberedw.

CHAPTER 33

12 December 1282

I T WAS DECIDED that at first light on the twelfth of December, the men who had accompanied Beth from Garth Celyn would take the prince's body to be buried at Cwm Hir. They could tell the abbot honestly that he had received absolution and could therefore be buried at the abbey. Beth insisted that she, accompanied by a few of her father's troops, would go with them.

As the group was about to leave for Cwm Hir, messengers sent out earlier by Beth's father returned, reporting that the large army they saw was engaging with Llywelyn's soldiers near Cilmeri. The speculation was that Llywelyn's men stood no chance because they were leaderless and the king, the Marcher lords and their commanders in the fields had given orders not to take prisoners.

After the cortege left Aberedw, Beth became concerned as to how they would convince the abbot to bury the body at the abbey, and even when the abbey was in sight she still had no answer to the problem.

However, when they arrived at Cwm Hir, they were shocked to see that the abbot was waiting for them. He was expecting to receive Llywelyn's body and assumed that they were Mortimer's men delivering the body to be buried.

The abbot explained that he had received a message from Madog, the Archdeacon of Anglesey, two days earlier on the tenth of December, delivered by a friar from Bangor requesting that he allow the burial of the body because Llywelyn had made a confession to an accompanying monk who regrettably had also died in the battle.

The abbot mistook Beth for Maud Langsbury, Llywelyn's cousin and wife of the custodian of Builth Castle, who wished to attend her cousin's internment in the abbey. He seemed to assume that Edmund Mortimer and the archdeacon were of the same mind, and was pleased to act in accordance with the archdeacon's wishes and had indeed already prepared a grave for the dead prince.

Beth was puzzled by these arrangements and asked the abbot to tell her again the date on which he had received the message.

He was quite happy to reply that he had received the message from the Dominican friar two days earlier, the tenth of the month, and had expected them to arrive with the body the previous day, the eleventh.

"Is the messenger still here?" she asked.

"No," he replied. "He returned to the north, but had to call with Edward Mortimer at Wigmore on his way with my seal on the message confirming that I had read it and agreed with the request."

Beth ventured one additional question. "What exactly did the message say?"

"In essence it was a simple message stating that there had been a battle and Llywelyn's forces had been defeated on the banks of the Irfon river. Llywelyn himself had been killed and the archdeacon was requesting that the prince's body be buried here and not taken to Gwynedd where it could, in years, be a place of pilgrimage for dissenting Welsh nobles and a point at which to gather and cause further revolts."

"Oh," she said, while those around her stood dumbfounded.

"The letter also stated that you might accompany the body of your cousin, Lady Maud."

Putting aside the insult to her in being confused with a

woman at least twenty years her senior, Beth was astounded by what was revealed by the abbot. She wasn't sure if all present realised the significance of what the abbot had said, but she knew exactly what it meant.

Perhaps the snow had slowed Llywelyn's journey south and the letter sent to prepare the abbot ahead of what happened had arrived at its destination before Llywelyn was killed. Clearly one part of the carefully planned plot had been delayed by the snow, while the other part had not.

More important to Beth was the naming of the chief plotter at Bangor. If Madog knew the date of the proposed meeting at Builth, then he must have been part of the plot.

Llywelyn had believed that Anian was his main foe at the cathedral, but Anian was what he was – he did not attempt to hide the fact that he was against Llywelyn, but Madog had encouraged Llywelyn and his court officials to believe that he was a trusted supporter.

Madog the Archdeacon, his supposed loyal friend, was the arch plotter against Llywelyn and he wanted to clear his conscience regarding their leader's death by ensuring a Christian burial for him, but in an unmarked grave and far from Gwynedd.

Having obtained the information she wanted, Beth shifted to the background, allowing the burial to take place without much ceremony, other than a brief mass for the dead and Llywelyn's body laid in the prepared grave.

Llywelyn's men stood silently by the grave and said their own quiet farewell to their brave leader. But Beth cried bitter tears for her prince, whom she could have loved if he had been free to love her in return and might have changed the course of history.

The abbot offered accommodation for them for the night, but the group knew that although there was not much daylight left, they had to depart the abbey as soon as possible before the other body would arrive for burial.

So, they bade farewell to the abbot who had been so helpful. They were desperate to get out of the abbey grounds and on the track northwards to Bwlch y Sarnau and well away from Builth and Cwm Hir.

CHAPTER 34

12 December 1282 and thereafter

B ETH NOW KNEW that Llywelyn had been betrayed by people he had trusted. The Mortimers had behaved as themselves – nothing else was expected of that family – but Archdeacon Madog had been trusted. It was a great disappointment to her and her spirits as a consequence were low.

Indeed all her companions that evening were tired and despondent. They had lost their leader in a most horrible manner, a man they had grown to admire and rely on – they were without hope and their world had collapsed.

In this state of mind, fright was the main influence on those who had been fearless in their support for Llywelyn. It influenced the path they had followed, their pace and even how they rode their horses in the descending gloom. They were afraid of being seen, of being heard, of being followed and of being found out. Like a hunted old fox, they kept as tightly together as they could to the sides of the hills. Beth and the three from Aberedw could not think of returning there in case they were confronted by the other cortege on its way to the abbey, hence their trek northwards.

There was still snow on the ground, which helped them as it muffled the sound of their horses' hooves, and the little light that remained was enhanced by the covering of snow which thickened the higher up the valley they went.

So, they moved northwards as quickly and as quietly as they could, up Cwm Hir to Bwlch y Sarnau and they were greatly relieved to pass over the rise and see Waun Marteg open out ahead.

The sun had set and darkness was closing around them fast – the outlines of the hills were no longer distinguishable. The birds were settling on their perches for the night. The occasional crow flew rapidly overhead to its roosting place. An owl could be heard screeching as it set off on its flight over the bog that lay in front of them. They were all used to the sounds of the darkness hours, but that night and in that place, these sounds generated more fear in them all. They seemed to sense that it was a very bad omen, much worse than on a normal night in the mountains of Gwynedd.

It was too dark to ride the horses now and so they dismounted and led them, instinctively taking the shortest path across the wide flat, wet bog that was the Waun. Keeping as close as they could to the trees, cautiously watching and listening, yet knowing they had to make progress and leave the abbey as far behind them as they could.

The horses were led away from the rocks and stones to ensure that their passage could not be heard. So, they progressed in total silence which in itself generated its own anxiety as they listened intently for the sounds of hooves behind them.

At the river Marteg, they saw the black, peaty water contrasting sharply with the snow on either side. As they were about to wade into the water, a disturbed hare rose noisily immediately in front of the leading horse and leapt along its own well-worn path but its sudden movement startled them and halted their progress. To Beth and her anxious companions, the sound of the hare's soft paws on the snow-covered grass sounded remarkably like a horse galloping.

The hare's image against the snow disappeared into the darkness. They recovered, and entered the river with its bitterly cold water reaching up to their knees. Once through they continued on their journey as quietly and as stealthily as they could, working their way slightly to the right and to the foot of the nearest hill until they came to the little stream that ran on their left from Pistyll y Geiniog.

The stream was in full flow, enhanced by the thawing snow during the day. It tumbled quickly down a steep gulley until it came to a point just above the track they were on, when it poured over a rocky face spreading its water wider and falling vertically into a small pool by the side of the track. It splashed into the pool and its sound could be heard becoming louder as they approached.

Their path crossed the little stream as it flowed from the pool. Instinctively the horses stopped to sip the water and all the men dismounted and went down on their knees by the pool.

Suddenly the area lit up; Beth could now see the outline of rocks and trees. She turned quickly to look behind her and saw a white light brightening the sky above Bwlch y Sarnau. It was the moon rising over the horizon – it was a wonderful moment for her as the lantern in the sky lit the surrounding hills, making them visible again. But, it shone on her too, causing her to feel very uneasy.

She remained mounted, knowing that they could continue to ride in the moonlight. She looked at the men on their knees by the pool. At first she thought her companions were praying, but on realising that they were not, she thought they were desperately thirsty and drinking the cold water – but no, they were washing their hands. They were rubbing and scrubbing their hands – they were washing off their prince's blood.

The men did not wish to be caught with blood on their hands – they were already preparing for the days ahead without their leader. The anxiety they had experienced on the journey to the abbey, at the burial, and immediately after, was dissipating fast – it was being replaced by a feeling of relief and they were preparing for their future life – protecting themselves, their families, their holdings and their well-being.

Beth was contemplating what she should do – go back to her father at Aberedw or go north and take her chance with these men. She looked down at them almost pitifully, ashamed that Llywelyn's most trusted men wanted to remove all traces of him because they were afraid of all the shadows around them and of the unknown future ahead.

Placing Llywelyn's body in the grave at Cwm Hir had been traumatic for all of them – they had taken great risks to ensure their prince was buried in consecrated ground just as they had risked their lives for him on many occasions. Seeing them lowering his body into the ground had been a painful moment in Beth's life also. She found it difficult to believe that it was only a few days earlier that she had returned to dreaming of marrying the prince and becoming a princess. All her hopes and dreams lay in the grave she had left behind at the abbey.

The cold, the glorious moon, the fear, the desire to live – all conflicting feelings were taking her from her wishes and dreams – more towards the course of reality. She wanted now to have a normal life – she wanted peace.

One of her men from Aberedw rose and came to stand next to her, "What will you do? If you wish we can escort you back to Aberedw now or in the morning."

"Prysgduon is just round the side of this hill – we will be welcomed there and no-one will follow us in the dark, even though there is moonlight," she replied.

"Shall we go on to Prysgduon now then?"

"Yes. I will make my mind up in the morning, but I think it would be wise not to return to Aberedw too soon. My father will be dispossessed by the Mortimer brothers and I might be better off away from there."

"I suppose you're right," he said glancing nervously at his

hands again. He must have thought he saw more blood on them and went back to the pool.

The moon, reflecting on the snow, was now throwing clearly defined shadows of the hills, the trees, the bare branches and of the horses and soldiers by the pool. The tops of the hills looked exactly like they did at dawn on a nice morning. It was a clear, cold December night with no breeze. Over the sound of the waterfall they heard a fox on the hill above them howling at the moon – at least they hoped it was a fox and not a dog – and it further raised the alertness of the men bent by the pool, with some rising to their feet feeling uneasy at the sound.

Beth stared at the falling water above the pool in front of her. The grey water flowed endlessly downwards, rimmed by snow. Beyond the dark trees, when the moon shifted slowly in its orbit, it shone a light into the falling water showing an old man on a grey horse in the distance.

Above the thundering noise of the falling water, she could hear the elderly man say to her, "I am Goronwy the son of Ednyfed. If I had been with the prince this would not have happened."

The men at the pool also heard it and, looking up at the tumbling brook, they had also seen something.

"Did you hear that?" asked more than one of the men. In shock they looked at each other.

"Yes."

"What did he say?"

Beth had heard it all, the first part she had heard clearly and understood and appreciated the truth in what had been said. But she also had heard more, but not clearly and not well enough to be able to understand and fully appreciate the meaning of what was said.

She told the soldiers the first part of what she had heard: "I am Goronwy the son of Ednyfed. If I had been with the prince this would not have happened." But, she kept his other words to herself.

"That's what I heard too."

"I definitely heard a voice," said another.

Beth had seen and heard the mounted grey knight speaking clearly, but could not believe it and glowered into the moonlight around her, searching for another explanation but could see no-one. She stared towards the waterfall, hoping to see the man on the horse again and hoping that he would repeat his words or even say more, but the moon had moved on and the knight and his horse had disappeared.

There was only the moon's rays reflecting on the noisy, falling water.

"It was definitely Goronwy, the son of Ednyfed, Llywelyn's old chancellor. I saw him when I was a child – it was definitely him," continued one of the soldiers.

"But he's been long dead."

"I heard him say that he was Goronwy the son of Ednyfed," another declared.

"He has risen from the grave to admonish us for not taking good care of our prince," explained one of the soldiers, returning to the edge of the pool to wash his hands again.

Beth kept her own counsel but was scared and frightened – she wanted to proceed to Prysgduon as soon as possible. "Come on. Let's leave here," she said, turning her horse's head northwards again. While some of the soldiers leapt into their saddles, others were slow to react. If they were frightened before they were petrified now and wanted to talk.

"He was right," they were agreeing.

"Llywelyn was let down. He was betrayed by many around him. Goronwy, if he were alive, would have warned him of the danger and steered him away from it," stated another.

"He would have told him not to meet and trust the Mortimer

brothers. I agree with him, if he were alive he would have prevented this catastrophe."

"He would have warned Llywelyn against Madog, that arch plotter," said Beth with venom, identifying the archdeacon as the one who had been the traitor in the belfry.

"Let's go," she urged them. "Let's leave here."

Beth was also pondering on what else the knight had said. She was sure that she had heard him say, "This war can't be won; Edward is determined to subjugate our people. Let time pass and the tide will turn for us again as it did at Moel y Don. Put down your arms, Llywelyn was betrayed and the future Princes of Wales will not be blessed."

She was surprised that the others had not heard these words, but was in too much of a hurry to leave the pool to raise the matter then.

At last they moved on and she was relieved that less than half a mile later, Prysgduon farmstead appeared in the snow below them on the left. The moon was still low in the sky, with the buildings in shadow of the hill but clearly outlined by the snow. Beth was pleased to see the familiar house, snuggling there at the head of a small valley and protected by the hills.

As they approached the dogs started barking and the door opened with a strongly-framed man filling the doorway with a long-handled axe in his hand.

"We are Prince Llywelyn's men and we've come to ask for shelter for the night."

"Identify yourselves by names."

Beth recognised him as Rhys, the son, and she spoke out, knowing that her voice would appease him, "I'm Beth, the daughter of Gruffudd ap Owain of Aberedw. We are asking for shelter for the night."

The man approached them with a lantern, holding it to their faces. Coming towards Beth he recognised her and was pleased to see her. Satisfied that they were no threat he said, "Come in. We'll see to your horses after you've warmed yourselves by the fire."

She did not sleep well despite the warmth and the comfort of the bed. Beth had too much on her mind. Should she return to Aberedw to her family or go north to Garth Celyn where six-month-old Gwenllian probably needed someone to ensure that she would be safe.

In the morning, the men of the north departed, leaving Beth and her three escorts to stay another day. Rhys and his parents persuaded her to stay, as the snow was still covering the land and also there was no news about what was happening at Aberedw.

The following day brought no relief from the snow and Beth, unsure of her future was persuaded to stay at Prysgduon for a few days and until the hunt for them was over.

Rhys was very considerate of her and promised to take her to Aberedw and to her father whenever she wanted to leave, but he continued to advise her to stay at Prysgduon. She liked Rhys and his naturally open character, his strength of character and inner calm. She spent many hours with him – she enjoyed helping him with the horses. She was thrilled to listen to his conversation and appreciated his humour.

She had been at Prysgduon for almost a week when she sent two of her escorts back to Aberedw to see what the situation was like there. They returned a few days later to tell her that her family was well, but her father was convinced that he would be dispossessed of his castle and lands. He advised his daughter not to return until things had settled. All the castle's traders, apart from the blacksmith, had left to continue with their trade in the west.

She cried at the news, but the Prysgduon family comforted her and encouraged her to stay. She was not reluctant to do so and was within days laughing again with Rhys and enjoying his company. They ate together, walked together, worked together and sat by the fire together.

As for returning to Garth Celyn and Gwenllian, a bard escaping from Gwynedd called at Prysgduon and, to Beth's horror, told them that the baby girl had been taken by King Edward to a nunnery in England and was destined to remain there for the rest of her life. Beth was crushed with sorrow for Llywelyn's child and the cruelty the king showed towards an innocent being. What was he afraid of?

As Christmas approached, the snow thawed and the white hills of central Wales and the Marches again became brown, orange and green. The peaks of the mountains of the north became more distinguishable from the clouds, but there remained lines of white in the crevasses and the shadowed parts of these bleak, rocky places.

There then followed a great storm of wind and rain; the worst in living memory with the rain falling as snow on the higher grounds of the north.

The branches of the oak trees were hurled against each other making a horrific thunderous noise. The rivers were swept up by the wind to form new waterfalls and whirlpools, overwhelming their banks and flooding the land around.

The sea at Aberogwen was in turmoil and the waves appeared like a forest of white trees bashing the land and dragging boulders from the shore into its belly. The reeds offered no resistance and disappeared under the swirling water, being uprooted and swallowed and then disgorged dead on a shoreline miles away.

The friary at Bangor was attacked by the sea, with it rushing over the embankment at Hirael. Many of the friars were drowned and the tidal wave, as it retreated, uprooted the trees and dragged them into the torrents, taking with them some of the skeletons and bodies of the dead.

For days the sun was powerless to penetrate the heavy, watery dark clouds turning the days into nights.

The storm washed the land of its goodness and its people's collective memory of their past, and left them confused about their history leading some to deny that they had a history – but not everybody. Some were not overwhelmed, their spirits remained strong and firm and they did not forget – Beth was one of these.

Through her bitter experiences, she matured into an astute, thoughtful and realistic woman and during the darkest moments of the storm, when it appeared that the world as she knew it had come to an end, she did not lose hope. She no longer dreamt of a prince, but more of someone she could share a happy life and who she could love and would love her. She wanted children so that she could tell them the story of her prince and his betrayal, and also to her children's children so that the story would be remembered from generation to generation.

NLW MS Peniarth 20: Brut y Tywysogion

Ac ena y gwnaethpwyd brat lliwelyn ene clochte en mangor y gan y wyr ef ehvn.

And then was effected the betrayal of Llywelyn in the belfry at Bangor by his own men.

NLW MS 872D

Koffadigeth am ladd lln ap gr ap lln
 Dywed i wyr Gwynedd gallon galed
 mae / mifi yw gronw gwirfab Ednyfed
 pe byasswn i byw gida / m / llew
 nis lladdessid gynn hawsed
Hynn a draythwyd wrth wasnaythwyr. lln ap Gr: ap lln pan oeddynt yn ymolchi ymisdill y geiniog yn ymyl y prysk dvon yn Sir fessyved wedi diank yn ol lladd I meisdyr mewn lle a elwir aber Edwy mewn pwyntmant a merch hwnnw oedd dwyssoc diwaithaf ynghymry //ysbryd gronw ap Eden: vichan a draethodd y geiriav hynny//

In rememberance of the slaying of Llywelyn ap Gruffudd ap Lln
 Tell the hard-hearted men of Gwynedd
 That I am Gronw, the true son of Ednyfed.
 Had I been alive with my leader
 He would not have been slain so easily.
This was spoken to the servants of Llywelyn ap Gruffudd ap Llywelyn when they were washing at Pistyll y Geiniog near Prysgduon in Radnorshire, having fled after the slaing of their master at a place called Aberedwy at an assignment with a girl. He was the last prince of Wales. It was the ghost of Gronw ab Ednyfed Fychan that spoke those words.

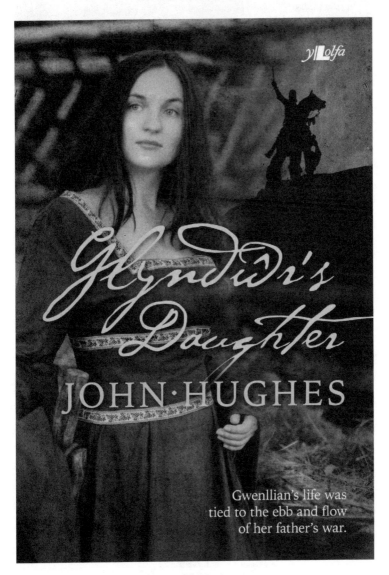

Glyndŵr's Daughter

JOHN·HUGHES

Gwenllian's life was
tied to the ebb and flow
of her father's war.

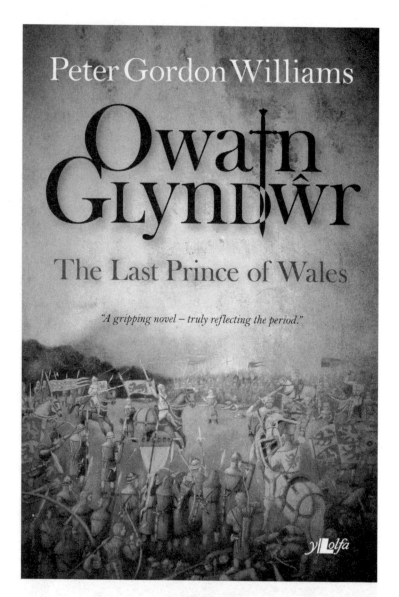

Peter Gordon Williams

Owain Glyndŵr

The Last Prince of Wales

"A gripping novel – truly reflecting the period."

y Lolfa

£7.95

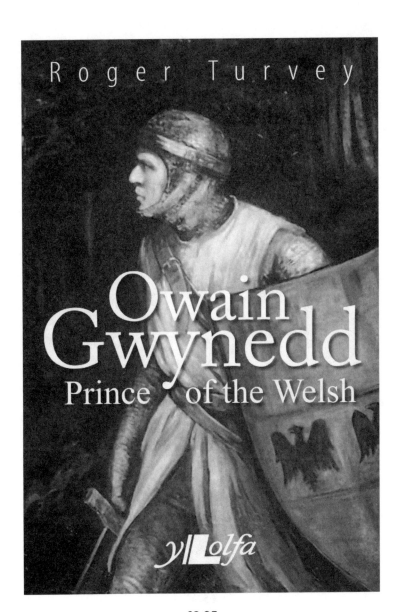

Roger Turvey

Owain Gwynedd
Prince of the Welsh

y Lolfa

£9.95

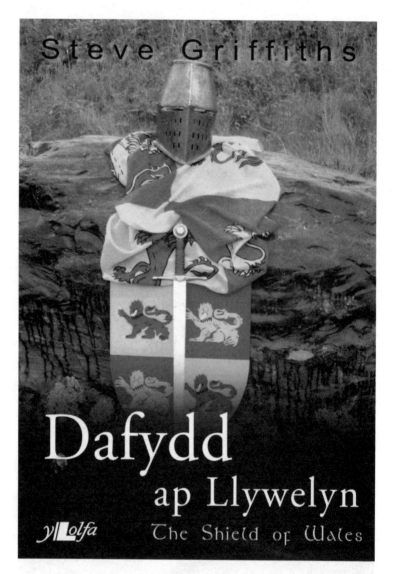

Steve Griffiths

Dafydd

ap Llywelyn

yLolfa The Shield of Wales

£5.95

Looking
for Wales

y Lolfa

An introductory guide
GERALD MORGAN

£4.95

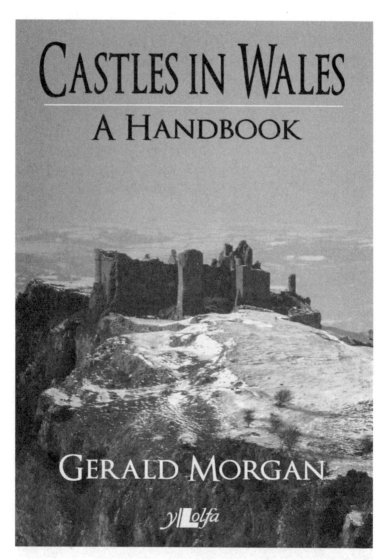

CASTLES IN WALES
A HANDBOOK

GERALD MORGAN

y Lolfa

£6.95

CASTLES
OF THE WELSH
PRINCES

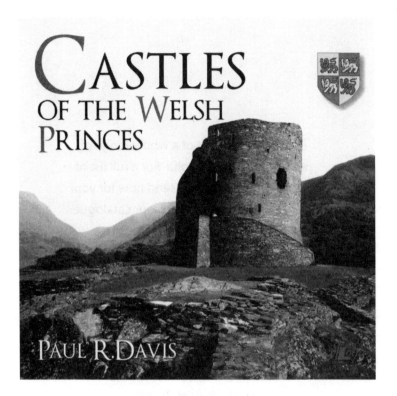

PAUL R. DAVIS

£7.95

Llywelyn is just one of a whole range of publications from Y Lolfa. For a full list of books currently in print, send now for your free copy of our new full-colour catalogue. Or simply surf into our website

www.ylolfa.com

for secure on-line ordering.

TALYBONT CEREDIGION CYMRU SY24 5HE
e-mail ylolfa@ylolfa.com
website www.ylolfa.com
phone (01970) 832 304
fax 832 782